VIKTOR

a novel based on a true story

by

Jo Calman

and

Casey J Smith

To Ed, with best wishes [signature]

ISBN 979-8-5155-6374-5

www.jo-calman.com

Authors' note:

The last time we both saw Viktor together we had lunch at an unpretentious but very good fish restaurant tucked away off Tverskaya Street in Moscow. At the time Viktor would have been in his mid-sixties, and unbeknown to either of us he was already seriously ill.

Before he died, Viktor discussed telling his story with my co-author and friend Casey J Smith. Over the years Casey had heard most of it, although I had heard only snippets. This book is part of it. We have based the book on his story as told to Casey by Viktor himself, and we have no reason to doubt it. To protect some living people, and to preserve the dignity of some of those who have passed, we have taken the literary liberty of creating some elements and some characters and situations. Conversations are mostly invented, although some are based on Viktor's own accounts of them. The historical characters named were in the positions stated at the time, but we do not wish to imply that they did or said exactly what we describe in the story.

This book is based on truth, but it is a novel, not an historical text. We have written it with great respect and affection for a remarkable man, unassuming as he was, highly intelligent, endlessly tolerant and polite. He planned to do dreadful things for his country, as many patriots do - we have no idea whether his plan would have worked; we're just grateful it was never tried. Viktor was too.

Jo Calman, Sussex, 2021

Casey J Smith, Moscow, 2021

Chapter 1 - Moscow, March 1981

The inaugural meeting of the 26th Politburo of the Central Committee of the Communist Party of the Soviet Union started on 3rd March 1981. The fourteen members of the Politburo, essentially the Cabinet, were all male and mostly old. The youngest of them was 50-year-old Mikhail Sergeyevich Gorbachev. The oldest was the Latvian, Arvids Pelše, who had just turned 82. Politburo meetings normally took days and days.

On the second evening the Chairman, Leonid Brezhnev, was closeted with three other members of the Politburo in his private quarters in the Kremlin. The three were Yuri Andropov - Chairman of the KGB, Andrei Gromyko - the Foreign Minister, and Dmitry Ustinov, Marshal of the Soviet Union and Minister of Defence.

"So, Yuri Vladimirovich," Brezhnev was speaking to Andropov, "you are bringing us alarming information. Please explain."

"Worrying, Comrade Leonid Ilyich," Andropov responded, "but I would not like to say alarming. You may wish to convene a closed session of the Politburo once we've discussed the matter between us. In essence, our agents are reporting that the Americans are preparing for war. More specifically, they are preparing for a pre-emptive nuclear strike on us, the Soviet Union."

Gromyko raised an eyebrow. He was an impishly astute and wily Belorussian, as well as a great survivor.

"Reagan is known to be hostile to socialism, Comrade Yuri Vladimirovich," Gromyko said, "but he is still in his first hundred days as president. Why do you think he would be thinking of such things now? Or are you saying it is not him who is thinking the unthinkable?"

"I think that determining his political reasons, Andrei Andreyevich, is a matter for your department," Andropov replied. "From our perspective, all I can tell you is what we are seeing: a newly elected president who is determined to recover some of the national dignity and standing lost by his predecessor. Carter was an appeaser, he had doves around him for the most part, but unfortunately our friends in Tehran made him unelectable when they burnt down the American Embassy and took his diplomats hostage. We know from our sources that Reagan is deeply distrustful of our motives in Afghanistan. Our favourable response to a request for fraternal assistance from a friendly government is seen in Washington as aggressive expansionism. We know that the Americans are actively supporting and equipping the lunatics who are attacking our troops."

"Only the Americans still believe the old saying that my enemy's enemy is my friend," Gromyko interjected, "we all know that my enemy's enemy is just my enemy of the future. They will be sorry for their misjudgement. I heard that they're also giving military training to a bunch of Islamic extremists called jihadists, whatever they are."

"Jihadists are a separate issue, Andrei Andreyevich," Andropov continued. "We know that Reagan is discussing an expansion of America's armaments. He wants to push the boundaries of the US's defensive area right up to our own borders. He also wants to go into space with new satellites and weapons that will sit in orbit above us. We don't yet know what those satellites and weapons will be or do. Some sceptics in Washington are calling it 'Star Wars', like the movie."

Brezhnev stirred. "Carter signed the SALT 2 treaty with me in Vienna in 1979. Are you saying that Reagan will dishonour it?"

"I can answer that, Leonid Ilyich," Gromyko said. "The fact is that neither the House of Representatives nor the Senate has yet ratified the treaty, so it is not technically in force. Their reason, as Comrade Andropov implied, is ostensibly their disapproval of our efforts in Afghanistan. Our ambassador in Washington, who you know well, is of the opinion that even within the Carter administration there were hard-liners who thought the treaty went too far, and they worked against him to delay it. The Tehran hostage crisis disempowered Carter, which worked in favour of the hawks. Even Brzezinski, who Reagan rates highly even though he was Carter's National Security Advisor, was unable to bring enough influence to bear to find a pragmatic solution. The Republicans never wanted the treaty in the first place. General Haig, Reagan's Secretary of State, who, by the way, thinks he still runs the Army, is delighted.

"Our experts sense a growing assertiveness by the United States Government. American politicians are shaken by the way the country is fracturing. There are too many factions and opinions, and they want a unifying force. I think hostility to us is becoming that unifying force. Since the 1950s the understanding between our nations was that if one side started the war both sides would perish, the doctrine of Mutually

Assured Destruction. That could not last - it was economically and politically unsustainable. All through the sixties and seventies we were in discussions about reductions and limitations in our respective nuclear arsenals. That has placated some of the more hawkish doves on both sides. We think it a reasonable assumption that Washington's preferred scenario now is to move the battlefield in our direction. Reagan wants any destruction to happen well away from the US, namely in Europe, right on our doorstep."

"I agree, Andrei," said Andropov, "our sources are telling us that there is to be a realignment of the disposition of tactical nuclear weapons to the eastern edge of Europe, even some strategic ones. I don't need to remind anyone here that the eastern edge of Germany is less than eight minutes flying time from the Kremlin for a NATO nuclear missile."

Brezhnev was silent for a moment. "Comrade Marshal Ustinov, your views please."

"Comrade Chairman," Ustinov said slowly, "if what I am hearing is correct, we are facing a clear and existential threat from the Americans. Our land forces are stretched, our navy is in a poor state of readiness, and our air force is structured and equipped for long-distance warfare. To adapt to a threat just a few minutes from Moscow will require new and different aircraft and weaponry. I am sorry to speak frankly, and I do not wish to seem pessimistic. There is no better, braver or more resourceful fighting man in the world than the Soviet soldier, but I fear that a close-quarters nuclear conflict will be beyond our capabilities to defeat, at least for now."

"Thank you, Comrades," said Brezhnev, "what we have said here will go no further than these four walls. I do not propose to discuss this with the full Politburo for the time being. We four need to give this matter our undivided attention. One question, for both Yuri and Andrei, when do you think Reagan will be ready to kill us?"

Andropov and Gromyko looked at each other. Gromyko nodded and spoke first.

"My thinking, Comrade Chairman, is that Reagan will need time to prepare, both militarily and politically. He will wait for an opportunity to exploit an invented threat before he launches a pre-emptive strike, and he has to have the forces and weapons in place to do that. The state of offensive readiness and defensive preparedness will be good indicators. Politically, I think Reagan will strike during the second half of his first term, so between the end of 1982 and the start of 1984."

"I agree with Andrei, Comrade Chairman," said Andropov.

"We do not have much time," Brezhnev declared. "Yuri, collect as much intelligence as you can get your hands on. We need to know what Reagan is thinking and how ready the Americans are for war. Andrei, please prepare a diplomatic strategy to use all our influence to make aggression more difficult for Reagan. Dmitry, prepare plans to increase our readiness for war, and to pre-empt the Americans. If we cannot beat them in a war, we may have to beat them before the war can start. I am sure you all understand me. Good evening."

Brezhnev stood and nodded at his three comrades. No one was smiling.

Chapter 2 - Moscow, Spring 1981

Viktor Gumnov stood on the train; as usual, there were no free seats, even at this time of day. It was not yet 7 in the morning, and the first signs of a late spring were just appearing. The forests beside the train tracks were turning from black to green. Once in a while a ray of weak sunshine broke free from the clouds. He liked to use the long commute to let his mind wander; to think, solve problems, reflect on life, or just dream of fishing. The journey from their little apartment in Chekhov to his office in the Lubyanka took nearly two hours. First on a regional train until he could connect with the Moscow Metro system for the Lubyanka station. From there it was only a short walk.

Today he was reflective, thinking back. He was a marine scientist by calling and education. He and his wife Natasha both hailed from the far-eastern seaport of Vladivostok. He had been in the Soviet navy and while serving as a cadet he had attended the Vladivostok Marine State University. On graduating from the Admiral Nevelsky faculty with a good degree in oceanology he joined the navy proper and served a further three years.

Natasha liked to tell everyone that she had fallen for the tall, slim and very handsome Viktor at a civic reception for new naval officers. She was working for the city council as an administrator, and being young, lively and attractive she was often invited to attend civic functions. She said that evening she shamelessly monopolised Viktor, who was more than happy to let himself be monopolised. A few months later they were engaged, and within a year of their marriage in 1964

10

they had a daughter, Alexandra - their Sasha. For a while they lived contentedly in naval officers' quarters, which were modest but comfortable, and while he was away at sea Natasha entertained her lovely daughter and took great delight in watching her turn from a baby into a small person. Fortunately, his sea trips tended to be quite short, so he too was able to watch his beloved wife and daughter flourish together. He was very happy. They all were.

By the time Sasha was five, he had been posted to Naval Headquarters in Moscow. The family had made the long train journey across the empire, leaving behind their parents and relatives, as well as their childhood friends. Rather than being a blow, the separation made the small family closer to each other; they really didn't need anyone else. Not that they were unfriendly or antisocial, far from it; they were outgoing and popular, with many friends. His HQ job was largely administrative, and while he was a loyal citizen and servant of the Soviet Union and would always do what the state required of him, he hankered after the intellectual stimulus of oceanological study and research. He let his feelings be known during a walk beside the Moscow River with his immediate boss, a veteran of the Great Patriotic War and a survivor of the Stalin years. Half expecting a lecture about being selfish, he had been pleasantly surprised to hear his boss commend him on his desire to serve the Soviet people the best way he could. A few months later he received a summons to attend an interview at the Shirshov Institute of Oceanology, a part of the prestigious Academy of Science.

Things moved slowly in that time, so despite being eagerly accepted by the Shirshov Institute it was a good year before a formal transfer came through. With it came a hefty pay cut, the allocation of a tiny, rented apartment in the distant town of Chekhov, and a commute of two hours each way. He was delighted. By this time Natasha was working as an administrator in a factory and earning twice the pay he made. Sasha was doing very well in school and was proving to be multi-talented as both an actress and a linguist. Life was as good as it got, even if he did have a permanent instruction from Natasha to buy any meat, butter, cheese or fresh fruit he saw in Moscow as there was never any in Chekhov, at least not for more than an hour after the shops opened.

Not long after he started work at the Institute, he began to get invitations to join delegations to other states, mostly within the Soviet orbit but occasionally in the West. He went to the United Kingdom going to Plymouth and Aberdeen. He visited Greece, going to Athens and the port of Piraeus. He also made two trips to America, a very rare privilege, once to the north-eastern area visiting Boston, Portland and as far north as Bar Harbor in Maine. The second trip was to the west coast: San Diego, Monterey and Portland, Oregon. All the trips were for conventions or research projects, and they were immensely interesting.

Unlike most of the other delegates, he had not been included in the trip as a reward or just because it was his turn, he was invited along because he could contribute and also fully understand the subject matter. He worked hard, drank sparingly, and was eternally diligent. He was also living the dream in his own mind, doing what he was interested in and good at, with a lovely loving wife and a beautiful, intriguing daughter waiting at home. He brought them back presents, but nothing outlandish or excessive. Small and interesting things that he always presented with a story about the place it came from, what it was for, how people used it.

Everything had seemed set for him and his small family. Eventually he assumed they would get a larger apartment with a separate bedroom for Sasha, maybe even a bit closer to the centre of town to cut down on the journey time, but all in good time.

The change had come early in 1976. Sasha was almost 11 years old. Natasha had been promoted again, as he had. They had a little more money, but not much. They acquired a very small *dacha*, little more than a hut, in the forest not far from Chekhov where he could indulge his passion for the *banya* (the traditional Russian version, much improved of course, of the Swedish sauna) especially in the coldest of winters. Then they'd sent for him.

He had been summoned to a suite of small offices deep in the bowels of the Institute. Like all Soviet citizens, he was aware of the *Komitet Gosudarstvennoy Bezopasnosti,* the Committee for State Security or KGB. It wasn't a secret; the KGB had a huge uniformed branch as well as many covert ones that operated in the shadows. Every army unit, vessel, airbase, factory and office had a KGB presence, as did the Shirshov Institute of Oceanology. It was they who had wanted to talk to Viktor Gumnov.

The room had been full of cigarette smoke. Two men sat in chairs behind a long table. They were polite and amiable; they offered him some tea. They asked about his family, naming Natasha and Sasha, and they asked him about fellow officers he had served with in the navy. They asked him about the people he worked with at the Institute, and about his trips abroad. Who had he met? What were his impressions of the English? The Americans? The Greeks? What was he working on now? Was he a truly loyal comrade?

He sat through it calmly and had replied as appropriately as he could. He had no secrets from the State, and he understood his responsibilities as a citizen and comrade. He did not fear the KGB.

"Well, Comrade Captain Gumnov," the elder of the two had said, "we think you could serve your country better if you left the Shirshov Institute and came to work with us. We have important work that you can do, and we think you'll be good at it. We've been watching you for some time. Your comrades all say excellent things about you; our reports of your conduct when you have been abroad have been exemplary, and I wish we could say the same about all Soviet delegates when they get let loose in the West. Will you join us?"

He remembered sitting quietly for a moment. He understood that there was only one answer he could give.

"I will serve my country to the best of my ability in whatever role I am assigned, Comrade Major," he remembered it word for word.

"Welcome to the Committee for State Security," the senior KGB officer said, extending a hand.

This time the move had happened more quickly. Within a few weeks he'd received his transfer orders and instructions to present himself at a run-of-the-mill military establishment mercifully close to Domodedovo airport and therefore less than half an hour from Chekhov. It was a regional KGB training school where he would undertake the statutory training and political refreshment required of new recruits of whatever rank. After the six-week course he would transfer again to a different training establishment, location undisclosed, where he would attend a residential training course for about three months to learn all the dark arts of espionage. If successful he would be transferred again to the Americas department of the First Chief Directorate, responsible for collecting and analysing foreign intelligence. Specifically, he would be assigned to the United States desk. And so it was that he, a former Soviet Naval Officer and excellent marine scientist, came to be a Russian spy.

He was still the same man. He still adored his wife and child; he still adored science and read all the oceanological journals from cover to cover. He still liked to fish. The area around Chekhov, where he still lived, had abundant streams, lakes and rivers deep in the forests where, depending on conditions and the time of year, he could try to outwit his scaly adversaries with worms, maggots, artificial flies or basic cunning. He would often wake before dawn at weekends and go off with his fishing rods in the rattly Lada that had been allocated to him to catch some trout or perch for lunch, or just to sit and think quietly.

Sasha still grew and was cheeky and charming. Natasha was blooming gracefully and beautifully and was always good company for her man. The only thing that had changed was that he could no longer talk to his wife about his work, not like he used to, only in general terms. And he could no longer answer Sasha's endless questions as openly and frankly as he wanted to. These things made him a little sad, but on balance life was still as good as it got.

The subway train came to a halt at Lubyanka station and he stepped off to join the throng on the platform. At work, he spent his days reading reports in American newspapers and reading other reports from Soviet agents deep inside the United States of America. It seemed there were a lot of them. Sometimes he found agents' reports that were exactly the same as articles in the Arkansas Enquirer or the Los Alamos News. He read and assessed a lot of reports, and he wrote other reports to tell his bosses what he had read. He also posed questions to be sent back to the agents, questions to fill in gaps in the centre's knowledge of what the Americans were doing or thinking.

He had been given free access to the KGB main library and the foreign language library so he could take and read any book or publication he wished, however prohibited and regardless of how heavily censored it normally was. He understood that this was a sign of the trust his KGB bosses placed in him. He found that he not only understood many of the arguments and statements put out by the enemies of the Soviet Union, he also agreed with some of them. However, he did not doubt for a second that such arguments and statements were just very clever capitalist propaganda, and no matter how compelling or tempting they were his faith in the socialist system was deep and unshakeable.

As he became more experienced, the importance of what he was reading and asking changed. It became more serious. The reports and questions were about political leaders, political thoughts and dogma. If Person X were to become president of the US, what would he (and it was always a 'he') think and do about Y aspect of Soviet policy? Would he be a hawk or a dove? What would be his attitude towards NATO? Would he accelerate or slow down the race for nuclear supremacy? He knew that these questions would not be answered by agents who retyped articles from the Arkansas Enquirer.

These questions could only be answered by brave and loyal people who risked everything to get into the hearts and minds of the American establishment, to get to know the Americans who made the decisions and who told the president what to do.

Chapter 3 – Moscow, April 1981

Two weeks after the secret meeting of a group within a group in the Politburo, Viktor Gumnov's concentration on a series of reports about leisure shipping in and around Cape Cod and Boston was interrupted by the telephone. It didn't often ring.

"Comrade Major Gumnov, please come at once to the office of the head of personnel for the First Chief Directorate," said a disembodied voice. Then a click.

He shrugged, put away the material he had been studying. He had to ask a colleague where the personnel office was, and eventually he found it.

"Major Gumnov," he announced himself to a uniformed NCO behind a desk. The junior motioned him towards a row of chairs, most of which were occupied by puzzled looking people. He took a seat next to a man a few years older than himself, a nondescript man of medium build, a bit shorter than average. He had seen him around the building and in the cafeteria. They had never spoken.

"Have you been summoned too?" the man asked him.

"Yes, are we in trouble?" He was smiling nervously.

"I don't think so, there's another personnel office for people who are in trouble. I'm Oleg. Oleg Gordievsky."

"Viktor Gumnov." They shook hands.

Before their conversation could continue, an officer in KGB uniform came out of a room with a folder.

"Colonel Gordievsky, please," the officer said.

Gordievsky stood, gave him a lop-sided smile and followed the officer. Twenty minutes later Gordievsky emerged, beaming broadly. He knew better than to ask him why.

"Major Gumnov, please," the officer called.

He rose and followed the officer into a large meeting room. He didn't know what to expect, but it wasn't the sight of a panel of senior officers, including the head of his own department, the First, which dealt with foreign intelligence concerning the US and Canada, together with the head of Directorate T of the First Chief Directorate, which dealt with scientific and technical intelligence, and the actual head of the First Chief Directorate (foreign intelligence) itself, Vladimir Kryuchkov. He stood to attention.

"Please sit, Comrade Gumnov," said Kryuchkov, the biggest boss in the room, "and relax. Some water, perhaps?"

"Comrade Gumnov," said his own department head, "you have been with us for some time now and we are very satisfied with your work. You will know that there have been changes in America, significant changes, and we need to address those changes by adapting our capacity. The Shirshov Institute reported very favourably on your knowledge and understanding of marine and maritime matters, and of various oceanological studies and principles." It was not a question, but he felt obliged to answer.

"Yes, Comrade General, I was trained and educated as a marine scientist, and I served in the navy before transferring to the Shirshov Institute. Oceanology is an abiding interest for me, a passion even."

"You've been to America?" asked the head of the First Chief Directorate, who must have already known the answer.

"Yes, Comrade Kryuchkov. I participated in two scientific conference delegations, once to Boston and Maine, once to San Diego and the West Coast."

"Is your English good?" Kryuchkov asked, in English.

"I'm told it is," he replied, also in English, "most foreign scientific papers are written in English, and it is better to follow conference discussions in English rather than needing to rely on interpreters."

"Excellent!" Kryuchkov nodded.

"What do you know of subsea tectonic movements, Comrade Gumnov?" this from the Head of Directorate T.

"It is a very broad and complex subject area, Comrade Colonel. Movement of the earth's tectonic plates can cause massive disturbances, earthquakes, both above and below the sea. The major effect of subsea tectonic quakes is the reaction to the movement of plates by water as opposed to land and air. Tidal waves, tsunamis, often ensue and can be devastating to structures on land. There is a great deal of research currently underway, mostly in the Asia Pacific region, where subsea earthquakes are increasingly common. It is not my specialist area, but I know where to go to if I need to find out more."

"Do you think subsea quakes can be predicted?" Directorate T asked.

"No more than any earthquake can. There are indications of impending seismic activity that can suggest that a quake is imminent, but I am not aware of any reliable prediction mechanism."

"Can human activity cause subsea earthquakes?" asked Kryuchkov, in English again.

"I don't know, Comrade Kryuchkov," he replied, "I would imagine that it is technically possible to initiate a relatively small quake as a research exercise. I think that the effects of a large earthquake, subsea or otherwise, are too unpredictable to risk starting one on purpose."

"Are you a 'yes man', Comrade Gumnov?" Kryuchkov asked.

"No, Comrade," he replied. Kryuchkov smiled and nodded.

"We have an assignment for you," his own department head then said. "We want you to go to Washington. We have many questions that need to be answered, but very discreetly, in secret. You have the skills and knowledge we need for this task. The assignment will nominally be for five years, and your family will accompany you - subject to the usual clearances of course. You are not to discuss this conversation with anyone at all, not your colleagues or anyone outside this room. If you do, you will be committing a crime of the most severe nature. Do you understand, Comrade?"

"Yes, Comrade General. What do I tell my wife?"

"Tell her you have been assigned to Washington as head of the SSOD office there, responsible for friendship societies, cultural research and exchange programmes. The details will be sent to you in internal mail together with a date for interview with the Central Committee panel which approves all international postings. Do you accept?"

"Yes, Comrade General. Thank you." He stood up smartly, waiting to be dismissed.

"You may go, Comrade Lieutenant Colonel Gumnov. Yes, the assignment comes with a promotion." Kryuchkov smiled at him.

Chapter 4 - Gander, Newfoundland, June 1981

The ungainly Ilyushin IL-62 airliner lumbered down the runway and climbed noisily into the skies above Newfoundland. It had been on the ground at Gander airport for hours, giving the midges and mosquitos time to feast on the assembled group of still drunk or newly sober and hungover Russians. The flight was already late. The final leg was just a couple of hours, southward along the eastern seaboard of the USA and then, just above New York, a slight turn to starboard for the final descent into Washington's Dulles International Airport - the entry point to the heartland of the enemy for him and his small family.

The Aeroflot direct flight from Moscow to Washington had been due to depart Sheremetyevo airport at 09.00 local time that Wednesday morning. That meant that he, his wife and their daughter had been collected at 04.30 by a service vehicle - an almost unheard-of privilege - from in front of their apartment block in Chekhov, some 50 kilometres south of the centre of Moscow and therefore more than 80 kilometres from Sheremetyevo, which was away to the north of the city. The roads were empty, but the vehicle was slow. It was 06.00 when they arrived, the appointed time to check in for the long flight. Natasha, who was Natalya to her friends and sometimes just Nata to her husband when they were alone, had been quiet on the journey across Moscow. She was even quieter now and had hardly spoken for several hours. Their daughter Sasha was not. The sixteen-year-old had hardly slept the night before, and apart from a brief doze as they flew over the Canadian tundra, she had kept up a continuous stream of chatter and questions to her father throughout the flight.

The plane was crowded; every seat was taken, and probably the lavatories too. Aeroflot was keen to squeeze every rouble from these transatlantic flights. The front of the aircraft was reserved for the foreigners who were prepared to pay the huge cost of business-class tickets, or the high-level party officials who were given them for free. Even with his rank of Lieutenant Colonel he was not entitled to one. In business class you got a bigger softer seat, a few drinks and a choice of fish or chicken. In the back the comrades got small hard seats, cold coffee and something quite similar to chicken - there was no fish. The few complimentary drinks grudgingly provided by Aeroflot usually ran out before the plane reached cruising altitude, so everyone who was sensible brought their own. It was officially prohibited to consume any alcohol not supplied by the airline, but everyone knew it was a citizen's right to get utterly drunk whenever he wasn't actually working, and Aeroflot didn't stock any vodka or enough cheap Krasnodar wine for all their passengers to do that. This meant that most of them consumed as much vodka as they could smuggle on board, sang as many songs as they could, and praised the greatest political system in the world until they fell asleep somewhere near the North Pole.

Although no teetotaller, he was unusually abstemious for a Russian; he didn't like being drunk or having hangovers. He was mightily relieved when they touched down at Gander for fuel and a change of crew. The foul smell of stale vodka breath, a thousand farts and as many Soviet cigarettes assaulted the Canadian ground staff as they opened the doors, and they stepped back blinking and coughing slightly. The passengers at the front were driven away to their comfortable lounge. The rest of them were directed towards the economy-class transit lounge, which was neither comfortable nor conveniently close. At least it was an opportunity for a walk and a stretch, and to take advantage of toilets designed for use by a human being of normal proportions.

Back on board after the three-hour wait he had taken the middle seat, Natasha the aisle. Sasha was by the window staring out at the ground below. An hour later Sasha gasped as the clouds parted and the bold outline of Manhattan showed itself.

"Papa! Look - it's New York! It's so big. The buildings are so tall and shiny. It's the most beautiful thing I've ever seen!"

He looked over the top of Sasha's head. The view of New York City was stunningly clear. He could see the oblong of Central Park and the shimmering waters of both rivers. The twin towers of the World Trade Center marked the far tip of Manhattan Island, while the majestic Empire State Building stood guard over mid-town. He had to admit it was a remarkable sight. He squeezed Sasha's hand and smiled at her pleasure.

The landing at Dulles was hard. The big Ilyushin almost seemed to shy away from the hostile earth, but the captain brought it under control. It rumbled its way across the airfield. Sasha's nose was glued to the plastic window as she looked at the American cars and trucks, at all the aircraft with flags and colours from all over the world, at the armies of miniature people who busied themselves attending to the needs of the humming planes and their hordes of occupants. The doors opened again and the mild air of an early summer Virginia evening flooded in. That it smelt of kerosene didn't bother Sasha. She was already on her feet itching to get out, despite the fact that her parents hadn't yet moved and the aisle was already packed with tired and grumpy Soviet citizens with headaches and raging thirsts.

"Wait a moment, Sasha," he said gently, "it'll take a while to disembark and get to the terminal. Just sit back and relax."

Natasha squeezed his hand. She was nervous and unsettled. She had never been outside the Soviet Union; the furthest they had gone together had been to Crimea for occasional holidays. Viktor had travelled with his work and was calm and strong; his English was very good. She knew he would take care of her and Sasha, but she also knew (as everyone did) that Americans hated Soviet citizens. She had never had to deal with hostility, and although she would fight like a lioness for her only cub, Natasha didn't know how she would cope with living among enemies for five long years. He squeezed her hand in return.

"Everything will be fine, Nata," he said softly, "once we've settled in."

Eventually he stood up. His family took the cue. He reached for their hand luggage and herded them towards the front door of the aircraft. Sasha looked around in awe as they moved through the business class cabin, strewn with blankets and magazines. The rows were as long as those in economy, but had only two seats, seats which were big enough to be small sofas. He nudged her gently from behind but said nothing. He smiled at Sasha's surprise when she found herself not in a corridor or on a stairway, but inside a weird-looking bus. It was level with the door but had long spindly legs down to its wheels. The passengers were loaded in until the strange vehicle was full, then it wheezed as the legs were half lowered and it trundled off across the tarmac. It swayed unsteadily and Sasha heard the sound of vomiting from somewhere near the front. Although she'd spent the last year fortuitously improving her English, she had no idea what the words yelled by the driver of the strange bus were. She could only guess what they meant, and he did *not* sound happy.

The weird transporter docked against an entrance to the passenger terminal. The driver opened a door at the front, then stood guard over the puddle of vomit which had been produced by the sheepish looking passenger who now sat forlornly on a nearby seat holding his head in his hands. He steered his wife and daughter towards the immigration hall, and once there towards the returning residents and work visa channel. Unfortunately, half the Aeroflot passengers also went towards it, including the one who had disgraced himself on the transit bus. The line was long and slow-moving.

"Viktor Vladimirovich Gumnov," the black-uniformed agent said it like a statement. "What is the purpose of your visit to the United States?"

"As you will see, officer, I am the new head of the Washington office of the Union of Soviet Societies for Friendship and Cultural Contacts, attached to the Embassy of the Soviet Union. I am here on a five-year assignment with my wife and daughter. It's in the letter I gave you, approved by your State Department."

"Wait here."

The officer waddled off with a bundle of green passports and the flapping letter, written in Russian but with an English translation attached.

Natasha stood quietly. Sasha's eyes were nearly bursting out of her head as she scanned the immigration hall. There were people of all shapes, sizes and colours speaking all kinds of languages. In the middle of Moscow you sometimes saw people who were Chinese or Indian or from the far east. Sometimes even a few black people, but not many. Out in Chekhov there were none at all. It looked so strange.

"Don't stare, Sasha," he said.

"But Papa, there are so many foreigners here!"

"We are foreigners here as well, Sasha," Natasha interjected. "People will stare at us too, so please try not to be rude."

"I'm sorry," Sasha said, "I didn't mean to seem rude. I'm just not used to seeing so many different looking people."

The Immigration Agent waddled back. Without looking at him or his family he started filling in a form.

"Fingerprints," he said, nodding at an inkpad.

As the agent supervised the rolling of fingers he also took pictures of the family's faces with a small camera. Natasha started to protest but Viktor silenced her with a glance. The Agent placed the fingerprint forms in a folder along with photocopies of their passports and Viktor's letter of appointment.

"Welcome to the United States," he said as he stamped their passports. He didn't sound like he meant it.

They passed through to the baggage hall and retrieved their suitcases. It didn't seem much, but the three cases contained all the possessions the family had. Their furniture had come with the two-roomed apartment in Chekhov, the clunky ZIL refrigerator they had saved for years to buy had been left outside the apartment and had disappeared as expected. It no longer worked in warm weather anyway, so it saved them the bother of trying to get rid of it themselves. All their other bits and pieces that weren't in the suitcases had fitted into two cardboard boxes which were now with friends of Natasha. It didn't matter to him, he had Natasha and Sasha. That was enough.

He wheeled the luggage trolley past a bored Customs Agent and they walked through the sliding doors into America.

A well-bult man of average height, a wrestler's physique, approached them. He had a sign with their family name on in Cyrillic.

"Comrade Lieutenant Colonel Gumnov, I am Leonid from the office," he said in Russian. "Technically speaking I'm your boss, but I'm here to escort you to your accommodation. Please don't talk about anything to do with work in the car on the way to the city. It will take about 45 minutes. Welcome to the land of the fat and the home of the crazy. Let's go."

Leonid led them to a waiting Ford sedan with Virginia licence plates. It was parked illegally and the driver, a tall elderly black man in a grey suit, leant casually against the door. Leonid spoke to him in English.

"Thank you, Travis. Please put the bags in the trunk." Then in Russian he spoke to Viktor.

"The driver is from a local car service we sometimes use if we're short of our own vehicles or drivers. Assume he will record and report everything that's said in the car to the Yankees. We would do the same to them in Moscow. Only say things you want the Yankees to hear, it can be useful to us sometimes. Your own vehicle will be delivered in a couple of days. Drive it yourself whenever possible, and every week or so bring it to the embassy motor workshop so we can see what they have put in it. We check all the vehicles every few weeks."

Viktor and his family all slid onto the rear seat; Leonid sat up front with the driver Travis.

"Landmark Plaza in Alexandria," Leonid instructed him in English. "Take the George Washington Parkway when we get to the Beltway Intersection."

Travis nodded but said nothing.

"You have an apartment in Alexandria, on the Virginia side of the city. It has three bedrooms and is big enough if you need to do any entertaining." Leonid was speaking in Russian again, so that Natasha and Sasha were included. "It has amenities nearby and it's convenient for the city."

They rode on in silence for twenty minutes.

"We're on the George Washington Parkway," Leonid was talking again, "heading north towards the Potomac River. The river is in Maryland; the Virginia state boundary is the riverbank on this side. You'll see something interesting soon."

A few moments later Leonid nodded towards an exit sign on their side of the highway. On the sign, in very large letters, were the initials CIA, the headquarters of the Central Intelligence Agency. The secret foreign intelligence service of the United States of America not only advertised itself to the entire world, but its location was also clearly visible from the highway. He had heard about this sign, but this was the first time he had seen it. In Moscow everyone knew that the Lubyanka was where the KGB headquarters were, but it didn't have its name in huge letters on a road-sign so you couldn't miss it. He looked at occupants of the steady stream of vehicles entering and leaving the complex as they drove past in the early evening rush hour traffic. How was he ever going to understand these people?

Leonid kept up a commentary of the tourist highlights as they neared Washington DC itself. Georgetown on the other side of the river, the Arlington national cemetery on this. The Lincoln Memorial on the other side, with the Washington memorial obelisk in the distance. They drove past the Pentagon, again clearly signed although it really didn't need it, and on to the suburb of Alexandria. This was where the first settlement in what was to become Washington had been built, using bricks that arrived as ballast on the ships from England and Europe which came to buy goods in the New World. The old quarter had the look of an 18th century English town. The Gumnov's apartment was further away from the river near the Landmark Mall, a large shopping complex the like of which the family had never seen.

They pulled up outside a modern-looking building. Travis opened the door for them and took care of the luggage. Their apartment was on the third floor. There was an elevator that worked and didn't smell of urine. The apartment had five rooms in all, plus a kitchen and two bathrooms. Each of the three bedrooms was bigger than their old apartment in Chekhov. It was furnished comfortably; the kitchen had equipment that Natasha had only read about in magazines. Outside there was a communal swimming pool. Natasha and Sasha could not believe it.

Leonid handed an envelope to him. It contained $300 in tens and twenties. He got the message.

"Natasha, why don't you and Sasha go to the Safeway store just across the street," Leonid suggested, handing her a wad of notes too, "you can have a look around and get a few groceries. Viktor and I need a few minutes to talk."

"It's OK," Viktor added, "it will be self-service and Sasha speaks enough English if you need to ask any questions."

Sasha was very keen, and she led her mother by the hand towards the door.

Leonid looked at them as they went.

"You have a nice family, Viktor," he said, "I hope they like it here. It's OK once you get used to it and can see through the pretence. You'll all start to feel tired soon, but I suggest you try to eat something and stay awake until around 10pm. If you sleep now, it will be days before you feel right again. It's jet lag - I never get used to it. You have important work to do, Viktor, vital for the Soviet Union. Your task is highly secret, no one in the embassy must know anything about it, except you and me - and I mean *only* you and me! I'll see you in the embassy tomorrow to brief you fully, but for now just remember that you are on active service and you need to stay alert and careful at all times. What have you told Natasha and Alexandra?"

"Nothing much. Just that I've been assigned to the embassy in Washington to work on cultural and scientific relations. Sasha doesn't care why we're here, she's just excited. She wants to see film stars and convertible Cadillacs and drink Coca Cola. Natasha thinks it's a good career move for me, and she's hoping to get a job at the embassy too, once Sasha's settled in school. I'll probably be away a lot and she'll need to make her own entertainment. It will be good for her to have friends from home."

Leonid nodded. "I agree; I'll arrange something for her. It's getting dark; why don't you go and find them? It's safe round here, but they might not know that. I'll see you tomorrow, comrade."

"Thank you, Comrade Colonel."

"Just Leonid unless we're in the office and someone important is listening, and even then it will be 'Comrade Second Secretary'."

Leonid's advice was sound. He had been in Washington for almost three years as head of the covert KGB station, unknown to almost all other embassy staff. He had seen newcomers arrive and leave, and he understood how overwhelming America and its inhabitants could be if you had spent your whole life in the Soviet Union. He found his wife and daughter standing close together in the doorway of Safeway. They were watching a group of black people of varying ages, but mostly young, who were watching them back.

"Good evening," he nodded at them.

"Yo! How you doin'?" one of them replied.

"We're fine. We've just arrived in town. Getting a few groceries in."

"We was wonderin'. Don't you got no car or nuthin'? Wid all dem bags of stuff? We was thinking they looked heavy and was goin' to lend a hand to the ladies."

"They'll be fine now, thanks all the same."

"You speak funny. You from Englan' or someplace?"

"Yes, someplace."

"OK. You have a nice day now."

The black group started to disperse and wander off. He turned to his wife and daughter. Natasha looked pale and was shaking, Sasha was subdued.

"It's OK," he said, "you're perfectly safe. It's just America. Let's go home."

He picked up the shopping bags and led his family back to their apartment, their home.

Chapter 5 - Alexandria, VA, June 1981

Thursday was a slow day. Neither Natasha nor Sasha had been able to sleep much during the night, and now that it was broad daylight they were both unconscious in their beds. He had fared slightly better and although he felt far from normal with the jet lag he was awake, showered and dressed. He made himself a light breakfast in the spacious kitchen of their palatial new apartment. He made tea for Natasha and took it to her. She stirred slightly but was soon asleep again. He wanted to explore his new surroundings so left a note for Natasha saying he'd be back around midday.

The new metro system hadn't yet reached Alexandria and he didn't understand the bus routes, so he strolled to the cab rank at the Landmark Mall.

"Scott Circle," he said to the taciturn taxi driver, who just grunted.

The cab was an old and shabby Chevrolet. It smelt musty and squeaked and rattled. The back seat springs were broken and the plastic seat covering was torn. It rumbled through Alexandria, turned northward towards the Pentagon complex and onward to the Arlington Memorial Bridge. They crossed the river and entered DC, skirting the Lincoln Memorial and the Reflecting Pool before turning left onto 17th Street. His eyes were drinking in the sights as he familiarised himself with the topography of Washington. He glimpsed the White House as they passed the Eisenhower Executive Office Building. On K Street they did a right turn, then a left into 16th Street. He stared out of the window at the Embassy of the Soviet Union to his right, at 1125 16th Street NW, Washington DC. A few moments later the cab stopped at Scott Circle. He handed over a $20 bill for the $17 fare. He waited for a moment, but no change was forthcoming. He shrugged and got out of the cab, relieved that his trousers hadn't stuck to the seat. The entire journey had taken less than 20 minutes.

He walked back down 16th Street; he saw the University Club, which was directly opposite the embassy and the ambassador's residence. From the outside they looked like normal Washington buildings, substantial and stately; the former homes of the tycoons and entrepreneurs who had, some would say, built the United States with their hands, their vision, and their ingenuity. On the other hand, some might also say, they had stolen America from its inhabitants, extorted even the sweat off the backs of slave labourers and gorged themselves on plundered profits. It was not an argument that he wished to join. Not yet anyway.

It was a pleasantly mild day. The sun was shining. There was a lightness in the air, people were smiling and talking as they walked. Excited tourists and groups of school students thronged the streets, taking pictures and talking ever more loudly to each other. 16th Street led directly down to Lafayette Square and Pennsylvania Avenue, 1600 Pennsylvania Avenue to be exact - the White House. Since January of that year its occupant had been a 69-year-old former movie star and very vocal anti-communist. Ronald Reagan's accession to the Presidency was one of the driving reasons for his move to Washington. Moscow remained concerned about Reagan's intentions, very concerned indeed.

He found a vacant bench in Lafayette Square and sat for a while. He watched the people; they didn't look like monsters. The White House shone, a huge Star-Spangled Banner waving slowly in the gentle breeze above the columned portico. He knew it had been built in the time of Napoleon, the upstart emperor whose vain attempt to defeat the Russian people had led to his eventual downfall and disgrace. Although it was in a different time, he was sure that the same fate would await any other upstart who tried to take on the Russian, now Soviet, empire. Reagan was the antithesis of Jimmy Carter, the thoughtful conciliator who'd had the misfortune to be in office when the Shah of Iran was ousted by the Mullahs.

That revolution had started because the Shah could see what was coming and he tried to ease some of the pressures that were causing many of his subjects to rail against him. He had tried to curb the excesses of the corrupt elites who ran Iran, the military officers, the wealthy bankers, the Tehran bazaar traders, but it was too little too late. The elites thought they could foment unrest and unseat the aging autocrat, intending to replace him with his young heir, a youthful and potentially more malleable monarch. It all went wrong for them and for the Shah, as everyone now knew.

Carter's problem was not of his making. To start a revolution there needs to be an object of hatred, to sustain the revolution the hatred of that object must also be sustained. So, the victorious Mullahs proposed the United States of America, naming it the Great Satan - most probably with a bit of nudging from Moscow, according to a KGB colleague who had worked in the region. The US Embassy in Tehran was stormed and burnt down. The diplomats and dependents inside were held hostage for more than a year, a year in which a rescue attempt failed spectacularly and miserably. Jimmy Carter, the leader who Moscow would have preferred to have remain in the White House, was a failed and unelectable president. So along came the Republican, gung-ho Ronald Reagan. A man who had already started referring in private to the USSR as 'the evil empire', something he would repeat in public a while later.

He roused himself from his thoughts. It was nearly 11 am. He decided to walk at least as far as Arlington from where he could get a taxi back to the Landmark Mall in Alexandria. His work would start tomorrow.

Back in the apartment he found his wife and child awake but groggy. He made them American coffee and suggested they take a look at the shopping mall. It was a beautiful day, he said, and maybe they should have a swim in the pool after lunch. They bought new swimming costumes at Sears, and some beach towels. The money Leonid had given them was pure spending money to help them get set up. Sasha wanted a milkshake and a hamburger, so they all had one. It was not to his liking, this bland and gloopy taste of America. They spent the day together enjoying the freedom and the warmth and the novelty. They swam in the pool under a clear blue sky. They strolled the streets of Alexandria Old Town, gazing at the quaint houses. Just normal sized houses, but very old, unlike anything in Moscow where the only old buildings were churches and mansions. Alexandria Old Town was like a film set; old-fashioned buildings made of old-fashioned bricks on cobbled streets. Natasha loved it. They walked beside the Potomac River and looked across to Washington. To the right, downstream, was the open countryside of Virginia and just a little further away the waters of Chesapeake Bay and the Atlantic. He was already feeling a pull towards the shore, and the need to start working on his task.

The apartment had a television set. They hadn't had a working one in Chekhov, just a radio. Sasha tried to find a music show or a movie, but the constant stream of advertisements and soap operas was confusing. Even when she did find a film to watch it stopped every few minutes for 'a message from our sponsors'. She soon turned it off. Privately she found the language very hard to keep up with. People on TV spoke very fast and used vocabulary she wasn't familiar with.

"Don't worry Sasha, you'll get used to it soon. The embassy has enrolled you in the International School. They teach in English, and you'll be meeting other people from different cultures. Your English will be fluent in no time," he told her.

On Friday morning the embassy sent a car to collect the family. The car was to take him to the embassy to meet the staff there and complete the necessary administrative formalities. While he was inside, the car would take Natasha and Sasha sightseeing. They were very excited. Leonid was waiting at the staff entrance. He asked how the family was settling in and was polite, but he clearly wanted to get on. Natasha and Sasha were driven off by an embassy driver who knew Washington well, having already been at the embassy for two years. Like all the other drivers and every member of staff, even the janitors and domestics, he had been sent from the Soviet Union on assignment. They employed no local staff at all. The driver's name was Denis, and he kept the ladies amused with funny stories and anecdotes as they drove around, stopping at the various sights to take them in. They had a superb day.

In the embassy Leonid started to brief him. They spoke as they walked the corridors.

"At 10 we will meet the ambassador and his deputy. The official head of the KGB station, the *rezident*, is away on leave. You'll meet him when he comes back but you won't have much contact with him. Your official function, as you know, is that of the head of the Washington bureau of the SSOD, which is how they refer to the Union of Soviet Societies for Friendship and Cultural Contacts. It is an unfortunate acronym, but it is what it is. SSOD has a small team here; you'll meet them and take an interest in their work. You're their boss in reality as well as in cover. As such you will engage in liaison with a great many contacts, American and others, some from government but mostly from cultural and educational organisations. Unfortunately, you will need to perform your cover role fully as well as your real one.

"You're going to be busy. Your VRYaN responsibility will be for the eastern half of the US - we'll discuss that when we can talk in complete privacy. Someone else, you don't need to know who, will be doing something similar in the west of the country from the consulate in San Francisco, but you're in charge of SSOD for the whole country. We already have regular contact with a number of sympathisers who can be tasked to collect specific information. You will meet some of those. In addition, you should try to cultivate sources of information yourself, but take great care. The Americans will be watching you closely, especially at first. Once they believe you're just a regular cultural diplomat they'll probably get bored with you and just follow you from time to time. We have a team of dispensable junior KGB officers who we can dangle in front of the Americans as decoys to keep them occupied and away from our real intelligence assets."

"So, who is it who's working on Operation VRYaN? If the KGB station isn't, is it just me?" He asked Leonid.

"No, it's not just you. Chairman Andropov has mobilised thousands of assets, some here in the US and others in Europe and at home; some know they're working on VRYaN, most don't. You don't need to know who else is involved. My job is to coordinate the activity here in America, and I never leave Washington for operational reasons. Even with my diplomatic status the Americans would not hesitate to use any tricks and methods to extract what I know if they suspected my true role, so as far as they know I'm a mere administrative official with additional responsibility for personnel who don't work directly for the embassy, such as yourself. You will have an allocated office here, but you don't have to use it every day. Your secretary will facilitate travel arrangements for you, as well as manage your SSOD operational budget and expenses. You should come in when you have something to communicate with me in private, or if I call you in for any reason. Other than that, you can work from home or from here when you're not travelling. Is that all clear?"

He nodded. There would be plenty of time for questions later.

"Let's go and meet Ambassador Brevnov and Minister Counsellor Kvartetov. After that we can take care of the admin."

The ambassador's office occupied a corner of the first floor of the building. It was surprisingly large, but very dark. He noticed that there was no telephone on the desk, and also that there were no windows. Ambassador Vladimir Brevnov stood to greet the visitors. He was a short man, probably in his mid-sixties. Viktor knew that he was a member of the Central Committee and a close friend of Brezhnev. He didn't smile or waste time on small talk.

"You have been sent to carry out vital work for the Soviet Union, Comrade Gumnov. The General Secretary has asked me to give you every assistance, and I will be seeing him in the next few weeks. I hope you will bring me good news on your progress so that I can share it with him. Now, if you will excuse me, I have matters to attend to."

The brief meeting was over. Minister Counsellor Boris Kvartetov had been standing beside the ambassador but had not spoken. It was Kvartetov who led them from the room to his own office nearby. If Brevnov was aloof and cold, Boris Kvartetov was the polar opposite.

"Welcome to paradise, Viktor Vladimirovich. Shall we have some tea? I saw you looking at Comrade Ambassador Brevnov's lack of telephones or windows. His predecessor was justifiably paranoid, and we know for a fact that the Americans have an observation post in a building right across the street. From the outside, the windows to his office look real but in fact they are fake. His walls are a metre thick, which is why the office is so quiet, and there is no natural light. If there was a phone in there the Americans would try to find a way to bug it, so there isn't one. He uses one we keep in a special metal box in the outer office, which is rarely unattended. We think it is beyond the prying eyes and ears of the Americans. You see, the embassy has two faces. One is for the Americans to watch, the other is just for us. Some of us, including you, are in both of them, but most of the people here are just in the one the Americans see. The ambassador was appointed by Brezhnev himself; he's a figurehead, and he likes to let people know he's well connected. The actual work of the embassy is driven by my office."

"He said the General Secretary is interested in my being here. Is this true?" he asked.

"Yes and no," Kvartetov replied, "the ambassador likes to drop the General Secretary's name into conversations. But it is true that we have been asked, if that is the right word, to give you all the help you need or ask for from a very high level within the Ministry of Foreign Affairs. It may be that Comrade Brezhnev does have a personal interest. Who knows?"

The tea arrived and the three men settled in armchairs in the Minister Counsellor's office.

"Now, work can wait. You must be tired after your journey and you need to settle your family. Leonid will take you through the admin and get you passes and such like, and also sort out your vehicle and driving permit. The Americans don't like us travelling around too much, although you will have to. Leonid will introduce you to your liaison officer in the State Department in the next couple of weeks. He'll be able to facilitate your official travel and head off any complaints from the FBI or police about having *Russkie* on their territory. You'll need to give them adequate notice of any journey further than 20 miles from Washington, except to the *dacha* at Pioneer Point. Having a liaison officer to talk to will simplify the process for you. Next weekend we're having a gathering at the *dacha*. We like to call it that, but in fact it is a huge capitalist mansion by the Chester River in Maryland. It's a little more than an hour by car. I've booked rooms for you and your family for the three-day weekend. Ambassador Brevnov will be away in Moscow for the Central Committee plenary so we can all let our hair down a bit."

Afterwards Leonid took him to the car park. There were ranks of small, quite shabby Ford sedans and a few larger, more impressive cars. One of these was a huge, stretched Lincoln limousine sporting a red hammer and sickle flag on its front wing.

"The ambassador's car, armour plated of course." Leonid commented. "This one is yours. It's brand new, delivered this morning."

Leonid was standing by a large, very shiny black Lincoln four door Town Car. He handed him the keys with a broad smile.

"I've asked one of the drivers to show you how it works and teach you to drive in Washington. It's a bit daunting until you get used to it. Now, enjoy yourself and have fun this weekend. Work starts on Monday."

He was speechless. He had never even seen a car like the Lincoln, let alone driven one. Two hours later, after a great deal of instruction from the very patient driver Denis, he was grinning from ear to ear as he piloted the huge car across the Arlington Bridge. He pulled up outside the apartment block in Alexandria and parked in his allocated space. When he showed them the car Natasha blushed quietly and Sasha squealed with excitement.

"Can we go out in it, Papa?"

They could, and they did.

Chapter 6 - Washington DC, June 1981

Leonid called at the Gumnov apartment on Friday afternoon. He was in his regular brownish compact Ford sedan, with his wife Katerina, Katya, in the front passenger seat. He was momentarily embarrassed by the opulence of his sleek and spacious Lincoln alongside the more modest transport of his boss. Leonid's grin told him he needn't worry; it was just theatre.

Leonid greeted Natasha and Sasha as if he'd known them forever, and he introduced his wife to the family.

"We've come to show you the way to Pioneer Point, the *dacha*. It isn't too far, but it's easy to get lost once you cross the Chesapeake Bay Bridge. If you take the wrong highway you'll get sucked into the places where the rich people from Washington go to shop and relax at the weekend. You'll end up broke, Viktor, but Natasha and Sasha will be happy! So, when we cross the bridge stay close to me and follow highway 301, not highway 50 to Ocean City where everyone goes by mistake at least once. We go to Centreville and then follow local roads from there. I'll make sure not to lose you."

Leonid guided them out of Alexandria and across the bridge over the Potomac. The easiest route from Alexandria took them along the 495 to the highway 50 intersection. In less than 45 minutes they were crossing the Chesapeake Bay Bridge onto Kent Island and then on to Centreville. He was glad to leave the highway and follow Leonid into Centreville itself. It was small, leafy and it looked almost artificially clean. There were very few buildings over two stories, and the predominant décor was weatherboard painted in various pastel colours. He had never seen this type of America before, having been mostly in larger cities. Centreville was certainly nothing like Alexandria, and downtown DC was another planet.

They arrived at the gates of a large mansion at Pioneer Point. Sasha was surprised to see a young Russian man, casually dressed in beige slacks, manning the gatehouse. He stated in Russian that he was KGB security and he examined their embassy passes, even though he clearly recognised Leonid and Katerina. He spoke into a radio and the gates swung open. Leonid led them to a parking area where both cars stopped.

"Welcome to Pioneer Point. I find it ironically fitting that this place was built for one of the men who created the DuPont company and General Motors, and who also built the Empire State Building. He established this place with its stables and grounds and the pool for his wife and family - he had 13 children - and he eventually died here in 1950. And what did his family do? Did they keep this as their home in his memory? No, they couldn't wait to sell it. We bought it around ten years ago, so now we can swim in his pool and keep our wine and vodka in his cellar. Americans have no sense of dynasty or history, only wealth. I'm sorry, Natasha, I'm forgetting myself, please forgive me. The steward will take you to your rooms, then Katya will show you round. I think Viktor needs to regain his sea legs so I'm going to take him out on the water. We have several boats here. I think we'll take a motorboat today. What do you say Viktor?"

They were shown to their rooms, which were in The Red House - the VIP section usually reserved for the ambassador or his guests. To his relief the surroundings were more comfortable than opulent; it was a place in which to relax. He left Natasha and Sasha to unpack and get changed. Sasha was dying to get into the large swimming pool, and unbeknown to Viktor or Natasha she had bought a new two-piece bikini for the occasion. He went off in search of Leonid, while Natasha went to find Katya, who was sitting under a parasol at a table near the pool. Katya waved her over and offered her a glass of white wine.

"This is lovely, Katya, *na zdorovie*." Natasha raised her glass and sipped the soft, delicate California chardonnay. "This is really delicious!"

"It's good to have the *dacha* to use," Katya said, "Washington can be a bit of a pressure cooker. You have to be careful all the time in case you say the wrong thing to the wrong people or do the wrong thing at work. I work at the embassy too. I understand you'll be starting on the new embassy project team next week. Didn't you know? I'm sorry to spoil the surprise, but don't worry, you'll enjoy it. There are some good people on the project. And believe me, you'll be grateful to have something to do. When we first arrived I spent six weeks in our apartment staring at the walls. I thought I'd go mad! Then Leonid arranged a job for me, helping out in personnel and administration."

"How long have you been in Washington?" Natasha asked.

"Coming up for three years now. We were in San Francisco for two years, back in the seventies. Leonid is an America specialist, but this is probably our last posting here. San Francisco is very beautiful, but the hills! So steep! And the weather is crazier than

Moscow. It's warm in the winter and cold and foggy in the summer. Full of strange people too! Lots of homosexuals and artists, and people who entertain in the street. I saw a woman once, she was juggling with live rats! Ugh."

"I don't think I'd want to see that," Natasha shuddered. "We're from the east, Vladivostok, that's where I've spent most of my life. Even when we moved to Moscow we didn't live in the city. I like visiting cities, but I've never really lived in one. Viktor likes the outdoors; he loves peace and quiet. He goes fishing a lot. He's travelled for his work, but this is his first foreign posting. He seems to find it interesting and Sasha is so excited all the time. She started at the International School last week, it's on Macomb Street near the zoo, and she's loving it. She finished high school in Moscow, so she doesn't really need to go to the International School, but we thought it would be good for her. She'll go to university when we get home; a few years in a different country is an education in itself, don't you think?"

"I do, Natasha. I wish ours had had the chance, but they're just the wrong age. The department puts them in boarding schools at home if they're younger than sixteen. Ours are fourteen and fifteen. We were late starters."

Natasha looked at Katya, who was gazing out over the pool. She was an attractive woman, maybe a few years older than her but still vivacious and bubbly. She had laughter lines round her eyes, but as Natasha studied her she saw other lines etched deep, signs of tension beneath the surface. Katya turned and reached for the wine bottle in its cooler on the table.

"Californian," Katya said. "They make the best wines in America. They have the climate, especially for whites. I still like the bite of a good Krasnodar white, and the richness of a Georgian red, but Californian will do nicely for now. Let me fill your glass."

Sasha emerged a towel wrapped around her shoulders. Katya poured her a small glass of wine. Natasha didn't mind; Sasha often tasted wine at home. What she wasn't expecting was the sight of her daughter in a revealing bikini as she dropped the towel, ran to the pool and jumped in.

"Sasha!" she gasped, even though Sasha couldn't hear her.

On the other side of the pool a group of three young men sat round a table. They were drinking beer and vodka. One of them was staring at Sasha's pale body as she swam up and down the pool. As Sasha pulled herself out onto the apron the young man stood and went towards her, a towel in his hand.

"Ilya Ivanovich," Katya called across to him, "how's your wife doing? I'm so sorry she couldn't come with you today. When's the baby due?"

The man stopped and glared at her, then returned to his seat, much to the amusement of his friends.

"You'll need to watch her. Ilya is a goat, as are most of the younger men here. Don't let any of the single ones near Sasha, and never leave her alone with a married one either! Sasha is a very pretty girl, so innocent too. You're so lucky."

******

Leonid guided him to a sturdy cabin cruiser moored alongside the *dacha's* jetty. He carried a shoulder bag, like an artist's satchel, and he climbed aboard. He busied himself in the cabin for a few minutes before emerging onto the deck. He gestured to Viktor to let go the forward mooring line as he started the outboard motor. Leonid untied the stern and deftly pointed the prow into the Chester River as he opened the throttle. Soon they were underway; he could smell the distant saltiness of the sea at the mouth of the estuary.

"Take the wheel, Viktor," Leonid called, and disappeared back into the cabin.

He came back a moment later carrying a wine cooler with a frosty bottle of Stolichnaya vodka in it, two small glasses and a tray with sliced dark bread and various smoked fish and meat slices. There was a bowl of pickled vegetables too. From his pocket he pulled a small square box which had a power lead and a red switch. He plugged it into a power outlet and pressed the switch. A hissing sound came out of it, but otherwise it didn't seem to do much.

"White noise," Leonid explained, "it's tuned to cancel out the frequency of normal speech. If the Americans have put a listening device on board all they'll hear will be humming. We can talk business safely here."

Leonid poured shots of vodka and raised his glass.

"*Na zdorovie*," said Viktor.

Leonid raised his glass.

"What did they tell you about VRYaN?" he asked, directly.

"Not very much," Viktor replied, "just that it was an important national defence project intended to assess the extent of American preparedness in the event of a conflict. I was told I'd be briefed on the specifics when I got here."

"They glossed over quite a lot," Leonid said. "Obviously they mean conflict specifically with us, the USSR. VRYaN is an acronym. It stands for *Vnezapnyoe Raketno-Yadernoe Napadenie* - 'Surprise Nuclear Missile Attack'. It's not subtle.

"Andropov has convinced Gromyko and Brezhnev that Ronald Reagan is intent on launching a pre-emptive nuclear strike on the Soviet Union. He has some supporting evidence for his theory, but we need a lot more to be sure whether Andropov is imagining it or if the unthinkable could actually happen. The Americans lost face in Iran; they'll almost certainly lose more face over Afghanistan. Reagan's economic policies are radical. If they work it will be good for the American people in the long run, but for Reaganomics, as they're calling it, to succeed a lot of poor people must lose their jobs and their homes first. Reagan needs a unifying enemy, and this is something I find personally worrying.

"We've seen threats and bluster before, but they were always just that. Now we're seeing quiet activity behind the scenes, which suggests the Americans are playing things for real, not for show. So, Andropov may be right. Your part in this is to examine and assess how prepared the Americans are along the Atlantic seaboard. Our friends in the GRU already study the US fleet, surface and submarine, but they don't look so much at the civilian side of things. Supply chains, maintenance programmes, transport infrastructure, all the secondary indications that the Americans are getting ready for war. That's where you come in. Build on our existing sources and contacts, and get more of your own, to discover this sort of thing. You were chosen because you are astute and inquisitive; you think sideways as well as up and down. We like that. But there's one more thing, or rather two more things.

"First, your glass is empty and you're not eating. Second, there is another element to your task. We need to be able to assess not only how ready the Americans are to start a war, but also how capable they are of withstanding one. Between you and me, the powers in Moscow are very worried that if a war starts, we won't be able to win it. So, we need to be sure that there *is* a way we can win, even if it means starting the war ourselves. We want you, looking at the Atlantic seaboard and the eastern states, to find weaknesses which we can exploit. Human, physical, industrial, even geological. Find us a way to win, Viktor."

He looked at Leonid, processing what he had just been told.

"What do you mean, starting the war ourselves?"

"Just that. It may come to a pre-emptive 'surprise nuclear missile attack' - VRYaN - if we are certain that the Americans are about to annihilate the Soviet Union with one of their own. If we wait too long everyone is going to die. If we start the war and don't win it, *we* are all going to die. If we can only respond with our dying breath the whole world is going to die. It could be that our only chance of survival, ours and the rest of the world's, is to start the war and win it quickly. Find us a way to do that, Viktor."

He drained his glass and refilled it. He took a piece of bread and some smoked fish, with a slice of gherkin on top. He drank and ate.

"Can we have lunch first?" he asked Leonid eventually.

Leonid laughed and turned off the white noise machine. He piloted the boat back to the dock at Pioneer Point. As they disembarked the smell of grilling meat was in the air. Some of the men had lit the barbecue in the fire pit and were busy cooking marinated lamb for *shashlik*. He looked around. There were about thirty people milling around, men and women, a few younger ones including his own precious daughter Sasha. He saw his lovely wife sitting, talking and laughing with Katya. Someone jumped in the pool. Another had put a record on the record player and *balalaika* music floated in the warm air. A stranger slapped him on the back and handed him a glass of deep red Californian cabernet sauvignon.

He thought for a moment about his parents back in Vladivostok, who he hadn't seen for three years, and about Natasha's elderly mother and her cousins. He thought about going fishing in the wilderness of Kamchatka, of the weekends at the little *dacha* near Chekhov. He was a Russian, a citizen of the Union of Soviet Socialist Republics. He would do it for his country, and for everyone and everything he loved.

Chapter 7 - Pioneer Point, MD, June 1981

Friday evening had rolled on. The *shashlik* had been good, the singing less so. Viktor and Natasha found a quiet corner together while Sasha chatted with her new friends Katya and Leonid. He observed that even with his lowly cover status as Second Secretary (Management), Leonid was held in high regard, especially by the members of the more discreet departments. Several came up to his table to exchange a few words, but they never presumed to sit alongside Leonid or his wife without an explicit invitation. Even the political enforcers who kept an eye on Party discipline and conformity deferred to him, such was the power of the head of the second, very covert, KGB station in Washington.

On Saturday morning he went for an early swim before anyone else was up and about. He thought he was alone, but when he climbed out of the pool he found Leonid waiting for him, holding a towel.

"Good morning, Viktor Vladimirovich. Another beautiful day," he said.

"Good morning, Leonid Petrovich, it is indeed. You're up early."

"I enjoy the few moments before the mayhem starts again, not that there's mayhem here, usually. You must be low on gasoline, I think. Get dressed and then let's go into Centreville for fuel and the newspapers." Despite Leonid's friendly tone, and the fact that his tank was three-quarters full, it was clearly not a mere suggestion.

"You're right, Leonid, it's a bit low. What's the rule? Never let the tank go below one third?"

"That's it. I'll have a coffee here while you're dressing."

Twenty minutes later he pointed the Lincoln down the road towards Centreville. He didn't really think of it as driving. He just sat in the comfortable seat and pointed the car where he wanted it to go, and it seemed to do the rest on its own. With his old Lada a constant war was waged between the driver, the gearbox, the engine and the steering. The dominant element always decided where, or if, the car would go. Leonid was quiet and pensive. He gave brief directions once they entered the town, then he started a vague sort of commentary. He spoke about the Queen Anne Courthouse and how the town was established in the 1780s on plantation land that had been worked by slaves. Now it was a small, affluent town in a nice part of the world.

They drove down South Liberty Street through the town centre to a gas station where they bought fuel and a selection of weekend newspapers. On the way back Leonid directed him to take a right fork and follow South Commerce Street. He pointed out the historic buildings in the town centre.

"You see in front of the Historical Society building? If you ever need to put anything in the post when you're at the *dacha* that's a convenient mailbox."

He said nothing, assuming that there was a point to what Leonid was saying. Back at the *dacha* Leonid explained once they were out of the car.

"That mailbox is a signal point for an agent, a very important agent, one who will be critical to you. He's a professional, not one of the mice. If he has something to communicate to you, he'll leave a small chalk mark on the side of that mailbox before 10 on Saturday morning. There was no mark today. If there is a mark, either you or I will see it - one of us will come to the *dacha* every Saturday for the day, if not the weekend. If there's a mark you must go to a place called Bethany Beach the next day, Sunday. Bethany Beach is on the coast in Delaware, about two hour's drive from here. You like fishing, so when you get back to Alexandria buy yourself some equipment. There's a Sears department store which is supposed to be quite good for that sort of thing. When you go to meet the agent, his code name is 'Jim', he'll come and find you if you go to the southern end of the boardwalk and find a place to fish from the beach south of that. People don't often go off the boardwalk so it should be easy to find a good quiet fishing place. I suggest you have a drive out there later today to get to know it, but I won't come with you."

"So, who's Jim, and what will he tell me?" he asked.

"He is a directable asset, a field agent. Like I said, a professional. We recruited him in Europe a long time ago and he's been a US resident for many years. He can blend in anywhere and he's very well connected with US Navy people, and a lot of others too."

"You said he wasn't one of the mice? What does that mean?"

Leonid laughed.

"People who become agents usually do it for one of four reasons: money, ideology, compromise, or ego. It spells MICE in English. None of those motivations is a guarantee that the agent won't turn against you, in fact they can be turned against you for the very same reasons, except maybe ideology - but who wants to spend time with an ideologically motivated Marxist? That's why I call recruited agents 'mice'. Jim isn't one because we recruited him in Germany after the Great Patriotic War. We saved his life. He would have certainly died, either at the hands of the allies, the black marketeers, or the Nazi dregs who were still holding out in some areas. Jim owes us everything. He also knows that he can't betray us. I won't say any more but I'll show you his file when we're back in the office."

He rounded up his wife and child and proposed a drive out to look at the ocean. Both he and Natasha were brought up by the sea, albeit the cold and remote northernmost region of Sea of Japan and the Pacific Ocean, and they missed the expanse of the water. Sasha had spent most of her young life in and around Moscow and had never seen any sea other than the Black one, which he felt was more a very big lake. She was very excited by the prospect of a real ocean. Natasha read the map while he drove. It was around 80 miles, mostly on highways festooned with billboards. They drove past towns with British-sounding names like Queen Anne, Denton, and Georgetown before turning off Highway 113 at Dagsboro (not so British-sounding) for the last few miles to Bethany Beach.

He parked in the Second Street parking lot and the family strolled along the half-mile long boardwalk, which was adorned by a handful of shops and food outlets. The place was quiet, and no one paid them much attention. The beach was expansive, edged with seaside plants in an attempt to keep the sand under some sort of control. Families and small groups were dotted around, sitting under parasols or lying on beach mats. They bought ice creams and sat on a bench, watching the rolling waves of the Atlantic. Sasha breathed in deeply, tasting the salty air.

"This is so lovely Papa, can we come here again?"

"I think that would be a good thing to do, Sasha," Natasha said. "Next time we must bring beach things and swim in the sea. I like it here; I think it will be good for fishing as well as swimming."

"OK," he said, "your wish is my command! I'll get a fishing rod for next time."

They bought hot dogs because Sasha wanted one, covered in mustard and ketchup and onions. They were pretty awful, but she loved it. After a couple of hours he said it was time to get back to the *dacha*. He had seen enough and had already identified three or four good rendezvous points for future encounters with the mysterious 'Jim'. Sasha and Natasha dozed in the car and he reversed the route. Going back to Centreville and Pioneer Point seemed to be quicker than coming to the beach, and it was just after 5pm when they pulled into the *dacha's* driveway. The younger men had clearly started drinking already, as had a few of the women - including Katya. It seemed churlish not to join them.

There was another barbecue, more *shashlik* but also shrimp and crab and fish, with salads and sweetcorn. The men were cooking and talking. The jokes about clever Russians and less clever Americans were flowing freely. They laughed loudly and drank more vodka.

Monday morning was a national holiday in the Soviet Union. It commemorated the fateful day in 1941 when Hitler had betrayed his pact with Stalin and launched an attack on Russia, effectively starting the

Great Patriotic War. In Ambassador Brevnov's absence, Boris Kvartetov and the Military Attaché had come to the *dacha* to give stirring speeches and a presentation about Soviet heroism. Attendance was compulsory. When it was all over the gathering slowly broke up and people started drifting back to Washington and a new working week.

In the embassy on Tuesday morning he first held a meeting with his SSOD staff and started mapping out a series of visits and trips to fit around current and future plans for renewed exchange programmes, academic partnerships, town and city twinning proposals and language scholarships. There were a surprising number of them, and in many places from Alaska to Florida. He was particularly interested in eastern seaboard opportunities, but also in the impending visit to Alaska by some Russian Orthodox bishops. It seemed that there was part of a tribe of native Arctic inhabitants, the Aleut, whose ancestors had inadvertently become Americans when Imperial Russia, the former owner of the territory of Alaska, sold it to the United States in 1867 for 2 cents an acre. The Aleut were ethnically and historically Russian; they still spoke an antiquated Russian regional dialect and followed the Orthodox faith, even conducting services in Russian. The bishops were always keen to grow their flock, and any visit to a new place was a pleasant diversion for them. He made a note in the file that he himself would accompany them. There was something in Anchorage he was eager to get to know more about.

At lunch time Leonid took him across the street to the University Club. The embassy had an arrangement with the club whereby diplomatic staff could obtain membership without going through the usual nomination, seconding and election procedures. He filled in the forms, paid his fees in cash and treated Leonid to lunch, his first of many at this convenient facility.

The afternoon was spent with Leonid in the subterranean vault with airtight doors, no outside communications and even its own independent power supply. They called it the dungeon, and it was the only place within the embassy that secrets could be spoken about and discussed openly.

"Tell me all about Jim," he said to Leonid, loosening his tie in the stuffy room.

"I was going to let you read it for yourself, but I might as well save you some time. He's originally a German, from the north, Hamburg. In 1945 he was in Berlin when the Red Army arrived, scraping a living on the black market. He'd been too young to be in the fascist military, but at the end of the war the Nazis were enlisting any kid over four feet tall and forcing them to fight in defence of strategic cities. Jim got caught up in that, but still kept his side-line of buying and selling whatever he could get his hands on. Even as the Third Reich was dying, the Gestapo and the SS were as determined as ever to hold on to whatever power they had. Jim was arrested and the Nazis were about to shoot him when the Red Army arrived. So Jim wasn't shot. Instead, he made friends with some of the soldiers who had saved him, and he was able to get them supplies of food, alcohol, cigarettes, women and so on. The Americans wanted to shoot him for that, as did the British and the French.

"A Major in the Red Army, who was actually one of us, saw some potential in Jim and suggested he should work for the USSR. If he chose not to, *we* would shoot him. Jim had no choice and nothing to lose.

"He joined us, quietly and without the others - the Americans, British or French - knowing about it. He went through the refugee and resettlement camps, reporting back on potential future allies and enemies for us in the new Europe. After he was 'de-nazified' he was given West German citizenship and settled in Stuttgart. He worked in the automobile industry and became an engineer, then ten or twelve years ago he had the opportunity of an engineering job here in the US. He started in Detroit, but eventually moved down to Delaware with DuPont. DuPont has lots of defence contracts and Jim has made lots of friends in the Department of Defense as well as the US Navy and the defence supply chain. He's a sociable guy. He's kept on working for us all the way through, reporting on German trade unions, identifying supporters and sympathisers in the German political system and so on. In the US he's done pretty much the same thing, and more. We've recruited several people who he's identified for us. His contacts in the military are particularly valuable to us right now, as I'm sure you'll appreciate."

"He sounds interesting," said Viktor, "I'm looking forward to meeting him. You showed me how he makes contact with me, but how do I make contact with him?"

"He's in regular contact, but if you, or we, need to see him urgently we put a small want-ad in the Delaware State News. It doesn't matter what the advert says, as long as it contains the words 'old' and 'German'. It's a daily newspaper. Two days after the advert appears he'll come to Washington. Go to Franklin Square Park, on K Street opposite the Washington Post building, and sit on a bench near the Barry statue. Jim will appear there at 11am, or within ten minutes either side, and you should follow him at a distance once you're sure he's not being tailed. If he goes into a subway station it means that he doesn't think it's safe and he's aborting. If he goes into a hotel it means he thinks it's OK and he'll find a table in the coffee shop where you can meet. If he goes into the subway make your way to Bethany Beach for 11am the next day - but be careful."

"It seems a bit one-sided, Leonid, always leaving it to him to decide where to meet."

"It's not in the text-book for sure, but it works here. Jim is good at what he does; I for one trust him. We've tested him over the years and he's never failed. We have other sources here and in Europe, and so far there's no suggestion that Jim is under any kind of suspicion or has been turned against us. If he was, we'd probably get to know. We have some very well-placed people who would tell us if the Americans thought they were on to a deep-cover Soviet agent."

"OK. I do want to meet him, and I hope he leaves a signal this weekend. I'm planning a trip next week up to New York and Boston and I'd like to meet him before that."

"New York and Boston?" Leonid asked.

"SSOD work. We have some academic exchanges coming up with Columbia University in New York, Yale in New Haven and Harvard in Cambridge. I thought I'd take the train up the coast and make a trip to introduce myself to the exchange programme teams, and take a look at the landscape, of course. I've read about a train called the Metroliner which goes all the way up the coast. It takes about three hours to New York, and I'll spend a couple of nights there. New York to New Haven isn't so far but I want to have a good look at the place, so that's probably night three. Night four will be Boston, and I'll fly back here on Friday."

"Sounds good," said Leonid, "but you'll have to clear it with your State Department shepherd first. He's a guy called Craig Durov, and he looks after cultural exchanges from the US side. He's got CIA connections, by the way, just so you're aware, but he'll fix your travel clearance. You're meeting Craig tomorrow morning at the State Department; it's at a place very appropriately named Foggy Bottom. The building is on 21st Street just south of E Street. Get to know Craig; he's not a bad guy and he likes to be helpful, and you should ask him for standing authority to go to the coast to fish without asking him every time. Say you want to go coastal fishing in Delaware and Maryland, mostly at weekends but at other times too, depending to your schedule. He should be fine with that, and he'll sign it off with the duty officer. One thing about US civil servants, though, they have very strict rules about gifts and hospitality, even accepting a cup of coffee can be a problem for them, so take it very easy to start with. They aren't being rude when they say no. They all bend a bit in the end, cold Stoli will see to that, but be patient."

Leonid looked at his watch. The afternoon had vanished.

"Talking of which, it's that sort of time. Let's get a drink upstairs in the bar."

Chapter 8 - Century House, London, June 1981

Summer had arrived in Century House, the tall and very ugly headquarters building of the British Secret Intelligence Service, otherwise known as SIS or MI6. The Soviet Section, which was always referred to as the Russia desk, had received the latest bundle of secret reports from Agent Sunbeam, a KGB officer also working for British Intelligence who was currently, and hopefully temporarily, filling an unimportant role at KGB HQ in Moscow. Sunbeam's reports were always good. He usually managed to find something interesting to talk about, something that London would want to know. This bundle of reports included some snippets emerging from the first meeting of the new Politburo, which had happened in March. A source had expressed concerns about the failing health of Chairman Brezhnev and had commented on possible succession plans. This was a matter that was never discussed in Russia, as forbidden as mentioning the possible death of Henry VIII had been in Tudor England.

The source was speculating that in second place to Mikhail Suslov, Yuri Andropov, the colourless Chairman of the KGB, was being mentioned as a possible interim Chairman and General Secretary while another more charismatic and less temporary leader was sought. The Russia desk at SIS was sceptical. Andropov, who had hawkish tendencies despite being an overt, and probably insincere, advocate of the policy of *détente*, would be a dangerous appointment - especially given the increasing animosity that President Reagan was expressing towards the Soviet Union. But this gloomy report was not what had brought sunshine into the halls of Century House. The good news was that Sunbeam was coming to London. He had been appointed to the KGB station at the London embassy, earmarked to replace the head of station, the *rezident*, who was due to move on at the beginning of 1982. The British Embassy in Moscow had received Sunbeam's diplomatic visa application, not that the clerks knew it was his, and had processed it favourably. Such was the excitement on the Russia desk they only skimmed through the rest of Sunbeam's messages, one of which commented on a sudden flurry of KGB staffing moves, something that was out of character for a routine-driven organisation. According to Sunbeam, the staffing moves were an indication that something unusual was happening, some out-of-the-ordinary intelligence operation or operations, but on a large scale. He expected to find out more in due course. Sunbeam's report mentioned some names of people involved in the KGB staffing moves, based on his observations while he was being assessed for the London role. Sunbeam's list included, among many others, the name 'Viktor Gumnov' with a note 'query Washington / USA?'. The list was delegated to an administrative assistant for routine research, as and when they had some spare time.

*****

Washington DC, late June 1981.

He got on well with Craig Durov. Durov was a middle-ranking, middle aged man wearing a cheap suit and a ready-made smile. He looked as if he should be a college professor at a small mid-West institution. They met in the State Department entrance hall and shook hands warmly.

"Hey Viktor, good to meet you," Durov said, "look, getting into this building's a nightmare. Why don't we go grab a coffee across the street?"

He readily agreed. 'Across the street' turned out to be a food kiosk not far from the Lincoln Memorial. The two men sat side by side on a bench looking at the Reflecting Pool.

"One of my favourite places in the whole of DC," Craig said, "it's particularly beautiful at night when the memorial is lit up. Of course, there's a pretty good chance you'll be mugged or shaken down if you come here after dark without a police escort, but I suppose that's the times we live in. Now, how are you finding Washington, Viktor?"

"Well, I've not been here long enough to know where to get mugged yet. We have a place over in Alexandria. My wife and daughter are here with me. My daughter, Sasha, is loving it. She's just started at the International School. My wife, Natasha, is setting up the apartment and she'll be starting work on the new embassy project in a week or two. Have you been to the Soviet Union, Craig?"

"Sadly not. I'd love to, but I'm not foreign service, even though I'm State Department. I just stay here. It's good to meet folks from all over though, especially places where Americans can't easily go, like Russia and China and East Germany. We plan to do some travelling once the kids are grown. We've got two, both in high school. We're originally from out west, Idaho, but we like it here. The work's good, even if life is a bit expensive. I'm not supposed to say that, I guess, in case you think I'm after something."

There was a bit more to this seemingly innocuous man than met the eye. He would treat him with caution, given Leonid's advisory warning about his CIA connections.

"Tell me, Viktor, what are your plans now you're here? SSOD doesn't seem to have been doing much these last few months, since your predecessor left. How's he getting on, by the way?"

"I don't know, Craig," he replied, "I've never met him. My brief is to revitalise the cultural and educational programmes, things which may have been neglected. I'm keen to restart the educational exchanges between the Ivy League and our universities in Moscow and Leningrad. I'm also interested in exploring the possibility of cultural and heritage exchanges, for example between the Aleut people in Alaska and their cousins across the Bering Strait. Theirs is a fascinating history. My family is from the north-east of Russia and there are still nomadic tribes of ethnic Aleuts living there. Some of our Orthodox bishops are planning a visit to Alaska to meet with the Aleut and other followers of the faith.

"I'm trying to set up a trip next week as long as I can get clearance from your people. I'd like to visit Columbia, Yale and Harvard. My office has set up provisional meetings with their outreach officers."

"If you let me have the details, I'll get that fast-tracked for you, Viktor."

He reached into his briefcase and extracted a slim folder with his draft itinerary and the names and contact details of people he planned to meet.

"I feel like I'm asking my parents for permission," he smiled at Craig, "but I suppose we'd do the same to you in Moscow."

"That's true, Viktor. Leonid said there was something else, something about fishing?"

"Thanks for reminding me, Craig. I like to fish, sea-fishing is my favourite. Someone at the embassy suggested that the beaches of Delaware and Maryland, out beyond the embassy recreation compound, are great for onshore line fishing. Flatfish, whiting, even small sharks. I'd love to give it a try, but it's outside the 20-mile limit. I wouldn't want to bother you every time I want to clear my head and spend a few hours on the beach, so I was wondering if there was some kind of permit I could have. You know, blanket permission for a limited area, that sort of thing?"

"I don't see why not, Viktor," Craig said, "it seems like a reasonable and harmless request. I can put it forward and let you know."

"Thanks, Craig, I appreciate that. Say," he said, "would you and your wife like to come over for a drink on Friday evening to meet my family? Nothing much, just a couple of beers and some snacks. Natasha will be thrilled to meet you. We're near the Landmark Plaza in Alexandria."

"Why, that's very kind of you Viktor. I'll ask Martha, she's my better half, but I'm sure she'll be delighted."

"Great. Let's say 5.30?"

"Sure thing. I'll give your office a call about the travel clearance, and we'll see you Friday."

The men stood and shook hands. He walked away smiling. He hadn't given the American his address, and he hadn't asked for it. It seems he knew it already.

******

A few blocks to the east, on the corner of 9th Street and Pennsylvania Avenue the weekly meeting of the joint intelligence and security group was taking place in the headquarters of the Federal Bureau of Investigation, part of which was concerned with counterespionage and national security issues. Once a week, a Special Agent in Charge chaired a meeting, usually quite brief, attended by representatives of the Central Intelligence Agency, the National Security Agency from Fort Meade out near Baltimore, and intelligence analysts and investigators from the Bureau. There wasn't much of interest this week. NSA reported an increase in encrypted traffic detection through the covert facility the Soviets thought the Americans knew nothing about. Not a huge increase, but nevertheless an indicator that something was happening.

CIA reported that there was no sign of any further increase of tensions internationally, but there had been some unconfirmed reporting about unspecified intelligence operations being initiated in Eastern Europe. Nothing for this meeting to be concerned about for now. The FBI analysts said that there had been some interesting personnel changes, including several new appointments, at both the Soviet and East German missions in Washington, and at the Soviet

Consulates and missions in San Francisco and New York. The analyst circulated a list of the relevant names to the meeting for routine research and checking out in the various databases held by each agency.

The SAC called the meeting to a close and promptly forgot all about it. Everyone left the room and the analysts' lists went on the bottom of piles to be looked at sooner or later.

Chapter 9 - Alexandria, VA, July 1981

Craig and Martha Durov arrived at the apartment at exactly 5.30. Craig carried a bottle of Californian red wine, Martha a modest bouquet of flowers. Martha was a shortish woman of about 45, quite plump and matronly, with a shy smile. She was clearly impressed with the size of the apartment but didn't mention it. Natasha had set up a table and chairs on the balcony overlooking the gardens and the pool, and had laid out a selection of Russian canapés, *blinis*, smoked fish, pickled vegetables, black bread and caviar, that sort of thing. He had a bucket of iced water in which floated a few beer bottles and a litre of Stolichnaya vodka.

"I've got something for you, Viktor," said Craig, passing a large brown envelope across the table once they were seated with drinks in front of them. "Your travel clearances for next week, and your standing authority to visit the Maryland and Delaware shore. Keep the document in your car and show it to the cops or Highway Patrol if they pull you over. They'll still report it, but they shouldn't hold you up if you show them the permit from State."

"Thank you, Craig," he said, "I appreciate it. I just love to fish; I need the peace and solitude sometimes. It helps me think and relax. Do you fish at all?"

"Me? No, I like my fish bought from the market and cooked at home by Martha. I'm not a typical American. Most of us love to shoot and hunt and fish; I'd rather be comfortable and read a book or watch a ball game with a cold beer in my hand."

"Hint taken." He passed Craig another bottle of beer. It was bland and fizzy, like most American beer he had tried. He would rather have had a *Zhigulyovskoe* beer from home which tasted of something and had a kick to it, but he was too polite to mention in.

"Are you travelling next week, Viktor?" Natasha asked.

"I'm going to see some people in New York and Boston," he replied. "I'm arranging some exchange visits with a couple of universities. I'm going on Monday, and I'll be back on Friday. Then we can go to the *dacha* if you like."

"I'd love to see New York," Natasha said, "can we go there?"

"Of course, but I'm going to be busy with work for a while. We'll arrange something in a couple of months." Viktor squeezed his wife's hand gently.

"I adore New York," Martha Durov said, "all those great stores, and the sights! You'll never forget your first sight of Manhattan."

"That's what I've heard," said Natasha, "our daughter Sasha is always going on about New York. She's out with her school friends this evening, but I'm sure you'll get to meet her."

He was rightly proud of the huge improvement in Natasha's English in just a few weeks, and by her new-found confidence speaking the language. Who would have thought a few months ago that he and his wife would be sitting on the balcony of their apartment in America drinking beer and chatting to real live Americans?

The Durovs left after an hour or so, promising to return the compliment and have the Gumnovs over to their house, which was on the other side of Arlington. Sasha came home soon afterwards, and the family agreed that a visit to the *dacha* and the coast at Bethany Beach would be a good way to spend the weekend before Viktor set off on his first trip away.

At 9 the next morning they were all in the roomy Lincoln heading for Centreville. In the trunk were fishing rods, beach mats and a parasol. He had deliberately let the fuel tank get low, so he went to the gas station for fuel and newspapers. On the way to the *dacha* they passed the mailbox. On its left side was a small dot of white chalk. Jim wanted to meet.

The *dacha* was quiet, only a handful of embassy staff were there. Sasha swam in the pool while he and Natasha read the papers and drank tea in the shade. July was warming up and it looked like it was going to be a hot summer. After a light lunch they took a boat out on the river until it was clear that Sasha was getting bored. By the time they got back Leonid and Katya had arrived, which cheered Sasha up. It was a pleasant evening and they had an early night.

On Sunday they drove to Bethany Beach. They chose a patch of sand and set up camp. Sasha went off with a handful of dollars to buy food and drink and be just like an American while Natasha went for a swim in the cool sea. When Sasha returned he said he was going to fish for a while and he walked off to the south, away from the beach in front of the boardwalk, which was fast filling up. A couple of hundred yards down he stopped and set up his rod, windbreak and a stool. He took a can of beer from his bait box and cast far out into the lapping waves. He sat contentedly and waited.

"How you doin'?" The voice belonged to a smiling man wearing the loudest Hawaiian shirt he had ever seen. "Caught anything?"

"Not yet. I've just arrived from Centreville," he said, continuing in English.

"Hey, me too. But I'm going back to Wilmington later."

This was the script he had been expecting.

"Good to meet you, Jim," he said.

"You too, Viktor, but call me Huey. Everyone else does. How are you settling in? I saw your wife and kid on the beach. They look happy enough."

"They are. We're getting on fine. What's happening?" He passed 'Huey' a beer.

"I've heard that there's a visit coming up later in the month. The *USS Saratoga* is going to be in port in Jacksonville at the same time the *Admiral Ushakov* is paying a friendly visit. The Americans do this all the time. The *Ushakov* is one of our, rather your, missile cruisers. The *Saratoga* is one of the biggest aircraft carriers the US Navy has, and it'll make your cruiser look like a rowing boat. One of my friends said that Admiral Crowe substituted the *Saratoga* for a much smaller warship that had been due to be in Jacksonville, just to make the point that size matters. They'll be having guided tours - you should go. I've heard that someone from Head Office is going to be on the *Ushakov* and he wants to see you, so you'll be there anyway. I might go along too. On these visits they always try to have a civilised drinks reception for the officers and crew from both vessels. It always ends in a fight. It's fun to watch."

"I'm going up north next week. New York, New Haven and Boston. I want to know about civil defence, supply chain resilience, fuel supplies, that sort of thing. Can you help?"

"I'll start working on it. I've got contacts at the ports in all those places. DuPont ships a lot of stuff through them. I'll let you have some names to look up, but not for next week. I guess you'll be pretty busy anyway."

"How long have you been in the US, Huey?"

"Me? Several years now."

"Do you like it?"

"Kind of. I like most of the Americans I know. Can't stand the government or the system though, or the poverty and prejudice. In the US you live with the hand your dealt when you're born. They say it's the land of opportunity, that anyone can make it. It's not true. If you get a good education and you're born in the right place and you work reasonably hard you'll probably do just fine. You'll make a decent living, get to live the American dream. The thing is you don't get a choice about where you're born or who your parents are, and to get a good education you've got to come from a family that's already made it, so living the dream is all you know. If you're a poor black kid from Birmingham or Baltimore or the Bronx the chances are you're going to live there all your life and die there as a poor black adult. If you're a rich kid and you're born out on Long Island you're going to live just about any place you want and live there very comfortably. Every now and then you get someone who says they're 'self-made'. There are a few of them, but only a few. There's more social mobility in Europe than here, not that that's saying much."

"So, you think life in the Soviet Union is better?"

"Don't start, Viktor. That's a whole other issue. I work for you guys, but I'm German, a European. I had my fill of totalitarians with Adolf and his bunch."

"OK, let's talk more about America. What do you think of Reagan?"

"The cowboy film star? He's popular, comes across well and he can talk to people. He's a communicator. He's also a Republican, which means he's out to look after the rich people. Democrats are too, of course, but they're more discreet about it. What worries me about Reagan is his economics. He's free market, with a capital 'free'. That means survival of the fittest, pure and simple. A lot of people who aren't so fit are going to fall by the wayside through no fault of their own. That's not so unusual for this country, but Reagan wants to do a lot in his four or eight years, no time for gradual changes. He's going to need to keep people on his side while he's throwing them out of their jobs and cutting their welfare. I think he's going to scare them into supporting him, which is where your team comes in. Reagan's going to make Americans so scared of what your side wants to do to them that they'll support him, whatever he does."

"You have some very strong opinions, Huey."

"Like I said, I've lived here a while. You've been here a few weeks; pretty soon you'll think like me." Despite his words, 'Huey' hadn't stopped smiling while he spoke.

"Let's talk about fishing and the coast," he said, changing the subject, "what are the seasons like?"

"Short hot summers, short cold winters. Spring and fall are really beautiful, the best times to be here. But with the heat and the cold we get extremes. Snow and ice storms in the winters - they can knock out power supplies and close the highways for days at a time. Some very small towns get cut off for months, but they get used to it. They're resilient. In the hotter weather we get the storms, the hurricanes. Hurricane season can run from June through to November, but it peaks around August and September. It's worst south of here, the Carolinas and Florida, the Gulf of Mexico, but storms can come north, even up to New Jersey. Tropical storms and hurricanes do a lot of damage. Whole towns get ripped up, flattened by the wind and flooded out. It's like an H bomb going off."

"How do people manage?" He reeled in and recast, listening all the while.

"They get used to it. State and federal government in regions where they get hit frequently are quite good at recovery, but it's a question of scale. One or two small towns they can handle; a big city would be a different matter. You know, New Jersey is the most populous state in the US. Five years ago Hurricane Belle hit Atlantic City. A quarter of a million people had to be evacuated from the seaboard area, there was about a ten-foot storm surge and the whole place was flooded out for days. Damage was in the tens of millions of dollars, just from one storm, and it took them months to get over it. Something like that in a big place, like Philadelphia or even New York City, would be a national disaster. Look, I've got to go. Let's meet again in a couple of weeks, I'll leave the mark. Good talking to you."

'Huey' drained his beer and gave the can back to Viktor. He gave a mock salute and wandered off, whistling tunelessly. He reeled in his line again. Unsurprisingly he hadn't caught anything. He packed up and strolled back to Natasha and Sasha. He was surprised to see Sasha standing very close to a tall young man wearing beach shorts and a tee shirt. They were looking at something in a bucket, talking earnestly to each other. He went over to them.

"Hi Papa," Sasha said, "Steven's showing me a horseshoe crab he's found. He thinks it's exhausted or something so he's resting it in this bucket for a while. Have you ever seen anything so strange?"

The boy Steven looked up. He was slim, with reddish hair and freckles. He smiled and nodded at him.

"It's not really a crab, even though it's called one. It's an arthropod, which means it has a bendy shell, and it's more like an underwater beetle. It's an ancient species, they were here before, during and after the dinosaurs. I was telling your daughter about them. Oh, sorry. I haven't introduced myself. I'm Steven Rourke, I'm studying marine biology and science at university in Boston and I'm working down here in Bethany for the summer."

"Viktor Gumnov, I'm with the Soviet Government." He shook Steven's hand. "I'm a marine scientist myself, by training, we should talk about what you're studying."

"Soviet? Wow, that's cool! Lexa didn't say. I knew she sounded foreign, but I thought maybe she's from Europe." Steven grinned broadly, and he started talking about the sea. Sasha was gazing at him, not hearing a word.

"Lexa?" he said as they walked away.

"I like Lexa," said Sasha.

He smiled to himself. His little girl was growing up.

Chapter 10 - New York City, July 1981

He picked up a taxi outside the apartment block at 6am on Monday morning. The cab was a DC one rather than an Alexandria or Arlington one, and as usual the driver was from Africa. He'd heard that just about all the taxis working nights in DC were driven by Ethiopian refugees; they were the only ones willing to risk the lawless streets of the capital of the free world after dark. He asked to be taken to Union Station. As always, the fare was $17 and also as always the driver didn't have any change. He was getting used to it.

The Metroliner is the fast train between Washington and New York. It hugs the coastline up through Wilmington and Philadelphia and goes through the heavily industrialised sprawl of northern New Jersey. The terminus was Pennsylvania Station in midtown Manhattan and the journey took less than three hours.

His first impression of Manhattan was overwhelming. Firstly, there was the noise, sounds of engines, horns, drills, whistles, sirens. Then there was the sheer size and height of everything. Buildings loomed up like giant geometric trees trying to thrust their concrete limbs into the sunlight far above them. Looking up at their slab sides he felt a sense of vertigo, almost panic. Then there were the people. Thousands of them, all hurrying this way and that, many eating sandwiches or drinking from tall paper cups, nearly all - male and female - wearing city suits with incongruous sports shoes in bright colours. His turn came and he collapsed into a battered yellow cab. The driver didn't acknowledge his presence or speak in any way, he just sat there. He looked at the name badge on the scratched plastic screen separating him from the driver. There was a blurred picture that could have been anyone; a photograph of the back of an angry-spotted neck would have been more useful. The name on the badge was Middle Eastern.

"Loews Hotel, on Lexington," he mumbled, temporarily rattled by the Big Apple.

"Which block?" the driver grunted.

"What?"

"Which block? The hotel? Lex is one-way going south. Which cross-street?"

He barely understood the words.

"I don't know. You're the taxi driver, it's your city."

"I'll go to Downtown and come back down Lex. You pay the meter. No' my fault you don't know where you goin'." The driver finished his short speech with something guttural, which he assumed must be some sort of insult.

What a place, he thought. He sat in silence as the cab turned right, stopping and starting at endless red traffic lights that seemed to be placed every 50 yards. He looked up at the Empire State Building as they passed alongside it; it was dizzyingly tall. After more than 40 minutes the cab jerked to a halt outside a hotel on Lexington Avenue that was shabbier than he had been expecting. He paid the exorbitant fare, more than $40, with a $50 bill. He knew there would be no change coming.

Inside the hotel it was like entering a slightly worn oasis. The receptionist welcomed him with a broad smile and she completed the registration process efficiently. His room wasn't ready yet, but he was welcome to leave his suitcase with her if he wanted to go out. He took her up on the offer and asked her for a map of Manhattan, and where could he get the Circle Line boat tour.

"It goes from Pier 83 on the West Side, on the Hudson River. It's between 42nd and 43rd. I'd say walk it, it's a nice day. Take a left out of the hotel and follow Lex until you get to the Chrysler Building, then take a right on 42nd Street. It takes you right up past Bryant Park and the library - a wonderful building - past Times Square and just keep going until you get to the river. Pier 83 will be on your right."

He thanked her and set off, grateful to be able to stretch his legs. The walk was good, it helped him get a measure of the city, come to terms with its size, chaos and energy. He paused at a sandwich shop, a deli, and after making some sense of the alien menu he ordered a turkey sandwich on sourdough bread and a coffee. The sandwich must have been 10 centimetres thick, with a wad of thinly sliced tasteless chilled white meat crammed into it. The dill pickle gave it a slight redeeming flavour, but only just. The coffee was appalling. He sat watching people, enjoying himself in spite of his lunch. He arrived at Pier 83 just in time to catch a departing round-Manhattan cruise, which would take about two and a half hours.

It was fascinating. He was absorbing information about this city, its buildings and its people. He was starting to understand its geography, and to see its strengths and weaknesses. The tour went anti-clockwise, down the Hudson to the southern tip of Manhattan, where Wall Street and the World Trade Center were, out to the Statue of Liberty from where he could see the commercial port of New York and New

Jersey. The port was vital to the economic health of the country, as were Wall Street and the Financial District. Rounding the statue and heading back towards the East River he looked south and saw the crammed-in houses of Staten Island and Brooklyn. In the distance he saw the borough of Queens and he saw planes landing and taking off from JFK airport. None of it was more than a few feet above sea level.

Up the East River and the boat captain was giving his learned and detailed commentary to the forty or so passengers.

"Some people wonder about the skyline," the captain was saying, "they wonder how so many tall buildings can be squeezed together in such a small space. If the buildings are so tall, how deep are the foundations? Well, the answer lies in Manhattan's geology. Millions of years ago two continental plates collided just about where we are today. The collision caused incredible heat, melting rock so that new, very hard dense rocks formed. These rocks settled in tight layers, and they're known as schist. Specifically, the bedrock here is called Manhattan schist, and across the island there are outcrops real close to the surface. You can see where they are because that's also where the skyscrapers are. The rock is solid enough to take the weight of these huge buildings, and to protect them from earthquakes. The Empire State Building is over 1400 feet tall, for any European folks on board that's about 440 metres, but its foundations are a mere 50 feet, or 17 metres. The schist enables that to work safely.

"The skyline of Manhattan is so spectacular because the skyscrapers are clustered together in bunches. It makes them look good, but it's also because the schist isn't everywhere. If it was there would be nothing but skyscrapers here. As it is, most New York buildings are much smaller and lighter. In Greenwich Village, for example, most buildings are just two or three storeys. That's because where the schist beds were formed when those tectonic plates collided there were gaps, fault lines, which formed deep cracks where the schist layers fall away sharply. At one time Manhattan was a lot of small schist islands with mud in between them. That mud became sedimentary rock, which is soft and friable, and prone to movement and erosion. It isn't strong enough to support the weight of tall thin buildings. There are concerns still that any significant seismic activity would probably unsettle the sedimentary layers and cause massive destruction in the low-rise areas, while most of the skyscrapers would stay upright. Mind blowing, isn't it?"

He was listening intently. The captain went on to describe the development of New York from a rural farming settlement - the Bronx was once a farm belonging to a family of that name - into one of the two most populous cities in the United States and probably the most famous city in the whole world. While it was certainly home to the rich and famous, it was kept running by ordinary working folks who lived in the poorer suburbs and over on the Jersey side. The city depended on these people getting to and from work.

The captain pointed out Gracie Mansion, where New York's mayor had his official residence as they forked left up the Harlem River. At the northern tip of Manhattan he commented on the huge New York subway train marshalling yards at 201st Street, and the massive sanitation plants that took care of the detritus of Manhattan's millions. He could see that the north end of Manhattan was a very different place to Mid-Town or the Financial District. He would be up this way again tomorrow visiting Columbia University, which was sited north of Harlem, and he was expecting a colourful day.

He was reflecting on the captain's words as they steamed briskly down the Hudson towards Pier 83. The captain didn't seem to have much to say about Harlem and the West Side. As they slowed near Pier 83 the captain took to the microphone again.

"Over there, behind the cruise liners, is one of the most notorious neighbourhoods in the whole of New York City. In the last century it was a horrendous lawless slum, populated entirely by Irish immigrants. It's called Hell's Kitchen. These days it's very arty and there's a thriving gay scene if anyone's interested. In the 19th Century it was murderous; even the police wouldn't go there - most of them were Irish anyway so they probably had a good idea of what the place was like. Strangers wandering into the area would never be seen again, they'd be robbed and killed. Life was hard and short. It wasn't much better until ten or fifteen years ago when people started seeing some commercial value in the loft apartments they created there in the older buildings. The Irish who still lived there and ran the neighbourhood were paid off to move out so Californians and Europeans could move in. It's still called Hell's Kitchen, but with pride now. No one really knows how the place got the name, but it does conjure up an image that seems to say it all. Anyhow, that's all from me, folks. You be sure to have a nice day and enjoy your visit to the Big Apple."

He made his way back to the hotel. Had he known he'd be walking through a place called Hell's Kitchen to get to the Circle Line he probably wouldn't have gone. Sometimes knowledge is an impediment, he decided. He had found the afternoon extremely interesting. He almost felt that he no longer needed to visit the outreach professor at Columbia University tomorrow after all, but he decided to keep the appointment anyway. What he had learned and seen already was leading him inexorably towards a way to fulfil his mission of finding the means by which the Soviet Union could win an unprovoked war against the United States.

He ate alone in silence in the hotel restaurant, still quite full and queasy after his deli lunch. He chose grilled shrimp, which were tasteless and the size of small lobsters, and sole, which came as an entire fish, but covered in some slightly sweet sticky sauce. A Californian pinot grigio helped mask the taste, and he was upstairs in his small room by 9pm. He called Natasha and chatted inconsequentially for a few minutes. All was well at home. She was looking forward to seeing him on Friday.

He said goodnight and hung up. In his cubicle at Headquarters in Washington the FBI agent made a brief note of the call to the target number in Alexandria and put the sheet of paper in a tray to be collected and typed up as and when. He had no idea who, if anyone, would ever read it.

Chapter 11 - Boston, MA, July 1981

He took a seat in the domestic departure area of Boston's Logan Airport. He'd bought a green tea from a coffee stall and he took a few moments to reflect on his trip, which had been interesting and rewarding but also exhausting. The final leg, the flight to Washington, was proving to be quite stressful. He wasn't a frequent flyer; to him there was still a mystique about the whole process of air travel. Here in the US, domestic flights were regarded in much the same way as a bus ride, and he found the casualness of it all a bit disturbing. He had another forty minutes before his flight boarded. It was a short flight, not much more than an hour or so in the air, to Washington's National Airport, which itself was only a ten-minute cab ride from his Alexandria apartment. He would be at home with Natasha by 6pm.

The first part of the trip to New York seemed a distant memory, although it was only a few days ago. On Tuesday he had risen early, woken by the harsh sounds of a midtown Manhattan morning. After a light breakfast he found a taxi on Lexington Avenue and he directed it to the main campus at Columbia University, on the Upper West Side at 114th Street and Amsterdam, or 10th, Avenue. The ride was remarkably civilised. They went uptown to Central Park and crossed over to the West Side. The journey took less than 20 minutes and he was pleasantly surprised to see that the fare was less than the usual $17 and he got change. He willingly gave the driver a $2 tip. The neo-classical splendour of Columbia stunned him. Off to the right he saw the crumbling slabs of Harlem's tenements; the graffiti, garbage and general decay of a deprived area which, in places, verged on the squalid. In contrast, Columbia's marble façade gleamed; its grass squares and quads and fountains were dotted with neat benches topped with well-polished students. The place reeked of wealth and privilege. He presented himself at the reception desk and asked for the professor in the Slavic studies department he was scheduled to meet. When he appeared, smiling broadly, he turned out to be a youngish-looking man in his thirties wearing a once smart and expensive jacket above blue jeans and brown suede boots. He was wearing a grey tee shirt emblazoned with the famous portrait of the deceased self-promoting Argentinian egotist Che Guevara. He could see why people like Guevara and Trotsky *et al* died violent deaths at the hands of people who should have been on their side. He hadn't known either of them personally, but he knew they would have been incredibly irritating.

The professor was impractically enthusiastic about cooperating with the Soviet Embassy to establish an exchange programme of mutual benefit. He gushed about the importance of international ties, and about the undying friendship between the US and the USSR that would inevitably emerge from the proposed exchanges. The professor concluded by inviting him to hold tutorials with his students any time he was passing. He had been pleased to leave.

The train ride to New Haven the following morning was short. He found the town to be pleasant and unhurried, and he was interested to see the port area facing onto Long Island Sound with its deep-water berths and many petroleum product tank farms. Yale

University was more self-effacing than Columbia, but not much. Again it boasted expansive open spaces and grand buildings, but with a more colonial feel to them. His welcome here was very different from Columbia. Instead of the esteemed professor he was expecting, he found himself subjected to an interview with a kind and matronly lady who ran the administration office of the Humanities School, which encompassed Slavic studies. She listened intently and made notes. After half an hour she said she would discuss his visit with the Dean at their next meeting and thanked him for coming. He decided not to waste a night in New Haven.

Back on the train, this time bound for Boston. He arrived in the late afternoon; the July heat was rising and the air was warm. He took a cab from South Station to his re-booked hotel on Boylston Street on the south side of Boston Common. The room was comfortable and more spacious than the one he'd had in New York. He dropped his bag, asked the receptionist for a map of the area and set off for a walk. Boston was easy to navigate, as well as being attractive and relaxed. He wandered past the tiny ancient church at the end of the Common, its image reflected in the mirror-glass side of a towering office building, and he headed for the waterfront.

He heard and smelt Faneuil Hall Market before he saw it. Music and voices filled the air; the aroma of cooking fish and meats wafted temptingly. He came upon a vast area full of bars, restaurants and food stands. People strolled, sat on benches and at tables; street musicians wandered among them playing and singing. He found that he was enjoying himself; he knew Sasha would adore it. He bought himself a cardboard tray of a spicy fried rice dish and a cold beer, and he had the best meal of the trip so far, sitting in the early evening sunshine listening to an *a cappella* vocal band and just watching all the people. He liked this place.

After a decent night's sleep he took a taxi across the Charles River to Harvard. Less showy than either Columbia or Yale, Harvard was nevertheless an impressive place. He found the Faculty of Arts and Sciences, which seemed to him to cover just about everything, and asked for the Slavic Languages and Literature professor he was scheduled to meet. The man was quite a lot older than he was, conservatively dressed and with a twinkle in his eye.

"So, Mr Gumnov, you're from the Soviet Embassy? You'll be with the VOKS, or whatever they call it these days."

"It's been the SSOD for quite a while now, but it's the same sort of thing."

"Ah, yes. I remember now. We say it stands for 'Secret Spies On Duty'. Just joking, of course, I'm sure you're not really with the KGB or anything."

The professor was toying with him, and he found himself warming to the man. They went to his room where he made them proper coffee and they talked for well over an hour. They agreed that it would be good to develop a programme of activities that could complement the curriculum for undergraduates as well as advance the studies of post-graduate students. On the matter of exchanges the professor was more reserved, saying it would have to be thought through and discussed at length. They shook hands and agreed to talk again soon.

"You should take some time to see Boston while you're here, Mr Gumnov," the professor said, "it's a very interesting revolutionary city. You can get a good sense of the geography from the top of the Prudential Tower; there's an observation deck and you can see for miles. I'll give you the name of a friend of mine down at U Mass, the University of Massachusetts. They have some interesting programmes there and you might get some traction speaking to them. Don't go near MIT, though, they're so tied up with the government they wouldn't let you in anyway."

He'd taken the advice and made his way back to Boston and the Prudential Tower. True enough, the observation deck at the top of the building gave him a panoramic view of the harbour, the airport, west and south Boston all the way down to Roxbury. All of it was low-lying, and vital to the survival of the city and the state. He decided to leave a visit to U Mass until the next time. He explored the city, did the Boston Tea Party tour, and killed time usefully until the next day when it was time to go home.

His flight was called, and he queued up with the other passengers to board the flying bus. The flight was uneventful; he watched the landscape unfold beneath him as they flew back to Washington. He had missed Natasha.

The apartment was full of cooking smells. Natasha poured him a drink, which he took out to the balcony. She joined him.

"Is Sasha out?" he asked.

"She's gone to see a film, a movie she calls it, with some school friends. She'll be back soon. She can't wait to hear about your trip, nor can I, especially New York."

"It's certainly a different sort of place. It takes some getting used to. I liked Boston, though, more than the last time I was there with the delegation years ago. We must put it on the list for a family visit as well as New York."

"Why do they call it 'The Big Apple'?" Natasha asked.

"I don't think anyone really knows," he said, "I've heard it might be an African American term for a city, or that it's just an advertising trick. It suits the place, though. You can imagine it as a huge piece of fruit, with some nice-looking bits and a few maggot holes. Do you want to go to the *dacha* or the beach tomorrow?"

"I said I'd go to the Smithsonian with Katya, but you go if you want. Take Sasha, I know she's very eager to go to Bethany again. There's that boy there, remember?"

"Steven? Is that his name?"

"You know it is!"

At that moment Sasha burst back into the apartment, chattering away about the *amazing* movie she had just seen: 'Raiders of the Lost Ark' with Harrison Ford. She paused to kiss her father hello and draw breath.

"How was your trip, Papa?" she asked eventually.

He started to talk them through the touristy parts of his journey, delighted to see that both his wife and his daughter were gripped by his descriptions. By the time he had finished Sasha was begging to go to New York first, then Boston.

The cumulative fatigue of the week caught up with him and the whole family took to their beds quite early. The next morning he was drinking tea in the kitchen when the phone rang. It was Leonid.

"Good morning, Comrade First Secretary," he said formally, "I'm sorry to disturb you on a Saturday. I hope your trip went well. I'm down at the *dacha* and I had a thought driving through Centreville. Could you please remember to bring all your receipts to the office on Monday? The accounts need to be sent off."

"Very well, Comrade Second Secretary. I'll see you on Monday." He hung up.

The message was disguised. It could only mean that Leonid had seen Jim's mark on the mailbox. In the whole of the Soviet Union the only people who did not need to submit receipts in triplicate were KGB officers on covert assignments overseas. Not only were they not required to produce receipts, they were actually forbidden from keeping them. The powers that be thought, quite rightly, that receipts and credit card slips were an easy trail for inquisitive foreign agencies to follow when they were looking for Russian spies.

"Sasha," he called, "do you want to go to the beach this afternoon? Your mother's going out with Katya and we can stay overnight at a hotel in Bethany."

By way of reply he heard a shriek of delight.

They drove down and booked into a small hotel a few streets back from the shore. It was clean and comfortable. As soon as they had checked in Sasha rushed off to find Steven, saying she would be back by 6.

On Sunday morning they both walked down to the boardwalk. He had his fishing rod, Sasha a couple of books and a sunhat. They found Steven almost immediately and he promised to look after Sasha, or Lexa as he kept calling her. He was a happy man as he strolled off to the south to find a quiet spot from which to fish while he listened to what his secret agent had to tell him.

'Jim' showed up at 11.

"Hey, Viktor. Good to see you again. How ya doin'?"

"Huey! What a surprise! How was your week?"

They carried on in this vein for a few minutes until they were sure no one was interested in them, then he pulled a couple of beers from his bait box.

"Cheers, Viktor," Huey said. "I've been asking around, about civil defence and emergencies. I said I was concerned about the hurricane season and the winter ice storms. The weather folks say both might be bad this year. I spoke to people I know in the navy and others up at City Hall in Wilmington. They're part of the north-east emergency management set up. What I heard, though not in explicit terms, was that emergency preparedness in the north-east USA is pretty fragile. Budgets are tight, especially with the economic situation, and they're having to let staff go. The smaller cities in the north-east can cope with a single incident affecting one of them, or at the most two, by combining resources like fire trucks and paramedics and engineers to support each other. Any more than two cities affected at the same time and they're screwed. They'd need to get federal support, and there isn't much of that.

"Their nightmare scenario is a series of tropical storms, not even hurricanes, hitting in quick succession starting in the south in Florida and moving up through the Carolinas. Flooding and storm damage along the coast as far as Cape Hatteras would eat up all the capacity there is along the whole eastern seaboard. If the storms continue into Virginia, Delaware, or New Jersey it's a major disaster. And God forbid a few big storms hit New York! It's happened before. My people say it could take several months, years even, to get back to any sort of normal. The scary thing is they're putting the odds on it happening at around twenty percent. It used to be a once in a century probability, now with weather patterns changing it's more like once every five years, and with limited resources... I don't know why you want to know about this, Viktor, and I'm not going to ask. But the people I spoke to are scared about this sort of thing. It keeps them up nights."

He had been listening carefully while baiting his hook and casting.

"Anything else on the naval visit to Jacksonville later this month?" he asked.

"No. I'm still thinking about going though. There'll be crowds, and that's good cover for catching up with some people who I'd rather not be seen talking with. Leonid can tell you about it. Will you be going down to Florida?"

"It's been a long time since I was on one of our navy ships. I want to remind myself about how bad they smell. I'll certainly be there."

"I'll be sure to say hi if I see you," Huey grinned. "Any more beer?"

Chapter 12 - Washington DC, July 1981

He and Leonid were in the dungeon where conversations could take place. He'd filled Leonid in on his trip and discussed some of his thoughts about fulfilling his mission. There was still a lot of thinking and talking to do before any proper plan could be formed. Leonid listened intently.

"I think you're right," Leonid said, "the east coast of the US is their weak underbelly. It has large cities and populations, as well as industry and finance and communications. Also, it's the seat of government. With the east coast out of action, the US is out of action. Let's take this further over the next few months. In the meantime, have you made plans for your Florida trip, your day out with the two greatest navies in the world?"

"Whose is the other one?" He laughed. "I've sent the travel request to Craig over at the State Department. He seems to be cooperating well."

"His friends at the CIA and FBI like it that way. It makes it easier and cheaper to keep tabs on you, on all of us."

"I haven't decided whether to fly or drive down to Florida. What do you suggest?"

"Fly! Driving takes forever and the roads are full of mad old Americans who retire to the south. They call them snowbirds, mostly because they've all got white hair but also because they fly south for the winter. They've all forgotten how to drive, at least with any regard to other people."

"Jim said there was someone from head office travelling on our ship."

"Yes, a Lieutenant General from the *Gruppa konsul'tantov pri Predsedatele KGB,* Andropov's own think-tank. It looks like he's given VRYaN planning and execution to them rather than the First Chief Directorate. He won't be using his own name, of course, but he's Sergei Baranov; I know him well. I've had a message instructing you to make yourself known to the Officer of the Watch who will be at the top of the gangplank, he'll tell you where to find Baranov. You just say to the officer 'It's not this sunny in Murmansk', nothing else. Not your name or where you're from. Clear?"

"Completely. Will you be there?"

"No, no need, no cover."

"Tell me more about 'Jim'. He seems to know a lot more than a field agent should. How did he know about 'someone from Head Office' being on the *Admiral Ushakov*?"

"He's more than just a field agent, Viktor. He's probably our most valuable long-term asset in the US. He's built up and runs his own network of agents, and he has his own communications with the Centre that don't come anywhere near the Washington *rezident.* Head Office keeps me informed, though. Most of Jim's people have no idea they're working for us. Some have no idea they're working for him, come to that. One thing, though, Jim knows nothing about VRYaN or about the real reason you're here. As far as he's concerned, you're my deputy in the covert station with the job of maintaining contact with him. Jim will take instructions from you, but he'll also do his own thing. He doesn't need to ask you or me for permission. He knows that if he blows it, it's down to him, no links back to us and no support either. If he goes to jail for anything he knows he's going to stay there. He's not going to appear on any swap list of captured agents."

"I met with him on Sunday, down at Bethany Beach after your call on Saturday. I'd asked him to do some digging on disaster management and preparedness up and down the coast. He's good. The answers were just what I needed. The east coast is fragile, and the powers that be know it and can't do a thing about it. Jim said it keeps them up at night."

"Good. Did you go there and back in a day?"

"No. Natasha was busy with Katya, as you know. I took Sasha. She's found a boy she likes. Steven Rourke. Nice kid, Irish origin I think, about 18 or 19. He said he's a marine biology student in Boston but works at Bethany as a beach patrol in the summer. Can we check him out?"

"Sure," Leonid made a note, "be careful, though. You know Head Office doesn't like us or our families getting too close to the locals on a personal level."

"Tell that to a 16-year-old girl with bouncing hormones and a head full of romantic ideas!" He chuckled, but he did understand the problems it could cause if a relationship did develop between the daughter of a serving KGB officer in the field and a US national.

"Right," he said, "I've got to get on. I need to organise some educational visits, and we've got the bishops coming to Alaska."

"OK," said Leonid, "by the way, has Natasha started work here yet?"

"This morning; I drove her in. She's very happy about it. She loved her day with Katya on Saturday, but she's starting to go stir crazy."

"Good, she'll need some distractions. I think you'll be away quite a lot until your VRYaN task is done. After that you'll find your SSOD work will move up a notch. Head Office has told us to get more involved with political intelligence. I'd like you to get to identify and develop some political contacts with the administration. With your time on the US desk in Moscow they, and I, think you can add a lot of value."

"Thank you for the vote of confidence. I was starting to wonder how keeping a bunch of bishops sober and out of the strip clubs in Anchorage constituted a valuable contribution to Soviet foreign policy. See you later."

******

A little after 4pm he went in search of Natasha.

"I thought we'd pick Sasha up," he said when he found her, "and let you have a look at the site on the way. I'll see you in the lobby in ten minutes."

Sasha was waiting near the International School entrance on Macomb Street. She looked distracted, not her usual sunny self. She got into the car but said little as they drove back towards Wisconsin Avenue. There was little to see at the site of the new embassy, just a boarded off piece of land, so he steered them all back across the river and home to Alexandria. He got a beer and took his usual seat on the balcony, enjoying the summer evening air. Sasha joined him while Natasha started making dinner.

"What's the matter?" he asked her.

"Am I stupid, Papa?" Sasha asked.

"What do you think?" he asked her back.

"I didn't think I was."

"Why do you ask? Has someone said you're stupid?"

"No. But I'm worried Steven might think I am."

"Has he tried to do anything to you?" He was concerned.

"No, nothing like that! I can take care of myself when it comes to boys. It's just that he gave me a book on Sunday. It's a kids' book, very silly, all about talking farm animals. He must think I'm stupid if he gives me a book about talking animals!"

He didn't know whether to be pleased or disturbed that his little girl 'could take care of herself when it came to boys'.

"What book is it?" he asked.

"It's here," she showed him, "it's called 'Animal Farm'. It's in English."

He smiled when he saw it.

"I've read this. It's not a kids' book, Sasha. It's by George Orwell, an English writer. His real name was Eric Blair, and he died a long time ago. You don't know the book because reading it isn't encouraged at home. Orwell was a socialist, but not like in our system. He was part of a movement known as democratic socialism. The book is what is called an allegory."

"What's that?" she asked.

"It's like a metaphor, or a fable. The message of the story is hidden inside it. The story is supposed to represent our revolution in 1917. The farmer is the old tyrannical Tsar Nicholas, and the humans in the story are the royal family. The farm animals all stand for the different revolutionaries, except the big carthorse, Boxer, who is supposed to be the proletariat, the people. The pigs represent the revolutionary leaders. The nasty one, Napoleon, is supposed to be Stalin, and the rats are chekists, the secret police. There's one line in it about equality, it says something like all animals are equal, but some are more equal than others. You can see why the authorities at home don't like it, can't you? The Americans wouldn't like a book that portrayed George Washington as a warthog or Lincoln as a vulture. It's a long time since I read it, so I forget some of the details. Why did Steven give it to you?"

"He said I might learn something from it. Which is why I thought he was saying I'm stupid."

"I suggest you give it back to him, but read it first and understand it, then you can discuss it with him. We can go back to the beach at the weekend, and you can see him then. It's good that you know about books like this; you should read the ones that aren't encouraged when you're a bit older and you can make your own mind up about them." He squeezed her hand.

He himself was an avid reader. His privileged position had given him access to marvellous books. He particularly liked French philosophers and wished his French was good enough to absorb Voltaire in his very original form. Now *there* was someone who understood allegory.

Later that night he was alone with Natasha.

"What do you think about Sasha and the boy Steven?" he asked.

"I think she's a young girl who is just becoming interested in boys. I think she'll get tired of him by the end of the summer and move on to someone else when the time is right."

"I hope you're right. It'll be difficult if she gets too attached to him. The office will disapprove - a lot. Goodnight, Nata." He turned off the light.

Chapter 13 - Jacksonville, FL, July 1981

He stepped off the plane at Jacksonville International and a wall of heat hit him like a hammer. In Washington that morning the humidity was building, here it had already built. He felt sweat form in the small of his back, despite his light cotton shirt and tropical weight linen jacket. The air-conditioning in the terminal building was a welcome relief, albeit a brief one. He waited in line for a cab along with a lot of other people who had come to 'Jax' to see the warships. A few other embassy staff were also due to visit the *Admiral Ushakov*, but he had chosen to travel separately in anticipation of some lively interest from the FBI and Defense / Naval Intelligence people.

As his taxi neared the Mayport Naval Base he saw the flags and banners proclaiming US / Soviet friendship, almost as if they meant it. The taxi was directed to an area temporarily set aside for the civilian invasion of the facility and he was dropped near the quayside. The *USS Saratoga* dominated the dockyard, a huge grey mass beneath acres of flight deck. It seemed ungainly and unbalanced, as most aircraft carriers do, and there was no doubt it was an intimidating sight.

He strolled around for a while, buying an iced soda from a stand and taking in the crowds. There were thousands of people there of all ages. Some with families and children, others wearing parts of old naval uniforms and medals on their blazers. He caught sight of the *Admiral Ushakov* moored on a smaller quay adjacent to the American monster. It was nearly two-thirds the length of the *Saratoga*, but with its lack of beam and height it seemed tiny in comparison. He was half-expecting to see his beach friend Huey and was looking for one of his characteristically garish shirts. There were many of them, but none on Huey. He didn't seem to be there.

He joined the queue to board the *Saratoga* on a guided tour. As a former naval officer, he had some residual professional interest in the ship and was curious to see just how many secrets the Americans had left on show. He was marshalled into a group of twenty others to be led by a young cadet officer up the gangway. The first thing that struck him was that every inch of space was utilised on the massive ship. Aviation fuel was stored in vast tanks welded to decks and ceilings, even above sleeping berths. There was no privacy anywhere except in the washrooms. Every section of the vessel was colour-coded according to function, so the engineers and engine room personnel had their own living and working area, as did the flight-deck crews, the aviators, the bridge teams, the weaponry officers and crew and so on. Even in port the noise was continuous and invasive, and he could only begin to imagine how it would wear you down if you were confined on board for any length of time. He guessed it would have been similar on the Soviet ships he had served on years before, but he had no clear recollection.

The climax of the tour was a visit to the flight control room where there were banks of screens showing images of the hangars and the flight deck, as well as a huge map table. The chart on the table was a large-scale map of the Jacksonville area with the *Saratoga* at its centre. On the map were small plastic model aircraft set out to represent their actual positions. A team of naval ratings and Petty Officers wearing headphones periodically moved the models around as they received information about aircraft movements, although this was clearly just for show as all the aircraft were securely on board. As a finale the tour-guide showed the visitors a broad canvas chute used by personnel to descend from the main deck to the hangar when scrambled. The visitors were invited to launch themselves down the chute as if they were fighter pilots racing for their airplanes. He gave it a go and regretted it immediately as he tumbled off the end and collided with a plump American ex-sailor.

He was glad to get off the *Saratoga* and he strolled towards the smaller Russian ship. It seemed less intimidating and, ironically for a guided-missile cruiser, more friendly. There was a line of people waiting to go on board, curious to see real live Soviets and Soviet war machinery. Tour groups were less formal and much smaller, reflecting the narrow corridors and a reticence on the part of the Soviet navy to have too much on show. He took his turn and shuffled up the gangway, sensing strongly that someone somewhere was taking pictures of him and everyone else visiting the ship. The photographers were almost certainly from both sides too. At the top of the gangway a junior lieutenant kept watch.

"It's not this sunny in Murmansk," he said softly in Russian.

"Certainly, sir, I can show you where the washroom is. Please take the corridor to your right and wait for me there," the junior officer replied in English.

A moment later a second officer appeared to replace the junior lieutenant. He nodded to Viktor, who followed him along the corridor and down a companionway to a lower deck. The familiar, half-forgotten, smell of cabbage, disinfectant, and too many warm bodies reminded him of the months he had spent on similar, if smaller, warships in Vladivostok. The officer stopped in front of a closed door and gestured for him to enter. He then nodded and left. He knocked and pushed the door open. Inside was a senior officer's cabin with a bunk and a small desk with two chairs. A second door led to what would be a shower room and head. The cabin smelt of tobacco smoke. The only occupant was a stout man in his sixties who was dressed in dark trousers and a white long-sleeved shirt. He wore no jacket, unsurprising given the heat in the cabin. There were sweat stains under his arms. He sat at the desk, upon which was a bottle, two glasses, and a small cloth pouch.

"Comrade Viktor Vladimirovich, welcome aboard. You may call me Comrade Baranov, but only in this room. I bring greetings to you from Yuri Vladimirovich, with whom I have the great honour to be working. First, have a drink. It is the finest Armenian *konjac*, very good for the heart and high blood pressure, or so my doctor tells me." Baranov grinned and poured out two generous slugs. "*Na zdorovie!*"

Baranov drained his glass and immediately refilled it. Viktor took a large sip and had to choke back a cough as the burning liquid hit his throat.

"Take another drink. It gets better, believe me, if you do it quickly enough," Baranov said. "I'm glad you were able to make it. Someone else was due to meet me today but he had to cancel. It seems the Americans are deploying a very large number of watchers today. You have a sound reason to be here, but my other visitor felt that he might attract some very unnecessary attention if he came along. When we've finished talking, I'll give you something to take to him. You know who it is, from the beach."

"I understand, Comrade Baranov," he said and waited. He took the second sip, and as predicted it was better than the first, if only just.

"We don't have much time. Unless you leave the ship within 20 minutes or so the watchers will assume you are up to no good, so I'll be brief. Comrade Grachev, Leonid, has already told you some of the details of Operation VRYaN, and about your primary role being to find us a way to beat the Americans. From what he has reported it is clear you are already thinking along the right lines, but there is more you need to know before you continue."

He sipped again at his brandy, waiting expectantly.

"It is imperative that we are able to defeat the Americans, and our analysis has shown us very clearly that if we are attacked at any time in the next five to ten years our chances of survival, let alone victory, are very slim indeed. Needless to say, these thoughts are not to be communicated to anyone at all, ever. Our immediate concern is that the Americans and their NATO allies now have sufficient capability, in spite of the Strategic Arms Limitation Treaty and the proposed Strategic Arms Reduction Talks, to utterly destroy Moscow and all that it contains within eight to twelve minutes of suspecting that the US or any NATO member is under attack. Their deployment of nuclear weapons in the eastern edge of West Germany has seen to that. After those eight to twelve minutes, we believe that intercontinental ballistic missiles will start to rain down upon our motherland within less than an hour, and we will be in no position to do anything about it, or to retaliate. So, a complicating factor in your mission is this: you need to find a way for us to win without the Americans or NATO knowing that we have attacked, at least for quite a while.

"While that sinks in, I will tell you about a heated argument in Moscow. It is between two groups of scientists who have been studying this problem. The thinking on both sides is focussed on making an attack look like a natural disaster. In fact, massive inundation caused by tectonic disturbance. Leonid suspects you are already thinking about this. The argument in Moscow is about whether it will be better to create tectonic disturbance along the Atlantic Ridge in the middle of the ocean, versus deploying warheads close inshore along the eastern seaboard of the USA. The modelling each side has produced inevitably tends to support their own theory and trash the other. Comrade Andropov does not know who to believe, which course of action he should advise the General Secretary to pursue. I have studied both arguments, and frankly I think they are both flawed - too much uncertainty. Whatever we do, it has to be sure to work, and work quickly enough to disable the US capability to respond. You can talk now."

He thought for a moment.

"Comrade Baranov, without being privy to the modelling or the data that has been produced, all I can say is I tend to agree with you. I think there is too great a chance of failure with both options. No one knows how, or if, mankind can intentionally create a sudden tectonic event of huge magnitude at a pre-determined time. The Atlantic is an ocean with enormous pressures at depth. The subsea tests that I know of suggest that nuclear explosions in very deep water lose most of their explosive force very rapidly. To me this says that we would need such a quantity of explosive material to achieve the desired effect, and to place it carefully at depths we cannot operate in, that the possibility of setting it up undetected is very small indeed. Several nuclear explosions in shallow water near the coastline would have an impact on shore through tsunamis, but not for long and not far enough inland to disable American responses. In addition, this course of action would almost certainly be detected as an attack and would initiate retaliation."

"So, are you saying that we are dreaming an impossible dream, Comrade Lieutenant Colonel? If we are, we have only one option, which is to roll over and say the Americans have won without a shot being fired. Is that what you are saying?" Baranov's easy bonhomie was slipping.

"No, Comrade Baranov," he replied, "I am saying we need more information to develop a third strategy, one possibly between the two you mentioned. The USA has several earthquake zones and it has experienced severe quakes, but none debilitating enough to disable the entire country. If I may have some time to research this subject, and develop some thoughts I already have, I may be able to help the appropriate bodies construct an effective plan that will possibly succeed. Maybe better than possibly."

"Time is an issue, Viktor Vladimirovich. We don't know how much we have. Our experts think that Reagan will want to make his move before he has to start thinking about the next election, which will be in November 1984. Not an auspicious date. We think we may have a year to finalise a plan, and no more than another year at the very most to execute it before it is too late for us. You don't have much time to do what you need to do, Viktor. But I think you can do it. If you can't, we will all pay the price. Now, another drink." Baranov poured to more huge shots. "To a red flag over the White House, comrade!"

Baranov drained his glass and refilled it. Viktor sipped his.

"One last thing before you leave. Give this pouch to your beach companion when you see him next." Baranov pushed the pouch across the desk. "It contains uncut diamonds, a lot of them. It is to finance his operation - he will have some major expenses coming up soon - and to reward him for his efforts. He knows exactly how many carats are in there, or how many there should be. Get them to him soon and look after them. They are not easy to replace. *Do svidanya*, comrade. Take great care and be successful."

Back on the quayside he avoided the hordes of sailors from both ships who were assembling for the buses to take them out to play in the bars and clubs of Jacksonville Beach. No doubt the bars and clubs had already removed anything breakable and had shipped in as many professional and enthusiastically amateur ladies as they could find. According to Huey, it was customary on such occasions for bar owners not to charge females for any food or alcohol, especially alcohol. Huey had also said the fighting would start at 9.30 pm precisely.

He hoped he would be back in Washington well before then, with his pouch full of diamonds and the weight of his homeland on his shoulders.

He was preoccupied, to say the least, as he made his way to the embassy the morning after his Jacksonville trip. He sought out Leonid as soon as the necessary business of his SSOD job was taken care of. He had a visit to Alaska to finalise, and the bishops were due next week. His travel authorisation had come through from Craig Durov at the State Department so he was able to book flights from Washington via Seattle for the following Monday. He planned to stop off in Washington State on the way back. Huey had an old friend who had a tourist boat there and who'd extended an invitation to Viktor to join him for some sea fishing. Had it not been for the feeling of immense pressure that was building in his mind he would have been looking forward to the trip.

"How was Jacksonville? Did you stay for the rioting?" Leonid was pouring tea. They had gone to the dungeon to talk.

"It looked like they wouldn't need my help, so I left them to it. I was home by 7 in the evening. I met Baranov."

"Did he give you a package for Jim?"

"Yes," he stirred his hot tea.

"Then I'm sure you won't need to look for the signal on the mailbox but check it out tomorrow anyway. He's bound to be at Bethany on Sunday morning. When you set up your fishing stuff hide the pouch under a rock or something nearby, don't hand it directly to him. If there's anyone on him, I mean the Americans, you'll both be grabbed if you're seen to pass him anything. Just indicate with your eyes where it is, and he can find it later."

"Seems easy enough. I'll go to the *dacha* tomorrow and we'll spend the night, then have a family day at the beach on Sunday. Natasha really likes it there. Baranov spoke to me about the mission."

"What did he say?"

"I'm guessing you know already. He said that the mission was a bit more complicated than you'd said. He told me that the objective is to cause a massive catastrophe that will cripple America before they know they're under attack, and also before their NATO allies work it out. He told me about the theories in Moscow about using nuclear bombs to set off an earthquake and a tsunami. He said it was my job to work out how to do it, and where, so the mission could achieve its objective."

"And what did you say to him?" Leonid's usual casual good humour had evaporated. He was continually reminding himself not to underestimate Leonid, who was after all a career KGB officer destined for high places, as well as being a true believer.

"I said it sounded like a high-risk strategy, which by coincidence had been among my various thoughts already. I told him that more research and thinking had to be done to work up a plan with a good chance of success. Between you and me, I'm not sure there'll be a plan with a cast-iron guarantee of working. If it goes wrong and the Americans work out there's been a failed attack the game will be up."

"It will, for all of us and everyone at home too. Tell me what's bothering you."

"The whole idea bothers me. If the plan, as and when it's worked out, succeeds even partially it will mean that tens of thousands, even hundreds of thousands, of people will die. Maybe millions. Ordinary people - not troops or combatants. The damage will be beyond imagination. Is this thing right? Should we even be thinking about it?"

"I'm glad you didn't mention such misgivings to Baranov; I would miss you, so would Natasha and Sasha. Look Viktor, I understand your feelings, and all I'll say is three words: Leningrad, Dresden and Hiroshima. Three among the worst crimes against humanity since the phrase was conceived. How many innocent civilians, Soviet citizens, were murdered by the fascists, or left to starve to death after they'd eaten every horse, dog, rat and mouse in Leningrad? After they'd eaten their own shoes, even each other? Why? How many innocent civilians were incinerated, had their lungs melted, had the air sucked out of them by the fireball at Dresden caused by British bombers? Who drowned without water? Why? How many innocent civilians were obliterated in an instant by Truman's atomic bomb at Hiroshima, and the next one a couple of days later at Nagasaki? If they survived the first blast and were not burned alive, their bodies were slowly eaten by radiation over years. Why?"

He didn't answer; he just sipped his tea.

"Well, I'll tell you. Leningrad was because of spite; because the fascists believed that we Russians were sub-human. There was no military or strategic reason for the siege; they did it because they could. The British carpet-bombed Dresden with incendiary bombs to see what would happen, to see if they could do the same to

116

Berlin. If it hadn't been for the unforeseen danger to their own bombers of having no air to fly in, Berlin would have gone the same way soon after. It was an experiment on a whole city of living people. As were Hiroshima and Nagasaki. There was no reason to do it, apart from to see what would happen and to frighten Moscow and the world. Japan was about to surrender anyway; they were beaten. The Americans firebombed Tokyo five months before they dropped their nuclear bombs, trying out the new napalm they'd invented. They killed more than 100,000 people, just as another experiment, the nuclear bombs killed 200,000 more. Japan was no longer a threat to the US, but the Americans tried out their evil weapons on live Japanese subjects anyway, just to see what they could do.

"There wasn't and never will be any rational justification for these callous acts of mass murder, these war crimes. But for us, Viktor, we do have a justification. If we don't do it to them first, they will do it to us. It will be our millions who will be dying, our cities in ruins, our survivors rotting and eating rats. We know this. This is what our intelligence tells us, what our experts know, and what our leaders believe. That is why we, you, must do what Baranov says. It is simple."

Leonid stopped talking and sipped his tea. Viktor looked at him for what seemed an age.

"And you believe that, Leonid?"

"I do, absolutely! I'd rather not be thinking about killing anyone or destroying anything, but we have no choice. We do it, or we die. All of us. Well?"

"I'll think about how to do it on my way to the beach. I'll make a plan and assess whether it will work or not. If there is a plan that will work, I'll tell you. And if I do you must promise me you'll help me convince them not to use it. If there isn't a workable plan you must tell them that too. I am a Soviet citizen, a Russian. I know what I have to do."

Leonid nodded at him; he stood up. Unexpectedly, Leonid approached him and enveloped him in a long wordless bear-hug.

"Go to the beach, Viktor," was all he said eventually.

******

After a tranquil Saturday at the *dacha* the family drove to Bethany Beach. The signal had been on the mailbox in Centreville, as Leonid had predicted. On the boardwalk Natasha and Sasha chose a shady spot at a beachfront coffee shop and ordered a late breakfast. Steven was sure to pass by and 'find' them. He walked off with his bait box and fishing gear, anticipating a quiet hour or two with his thoughts and a mental tussle with unseen fish.

Just after 11 Huey turned up. After the usual banter of greeting, he squatted on the sand next to him and accepted a can of beer.

"You saw the man from Head Office, I take it?"

"I did," he moved his eyes to the left, indicating a small pile of pebbles and shingle. Huey nodded.

"How was he?" Huey asked.

"Hot, tired. I don't think he's a naval man. He has a lot of brandy, though. You didn't go?"

"No, I'd heard that the other side were going to be out in force, checking out visitors. They had CIA, FBI, the defence intelligence people, everyone. I'm surprised there was any room for ordinary folk. I stayed home and watched TV."

"I'm going away next week. I plan to visit your friend in Seattle after Anchorage. Is that still OK?"

"Sure, Mike's expecting you. He's got a boat, the *Zephyr*, moored at Anacortes, the Cap Sante Marina on Fidalgo Island. It's on Padilla Bay. You'll find the boat on the southernmost dock, so you can park on Seafarer's Way. Just turn up around 11 on Saturday morning, he'll be waiting. Anacortes is 60 or 70 miles north of Seattle, but it's a fast road, and there's a bridge to the island."

"What does Mike know about me?"

"Just that you're a friend of mine from here. That you work for the Russian government at the embassy, but you're a regular guy. You were a navy man, you like to fish, you love being on the water. You like to hear and tell fish stories. And of course, you always have real Russian vodka."

"So, what's Mike's story?" he asked.

"He was an officer in the Coast Guard, in command of a cutter. He's a good sailor, but he liked a drink and there were a couple of unfortunate incidents. Nothing too serious, but enough to make the Coast Guard not want him on one of their boats anymore. He didn't want to drive a desk ashore, so he quit on a medical pension. He's got himself a decent boat and he does whale watching and sea fishing trips when the weather's right."

"How do you know him?"

"I met him in a bar in Seattle. I go there for work quite a lot, both my DuPont work and my other work.

119

Mike had just been to the bank for a loan to buy a boat. They turned him down. He looked like he wanted to talk, so I sat with him and he talked and talked. I said I'd see him the next day, and when he was sober I got him to talk me through his plans. I said I'd stake him the boat money. He's paid back every cent, and the business is doing well. He's a good contact now, he knows everyone who's anyone on the northwest coast. There are some interesting things up there, aircraft, aerospace, and there's a new thing he's talking about. A couple of kids who know about these things have set up an outfit making an operating system for business computers. Mike says they're undercutting IBM, so much so that IBM are now buying their operating systems from them. He thinks that they're going to revolutionise business and information flows and put personal computers in every home in the country. I can't see it myself, but Mike's convinced. I've told Moscow; I'm not sure if they're interested. The outfit's called Microsoft, which doesn't sound too impressive. Anyway, Mike is now my biggest fan and he'd do anything for me. You'll have fun with him."

"I'm looking forward to meeting him. I've just got the bishops to look after first."

"Are there any married ones?"

"No. I don't think you get to be a bishop if you're married."

"Oh boy! I suggest you either lock them up at night or go to sleep early and leave them to it so you can say you didn't see or hear anything."

"Are they that bad? I don't know much about the Orthodox Church."

"If they're anything like the group that visited New Jersey a few years back they are definitely that bad. Enjoy!"

After a while he reeled in his line, the hook unoccupied. He packed up his things and bid farewell to Huey, who remained on the sand with a fresh beer.

"See you in a couple of weeks?" He asked.

"Sure. Have a good trip."

Back at the coffee shop Natasha and Sasha were with Steven, who stood politely when he approached.

"Steven, how are you?" he asked.

"I'm fine, Mr Gumnov. I'm just enjoying the sun and the company. The season will be over soon and I'll have to go back to college in Boston. It's been really great meeting Lexa and you all."

"Call me Viktor. Why don't you give Sasha your address at college? I have some business up there from time to time and she may want to come with me. She can let you know when we're coming and you two can meet up."

Sasha blushed scarlet. Steven grinned from ear to ear.

"I'll do that. Thanks, Mr, er, Viktor."

Chapter 15 - Anchorage, AK, late July 1981

On Monday morning he was driven in an embassy car to Dulles airport to catch a North West Airlines flight to Seattle and on to Anchorage. It was early when he left his apartment, Natasha and Sasha were still sleeping. Natasha would get a bus to work later, Sasha would meet up with friends and no doubt dream about Steven Rourke all day, every day, until she was back at school after the summer break. As the plane climbed through the low cloud over Washington he looked out of the window and stared at nothing.

With the three-hour time difference, it was still morning when the plane touched down in Seattle. A two hour wait, then a further three hours in the air and one more hour of time difference saw him walking out of Anchorage's International Airport a little before 6 pm in broad daylight. In Washington it would be the dead of night. Here the sun would shine until after 10 in the evening, and it would still be twilight as midnight approached. Dawn broke a little before 4 am.

The bishops weren't due to arrive until Wednesday morning, and their official programme, which was the only part of the visit that he was concerned with, ran until Friday morning. That Tuesday morning he put on some comfortable shoes and went for a walk. One block up from his hotel and three or four blocks to the west he found the Coastal Trail. It was a gentle pleasant walk along the Knik Arm seashore, and after about three miles he came to the entrance of the place he had been seeking. The Anchorage Earthquake Park was created to commemorate and record the massive earthquake that had struck Alaska on Good Friday,

1964. It was the largest and most powerful earthquake ever to hit the US, and as such it was the subject of extensive studies by academics and seismologists. The sparse population of Alaska meant that the death toll was just 131 in total - a lot, but nowhere near the number who would have perished had the quake struck San Francisco, for example, or Los Angeles. The quake on 27th March 1964 was centred south-east of Anchorage. The downtown area of the city was flattened, as were hundreds of acres of forest and wilderness. The shoreline shifted and changed forever. In the Earthquake Park visitor centre he found an earnest looking young man wearing a jacket with the park's logo.

"It was quite a shake," he said to the park guide, "I was in Russia and I felt it. Do you remember it?"

"I was just a little kid, but my parents told me about it. You say you felt it in Russia?"

"Yes, I was visiting family in Magadan, that's up in the north-east, when it hit. It didn't do any damage, but we felt it. Then we saw the tsunami a few hours later."

"Here in the US they say the earthquake was felt in nearly every state, except a few right down on the south-east coast. You saw the tsunami? What was it like?"

"It was quite scary, even though Magadan is over 3,000 kilometres from here. It was still light; Magadan is quite sheltered, but the tide suddenly went out very quickly. Then after a few minutes it came in again, moving very fast. The wave was only three or four metres by the time it hit, like a bad winter storm, but it was the suddenness of it that surprised everyone. I'm here on business, so I thought I'd look in at the Park to see for myself where it all happened."

"Well, if you're interested there's a department at the university which has a big display on the quake. It's open to the public by appointment. I could give them a call if you want, if you have time while you're here to visit with them. I graduated last year from the same school, so I know them."

The friendly young man made the call and told him that he would be welcome to visit the university that afternoon. He wrote down a name and a phone number and drew a map showing where the campus was. He even told him that he could take a bus that ran all the way along Northern Lights Boulevard to the campus and would drop him right by the Natural Science Building. He was endlessly amazed by the helpfulness of most Americans. He had to suppress the thought that they wouldn't be quite so helpful if they knew what he was really doing.

He had a light lunch at the Earthquake Park cafeteria before catching the bus. He found the Natural Science Building easily enough and asked for the person whose name he'd been given, a Professor Ellerson. A few minutes later an older man appeared in the lobby. He was weather-beaten and wearing a tweed jacket. There were pens in his breast pocket and a broad smile on his face. He introduced himself and they shook hands.

"The Soviet Embassy in Washington, hey," the professor said, "what brings you to our fine city?"

"I work with friendship societies, trying to build bridges between our different cultures. We have a delegation of Russian Orthodox priests arriving tomorrow who will need looking after, and I'm speaking to City Hall about the possibility of a 'sister city' relationship between Anchorage and Magadan in Kamchatka, across the Bering Sea. I'm only here for a few days. It's wonderful to have such opportunities."

"Russian Orthodox? That's interesting. I have many friends in the native Alaskan community. Some of them are members of the Orthodox church."

"If you have time, why don't you join us for dinner on Thursday? The local dean has invited some of his Aleut congregation along to meet the Russian priests, they're mostly bishops, and there'll be a talk on the history of the Orthodox church in Alaska. Archbishop Gregory will be the guest of honour."

"Great, I'd love to."

"I'll call with the details tomorrow."

"Now, what can I tell you about the earthquake? Luke said you'd actually felt it over in Russia. Not surprising, but it's unusual to meet someone from over there who's a real live witness. Tell me about it."

"There's not much to tell," he said, "I hadn't been married long and my wife and I were visiting her cousin in Magadan. Over tea early that morning my wife asked me if I felt the earth move. For a minute I didn't know what she was talking about, then I looked at my tea glass. The surface was rippling and then I felt the house trembling. It went on for a few moments, maybe no more than a minute, then the house seemed to let out a quiet sigh and slump. It was very strange, unmistakeable. I've experienced one or two small earthquakes since then and I've no doubt that's what I felt that day, but a long way off. Then there was the tsunami. We went to a headland on the waterfront for a walk maybe three or four hours after we felt the quake. We saw the main wave strike, it was three or four metres high, like a winter storm, but the sea was calm and it was springtime."

"Interesting. That's around 2,000 miles, give or take. I'm not surprised you felt it. It was a very major earthquake. Shall I'll tell you how it happened?"

"Please, I'm interested," he said.

"As you probably know, the earth's crust isn't a solid continuous layer. It's made up of separate parts, plates, which sort of float. They're important because they provide pressure valves for the earth's core. If the plates were fused together and rigid the earth would have died millions of years ago, melted or exploded. The plates move, allowing heat and pressure to escape through cracks. As a plate moves laterally or vertically it rubs against the adjoining one, generating enormous friction force. Every now and then the force is released when one or other of the plates gives way and moves. Mostly this movement is sudden and violent, and it releases energy on a huge scale. What happened in '64 was the result of millions of years of pressure building up between the North American and Pacific plates. A stretch of the North American plate, over 600 miles long, was displaced. It pushed up, lifted by about 60 feet, and everything on top of it lifted 60 feet too. Sea, land, everything. And of course it tried to come down again. Movement of this nature generates enormous heat and can cause solid ground to turn to liquid, so anything on it sinks. All that happened in less than five minutes, which seems short but believe me it didn't feel short at the time. I was there. That quake measured 9.2 on the scale, the biggest one ever recorded. If it had

126

happened anywhere else, anywhere with higher density population, it would have been a total catastrophe, millions killed. Here the casualty numbers were small. The biggest single loss of life was at Valdez port; 32 people in one building died."

"Could it have been predicted?" he asked.

"Good question. The short answer is yes and no. Yes because it was going to happen one day; no because we don't have the means or know-how to measure and fully understand the pressure scales and distribution. We knew it had to happen, but not when."

"Everyone talks about California and the San Andreas fault when they mention earthquakes. Why was this one so big compared to earthquakes further south?"

"Well, in my view it's the pressure cooker effect, as I mentioned. If you release pressure fairly often it doesn't get to build up too much. In California there are tens, hundreds, of small earthquakes every year. They take the edge off the pressure build up. Also, the movements down there are more lateral than vertical, a shimmy if you like rather than a hop. The one we had was a sudden and very forceful vertical shift, harder to withstand in terms of architecture and engineering."

"Has anyone ever looked at artificial ways of releasing pressure? Is there any way to do that?"

"We talk about that all the time, we seismologists. In theory, it's feasible. They've thought of using fracturing technology, like in oil and gas extraction, to prise plates apart hydraulically. No one's contemplated fracking on anything like the scale that would be needed. The plates are up to 20 miles thick - that's a lot of rock to push apart with fluids. With the types of nuclear energy devices available these days there's a school of thought that says it should be possible to release tectonic pressure through controlled nuclear explosions. No one's tried it, of course. The authorities go very pale whenever it's mentioned. When and if we get the ability to do experiments, even some extensive accurate modelling to look at the likely outcomes, someone might give it some serious attention. But if you ask me, it should be possible. The right technique in the right place could potentially defuse something like the San Andreas fault, or other smaller fault lines in places where a major earthquake would cause untold devastation. There are plenty of those just in the US, not to mention Europe and Asia."

"Other smaller faults in the US? I just assumed faults were just where the tectonic plates met," he commented.

"They're not all neat and tidy. You get jagged edges, smaller cracks, transverse faults, other places to get frictional build up. Over in the east especially there's seismic activity around some minor fault lines within the North American plate. Quakes there are less frequent, and to date they haven't caused major damage or disruption, but I think it's building up. For example, there's the Ramapo fault in northern Pennsylvania and New York State. It runs south-west to north-east along a line roughly parallel with Long Island Sound but a few miles west, inland. If it went, it would be catastrophic for the north-east USA. And there are smaller faults diverging off it that go right under Manhattan. There are a lot of small movements going on most of the time, but my feeling is that pressure along the main fault is increasing. The releases

128

from the small quakes aren't enough to ease the pressure build up. If it was my call, I'd be looking seriously about how to conduct controlled pressure release operations to stabilise the fault before nature decides it's time to do it her way."

"Interesting," he said, "why do you think people aren't considering it?"

"Beats me," said the professor. "I guess no one knows enough about how a pressure release would work. If it went wrong, it could initiate a very major earthquake, the first man-made one in history. Who'd want that to be their legacy?"

"Thank you, professor. I'm living with my family in Washington for a few years. I hope, selfishly, that Ramapo stays quietly asleep for a while longer. I'm not sure I'll be doing much sleeping after this conversation. I've taken up enough of your time, and I need to get things ready for the bishops. I look forward to seeing you again on Thursday, I'll phone through the details."

Chapter 16 - Anchorage, AK, late July 1981

The bishops turned out to be a lively group. There were five of them, aged between late 40s and early 60s, all with long hair and beards, and dressed head to toe in black. The only thing that lifted their sombre image was the bright gold cross on a chain round each of their necks. They had a young man in a cheap business suit with them, their interpreter, KGB out of Moscow for sure.

He met them at the airport. He'd rented a minibus with a driver, and on the way to the hotel he explained their itinerary. He opened a window slightly to let in some fresh air. It was obvious that the bishops had availed themselves freely of the complimentary drinks on the North West Airlines flight from Chicago to Anchorage. When they got to the Hilton the senior bishop spoke for all of them, saying the journey from Moscow had been long and arduous, and they all needed some rest. The KGB man / interpreter seemed relieved. With Huey's words echoing in his mind, he decided to linger a while in the lobby.

Sure enough, within fifteen minutes they were back, dressed in 'civilian' clothes and without their gold crosses or their KGB minder. The senior bishop saw him and winked as they headed out of the door onto 4th Avenue towards the downtown bars. Fortunately for them, the sight of middle-aged men with long hair and beards wearing poorly fitting denim jeans and plaid shirts is a common one in Anchorage. Oil workers and fishermen flock to town on R and R, and in the unshaven summer months are virtually indistinguishable from off-duty Russian Orthodox priests. He didn't follow them. At breakfast on Thursday the bishops were all present and correct. One of them was very quiet and had a black eye, but the rest were cheerful, dressed for work and evidently hungry.

Their first appointment was at the Cathedral of St Innocent, the Russian Orthodox church on Turpin Street. They were to meet the Orthodox Archbishop Gregory and conduct a service commemorating 175 years of the faith in Alaska. The cathedral was modest, but one of the local priests said that they had plans to enlarge and beautify it as and when funds allowed. The archbishop was waiting for them. He was a kindly-looking man, grey haired with a well-trimmed beard and an intelligent look in his eye. He greeted them in Russian.

"Brothers, gentlemen, welcome to Alaska. You're lucky this isn't wintertime, I assure you. I hope your accommodation is comfortable. We have a full devotional programme this morning, but after lunch one of our congregation has laid on a helicopter tour of the city and the glaciers nearby. They are truly spectacular! I have reserved a seat for myself."

The Russian bishops laughed politely, and he switched off as the ritual exchanges between the priests and bishops droned on. While he had little interest in religion, he did have a keen interest in cultural history and was eager to understand how and why the Orthodox church was thriving here in the far north-west of America. While he sat quietly waiting, he was surprised at the number of people who came into the church, lit candles, prayed, and left again. Many of them appeared to be native Alaskans, 'Eskimos' as one of the underlings in the SSOD office had referred to them. Lunch when it came was a modest affair, and once it was over the group, including Archbishop Gregory, piled into the minibus. He was surprised when the archbishop chose to sit next to him, rather than the senior Russian bishop.

"Well, my friend," Archbishop Gregory started, in perfect Russian but with a Ukrainian accent, "what do you think of our city so far? It's not so pretty, but the scenery is wonderful."

"It is, sir, wonderful indeed."

"What brings the head man from SSOD in Washington to Alaska to babysit priests who your government does not approve of?" The archbishop's smile remained in place, but his eyes were not smiling.

"The visit interests me, I took the opportunity to come along. I'd like to know more about the cultural links between Alaska and Kamchatka. I'm from the region myself and I know the north well. I can see the physical resemblance between the native Alaskans and Kamchatkans."

"Well rehearsed, Comrade Gumnov, but I wasn't born yesterday. My good friend Professor Ellerson from the university called me last night. He said he'd spoken to you at length about earthquakes on Tuesday afternoon, and that you'd invited him to the dinner tonight. He's delighted, of course, and he will be coming. Look, I understand how things work. I'm from Ukraine, Kyiv originally, as I'm sure you can hear. My family didn't do well under Stalin, and even less well under Hitler. By the time the war was over there weren't many of us left. Stalin hated the church. He tried to obliterate it, but nevertheless it lives on. His successors have continued their persecution of us. I managed to get to the US in 1946 and I've lived here ever since. All I've ever wanted is to serve the faith, which is what I've done. From sweeping the floors of the church in New Jersey to becoming Archbishop of Alaska. The church in Russia, the USSR, is a pale shadow of its former self. I know full well that the only reason it still exists is that the Metropolitan has made some Faustian pact, not with the devil but with the KGB, in order to survive until things get better. Which they will.

"I fear, Mr Gumnov, Viktor, that you are here for an underhand purpose. This saddens me as you do not seem a bad man. Saint Innocent, the patron saint of this church - I don't like to call it a cathedral yet, but it will grow into one soon - brought the faith to the Aleut people who were living here years before any foreigners came. He developed the written Aleut language, which they hadn't needed before, and translated the bible so they could read it in their own tongue. Of course, many words had no equivalent in spoken Aleut, so they stayed in Russian. It makes me smile sometimes to see a Russian word in the sacred texts in Aleut. When the Tsar sold their land to the Americans the Aleut weren't consulted. All they knew is that they were suddenly cut off from their families across the sea. And after the revolution, enmity between the Soviets and the Americans meant that they were never again going to be able to see each other. They took the separation hard, keeping the faith and traditions of the church have been important to them. It is part of their culture, the culture you claim to be interested in.

"There is no *resemblance* between native Alaskans and native Kamchatkans for the simple reason they are the *same* people. One day, when communism and capitalism have made their peace, they will be able to be one again. Until then, my friend, be careful what you do. These are good people who have paid a heavy price already in a fight that has nothing to do with them.

"Now, my lecture is over. We are nearly at the airfield. I hope you enjoy the flight. I would be honoured if you would sit next to me at dinner. I want to tell you all about the culture and the history of the church in Alaska, it is a fascinating and humbling story."

"I'd like that," he said. He couldn't think of anything else to say.

The helicopter trip lived up to the archbishop's expectations as they soared over the glaciers and mountainous wilderness to the east of Anchorage. The dinner was back at St Innocent's, the food having been prepared by the congregation and parishioners. Apart from the bishops and local priests there were dozens of guests, including Professor Ellerson who shook his hand warmly.

"I mentioned to Archbishop Gregory that we'd spoken. He was pleased you'd invited me along. It's a shame you're leaving tomorrow; I'd like to have a chance to continue our conversation. Maybe next time." The Professor smiled again and went off to find his seat.

The dinner was a traditional Russian feast, with liberal doses of ice-cold vodka, herring, cucumbers, *kasha* (a sort of wheat porridge), *borscht*, caviar, various smoked and dried and pickled meats and vegetables, cheeses, and a deliciously sweet *Guryev kasha* as dessert. His head was spinning slightly as they stood to leave. True to his word, Archbishop Gregory had given him a lot of attention and he now had chapter and verse of not only the Orthodox faith in Alaska but also the story of the colonisation of the Aleut lands in northern Russia. He wished he could have stayed in Anchorage longer to talk with the enigmatic cleric, but he had a catastrophe to plan.

Chapter 17 - Anacortes, WA, late July 1981

He collected a pre-booked rental car from Hertz at Seattle's Tacoma airport. The process was quick and efficient, and within 40 minutes of the flight from Anchorage landing he was heading north on Highway 5 towards the Canadian border and Anacortes. He was thinking back over the last few days in Alaska and making a mental list of things he still needed to know, people he still needed to speak to. He was also listing tasks that he would want the useful and resourceful Huey to help with.

He drove steadily, enjoying the luxury of not needing to be anywhere in particular. He had a room booked at the Ship Harbor Inn near the ferry port in Anacortes and he took an hour or so just driving round the beautiful small island. From a headland near Washington Park he looked out across to the San Juan Islands, and in the distance Vancouver Island. It was a stunning place to be, yet another unexpected American surprise.

He slept well and soundly and luxuriated in a warm bath before a leisurely breakfast. At 11 he was strolling along the southernmost dock at Cap Sante marina looking for Mike and his boat, the *Zephyr*. He found it easily. It was a solid-looking 40-footer with good weather protection and a sturdy flying bridge. The vessel was not swanky or plush, but it looked well cared-for and extremely capable. A man in his fifties, presumably Mike, sat on a bench on the afterdeck whittling a piece of driftwood.

"Permission to come aboard, sir?" he asked.

Mike looked up. "Viktor? Huey's pal? Welcome aboard, friend," he said. "Coffee?"

Mike busied himself in the galley brewing coffee and toasting bagels.

"Do you have somewhere to keep these cool?" he asked, handing over a bottle of Stolichnaya and a tin of caviar. "I have some blinis too, for the caviar. I stole them from the dinner last night in Anchorage. Nice boat."

Mike smiled and put the vodka in an ice box.

"That's good stuff! We don't often see proper Stoli here. Once we're ship-shape I thought we'd take a run out to show you the islands. Later we'll see if we can find some salmon. We'll get back to the dock by around 6. That OK with you, Viktor?"

"It sounds perfect. I'll be your crew, just give me my orders."

They let go the boat a few minutes later and set out to sea. They stood in the wheelhouse sipping coffee and chewing on bagels. He was struck dumb by the beauty of the islands against the deep green cold Pacific water.

"Have you always lived around here, Mike?" he asked.

"I wish! I'm from the plains, Sioux Falls, South Dakota - about as far from the sea as you can get in the USA. Pretty place, though. By the time I graduated high school I was going a bit off the rails in the middle of nowhere, so I struck out for the West Coast, California. I didn't want to go to college, my folks couldn't have afforded it anyway. First stop was LA. I was interested in the movie business - not the acting, the technical side. I thought I could get a job, parking cars or something, while I looked for an opportunity. The thing is so did everybody else. I nearly starved.

"I moved north, ended up in San Francisco, again looking for casual work until something better came along. But all the casual work was being done by Mexicans and Chinese. I just about scraped by, then one day in Union Square there was a US Coast Guard recruiting booth. I got talking, they were hiring, I signed up. After a few weeks I got a letter and an air ticket to Connecticut to go to the training school and that was that. For some reason they put me forward for officer selection; I passed, got selected, and at the age of 21 I was a midshipman on a cutter out of Miami. After a few years I climbed the ranks. I got my own command in the late sixties and got sent to Vietnam. That was something, not as bad on a Coast Guard cutter as being an infantry grunt in a trench, but interesting, nonetheless. I saw some pretty dreadful things.

"After the Vietnam tour I was assigned to the Pacific Command and got to know this part of the world. I really liked it. I don't know if Huey told you why I left the Coast Guard. If he didn't, it was because all the years at sea had taken a toll. I'd never married, I had a few girlfriends here and there, but nothing serious. I got my fun in bars, started drinking too much. One thing led to another, a few fist fights, some money troubles, various confused and confusing situations. It all added up to me being told that my seafaring days were over. I could get a desk job someplace, but if I wanted to leave on a medical discharge it could be arranged. I'd given good service.

"So, here I am. Fifty something years old, still not married. My boat is my home, the *Zephyr*, but I do have a small apartment here in town for the winter months and to keep some stuff in. The storms in these parts are spectacular, but I'd rather be watching them from dry land. It's the most wondrous part of the world. What's not to like?"

Beneath the words he sensed a deep sadness and fatigue, and loneliness of course. He tried to keep things light and cheerful.

"You should write a book, Mike. Tell me about salmon. In Russia you only ever see them in tins these days. How do you find them?"

"Out in the ocean you'll never find them. When they come towards the shore you have your chance. They come to rivers to spawn. It makes us fishermen, amateurs like me and the professionals, and the bears and the seals, very happy. I always look for the seals, they find the salmon better than I can, and other interesting things too. Pacific salmon come in different species. The best of all is the Sockeye, or red salmon. Delicious, expensive, and very hard to catch. Then there's the Masu, it's a bit smaller than the Sockeye but can be heavier. It's sort of pink but has dark marks on its sides. I'd say the Masu is second best, also good eating and good money. Then there's the Coho and Chum. The Coho is good game, it fights; people pay well to go fishing for them, even though they're quite common. The Chum is a pretty fish. The native Americans round here are the Chinook, they named it Chum as it means 'spotted', which kind of sums it up. The most common salmon in these parts in the Pink salmon, which is actually mostly silver but has pink flesh."

"In Russia, pink salmon is a rare delicacy. We stand in line for hours for a few cans of it."

"Here we feed it to cats or give it to homeless people. Nothing wrong with it, though."

They set out their lines and chatted quietly, just enjoying the water and each other's company. As the day wore on he suggested a snack.

"Sorry to have to ask, Mike, but is drink an issue for you?"

"Not anymore, I'm in control now. I enjoy it, but on my terms. Look in the cabin."

He went inside. In a cupboard a small but well-stocked bar was set up, along with a small freezer for ice and a fridge for beer and sodas. He retrieved the Stolichnaya and opened the caviar. Back on the deck he set out a plate of blinis beside the caviar, with two small spoons. He opened the chilled vodka and poured shots into two glasses.

"*Na zdorovie!*" he said.

"*Na zdorovie!*" Mike replied.

The shots were downed as his line went taut. Mike watched, ready to lend a hand as he skilfully reeled in his catch, playing it to avoid stressing the fish and keep the hook secure. It was a five- pound Masu; he pulled it on board and Mike quickly dispatched it.

"That's lunch fixed, Viktor. You like *sashimi*?"

"Is Ronald Reagan orange?" he replied. Mike laughed.

More vodka flowed as Mike expertly skinned and sliced the fresh salmon. In the galley he mixed a light marinade of soy sauce and finely sliced cucumber. It was ready to eat in a few minutes, and with a caviar accompaniment, a few blinis and liberal doses of Stolichnaya it was one of the best meals he had had in a long time.

Afterwards Mike rinsed the plates in the sea and made more coffee.

"Huey said you might have some questions for me. Shoot," Mike said.

"Not questions so much, I'm just interested in a few things. I was in the Soviet navy; did Huey say?"

"No, but you have the look."

"I was a cadet, then a junior officer for a few years. I enjoyed it but got married and we had a daughter. We decided being away at sea for months at a time wasn't so good for family life, and I got a move to a research institute as a marine scientist. I'd studied oceanology at university, so the authorities were happy with it. Anyway, a couple of weeks ago I went to Jacksonville in Florida to see the *USS Saratoga* alongside one of our ships which was on a goodwill visit. I got me thinking about the peacetime role of navies. I know the Coast Guard has safety and search and rescue functions. In the Soviet Union the navy carries out research and does experiments for institutes, and patrols for security of course. I'm not looking for secrets, but what does the US navy do?"

"Mostly it tries to manage itself. It's enormous," said Mike. "The US Navy is geared up for war; it leaves all that other stuff for someone else, like the Coast Guard. No way does it do research for marine science. It doesn't do defence, either. You only have to look back to Pearl Harbor - the fleet was a sitting duck. No, the US Navy is about offensive operations. The fleets are at sea much more than most navies."

"So, just theoretically, if the US suffered a severe natural disaster, say two or three big hurricanes in quick succession, would the US Navy play a part in rescue operations or the recovery?"

"I guess they'd try to, but they're not trained, prepared or equipped for that sort of thing. Military response would be led by the Coast Guard and the National Guard, in support of FEMA."

"FEMA?"

"The Federal Emergency Management Agency. Carter set it up as an over-arching agency to take charge of the sort of thing you're talking about. Doesn't work, though."

"Why not?"

"Not enough money, no teeth, no political clout. I'll tell you something, Viktor, if a really major disaster strikes, anywhere in the US, but especially somewhere where there are a lot of people, it will be a long, long time before FEMA or the Coast Guard or anyone else will be able to get things back to anything like normal."

"That's worrying, Mike. I would have thought the US would have it all planned for and nailed down."

"That's what the American people like to think too." Mike knocked back another shot of Stoli, his words were beginning to slur. Mike helped himself to the bottle and refilled his glass.

"If only they knew! It's time to turn around and start heading back. I fancy a beer; the *sashimi* had a bit too much soy on it. Makes me thirsty."

"Best thing about it," he said, going into the cabin and emerging with two cold beers. "Let's go home."

Chapter 18 - Washington, DC, August 1981

August is a dead month in Washington. Anyone who's anyone leaves the hot and humid city for somewhere cooler and dryer, or at least more entertaining. Government practically closes down, and most DC-ers take their annual vacation in August. Even the Soviet Embassy was depleted. Many of the staff had gone home for leave, others had taken up residence at the *dacha* or had gone to the seaside. Natasha and Sasha were happily holed up in a rented room at Bethany Beach for the whole month, while he stayed behind in the Alexandria apartment and joined them for weekends. He had work to do.

In his SSOD office he worked alone, his secretary having gone on leave. He told the administrator that he was not to be disturbed and locked the door. He took the framed photograph of Brezhnev off the wall and removed the glass. He laid a single sheet of paper on the glass and started writing in pencil, his handwriting neat and precise. As each sheet filled up he moved it aside and started on a fresh one. There would be no pads of paper with ghostly imprints of words or diagrams for an inquisitive person to find and pass on. By the time he had finished he had a list of information he needed and which he knew must exist somewhere, but he had no idea where to find it.

The first two weekends in August he drove down to Bethany Beach via Centreville. There were no marks on the mailbox, nor was there any sign of Huey on the boardwalk or the beach. He needed to speak to him. Soon.

On his way back to Washington after the second weekend he made a diversion to Dover, Delaware, to visit the offices of the Delaware State News. He had already drafted an advert, not long or particularly good, offering good prices for old German carved wood pieces. He added a fictitious Wilmington Post Office box number and paid cash. He was assured that the ad would go in the Monday edition.

At 10.30 on Wednesday he left the embassy on foot. It was a hot day, so he left his jacket behind and strolled along K Street towards Franklin Square. The only people he saw seemed to be tourists. He picked up a Washington Post and found a seat near the Commodore Barry statue in the park. Shortly before 11 he saw Huey's stocky figure. He was wearing a baggy tee shirt and khaki slacks, topped off with a blue Kansas City Royals baseball cap. He had a battered SLR camera on a strap round his neck. Huey stood in the park and took a few pictures of the statue before walking away whistling in his tuneless fashion. After a couple of minutes, when he was sure no one was following Huey, he stood and strolled off after him. Huey wandered south to New York Avenue before turning right towards the White House, where he took more pictures. Across Lafayette Square then another right towards Connecticut Avenue. He checked his watch outside the Mayflower Hotel and went in. He found him sitting in a quiet corner of the bar with a cold beer in front of him. Viktor greeted him and ordered the same.

"I've missed you, Huey," he said, "have you been away?"

"Just a short vacation, Viktor. It's good to get away from the area from time to time. You'll get to appreciate that when you've been here a while longer. How have you been?"

"Good. Natasha and Sasha are at the beach for the month. I'm here working. I need a couple of things, and I thought you might be able to help."

"Fire away."

"I'm guessing the navy has some detailed charts of US coastal waters, complete with very accurate sea-bed data. They'd need them for submarine operations. It's the sort of thing the US Geological Survey and the Coast Guard might collaborate on. I'd like to see them, the charts, for the eastern seaboard from the south of Florida to Newfoundland. Can you get hold of them?"

"I've got some friends at the Department of the Navy. I can ask some discreet questions. Leave it with me. Anything else?"

"The Federal Emergency Management Agency. What do you know about it?"

"FEMA? It's new. President Carter only invented it a couple of years ago. As it happens, I have a friend who was in at the birth of FEMA, but they fell out. He's down south in Mississippi or Louisiana someplace, running a crab and crawfish place. I'll give him a call. It's probably best if you speak to him yourself."

"One last thing. If I wanted to read up on current scientific research in the US, or find out which visiting scientists are giving talks and where, where would I look?"

"Mmm," Huey paused for a while, "I know from an engineering perspective. There are regular periodicals, magazines and such like, that you can subscribe to;

they come in the mail. Or if you're smart you can try to get a reader's card for the Library of Congress - they get everything there. Why don't you go and ask them? It's just east of the Capitol complex, off Independence Avenue. They'll probably have anything you'd want and being American they'll help you find it too."

"It's a crazy country, Huey. They seem to be doing their best to make it easy for people like us. Another beer?"

"Don't mind if I do. How was Mike?"

******

In Century House in London August was as dead a month as it was in Washington. In Britain almost everyone was on holiday. The upper classes chose the homes of lower-ranking people and invited themselves to stay. The benefit of this was that the slightly lower-ranking classes tended to want to impress their social superiors and were happy to feed, water and entertain them whenever the opportunity arose. They also tended to have nicer houses with better furniture, facilities and plumbing than the upper classes. Lower down the social ladder people paid to go to hotels and on package holidays. Only the diligent few were left in London in August, with its leaden summer skies and dirty underground trains.

One of these was a semi-retired spy, a man who had worked the Russia beat for the Secret Intelligence Service for years, both in the field and at HQ. He spoke and read Russian, of course, and his knowledge of Russian intelligence operations was encyclopaedic. He was spending the week meticulously reviewing the intelligence product emanating from the Service's current star agent, Sunbeam. Sunbeam was now installed in London as the *rezident* designate - the next head of the London KGB station - at the Soviet Embassy in Kensington Palace Gardens. Sunbeam's product was unpretentious - clear, factual, and usually apposite. What commentary he added was invariably insightful and as valuable as the actual intelligence. His handlers in London had only just started meeting Sunbeam regularly, but already the flow of copied documents appearing on the expert's desk was impressive.

He was looking at material from a little further back, though. His attention had been grabbed by a passing reference in a Sunbeam report from Moscow made earlier in the year. In his report Sunbeam mentioned an unusual number of KGB staff moves, something the source had become aware of when he himself was summoned to the KGB Personnel Department to get his posting to London confirmed. Sunbeam had provided a list of some of the agents being posted, one of whom was a Viktor Gumnov, at the time a KGB Major with a desk job in Moscow. Gumnov was one of several whose profile didn't sit well with the expert. He knew that the KGB was nothing if not a creature of habit when it came to posting agents to the West.

Gumnov wasn't career KGB. He'd started out as a naval officer with a marine science background and had later worked at the prestigious Shirshov Institute. The expert had found a few routine reports naming Viktor Gumnov as a delegate on various conference trips. Nothing unusual, in either a good or bad way, and certainly nothing to indicate that he had been on active service for the KGB on those trips to Plymouth or Aberdeen, or to the US. How then, wondered the SIS expert, had Viktor Gumnov come to be the head of the SSOD bureau at the Soviet Embassy in Washington DC? He started drafting a telegram to the SIS station in Washington requesting tracing with the CIA and FBI, as well as some discreet background research by the station's own people.

******

He was relieved to get to the fresher seaside air of Bethany Beach on Friday evening. He gave the *dacha* a miss and went straight to the beach-front guesthouse where his wife and daughter were staying. On the terrace overlooking the slow swell of the Atlantic he sipped a chilled beer and let the words pouring from his lovely daughter, just turned seventeen but still chattering like a toddler sometimes, wash over him. She spoke about Steven a great deal. He thought to himself it might be time for him to get to know the young American better.

They ate fresh fish and drank dry white wine. A separate room had been acquired for Sasha, so he and Natasha enjoyed time in each other's private company for the first time in quite a while. He rose early and went fishing, just fishing. No conversations with Huey, no hidden meanings or movements.

The junior officer from the SIS Washington station in the British Embassy watched and later wrote down everything he'd seen. A normal family weekend. No unusual contacts or behaviours, everything just normal. It had been an easy follow from Alexandria. The target's distinctive Lincoln stood out, as it would even without its diplomatic licence plates. His own rented Ford Escort blended in with the early evening traffic. The British agent relaxed and decided to enjoy an expenses-paid weekend at the beach and went looking for an American girl to play with.

He didn't get lucky, but that was fine. He observed the target on Saturday and on Sunday. Again, nothing out of the ordinary. On Sunday he went fishing alone and didn't meet or speak to anyone. The British agent would report back accordingly on Monday. Another wild goose chase from London.

Chapter 19 - New Orleans, LA, September 1981

His flight from Washington touched down at New Orleans early on a steamy Wednesday afternoon. In Washington the weather had begun to cool; here it was a good 20 degrees hotter and very humid. He didn't like it at all. He found the Hertz desk and collected his rented Buick from the parking lot. Driving from the airport his first impressions of the city, the 'Big Easy', weren't good. It was dirty, tired and run down. It was also too busy and chaotic, not at all American.

His mission was twofold: first was a discreet rendezvous with one of Huey's 'special friends', a clerk at the Stennis Space Center across in Mississippi. The US Navy's Meteorological and Oceanographic Command was based at Stennis, and it seemed that Huey's contact had come up with exactly what he needed. All he had to do now was have the clandestine meeting, retrieve the documents and get them back to the embassy in Washington without anyone knowing. After that he was heading for a town called Gonzales, roughly mid-way between New Orleans and Baton Rouge, the Louisiana State capital. There he would meet another of Huey's friends, one with a lot to say about the US Government's emergency management preparations.

It would be a busy couple of days. He just wished the air conditioning in his rather basic two-door Skylark was better. He had to smile; not so many months ago he had been grateful for any sort of independent transport, now he was criticising the air conditioning in an American car with power steering and comfortable seats!

It was his first visit to the deep south. It was unlike anything he'd experienced before, steamy, hot, and swampy. From the highway he caught glimpses of run-down shacks built of timber with rusted skeletons of pick-up trucks abandoned outside. From time to time there was the carcass of a dead animal on the shoulder, including a headless alligator. Off to the right, the lazy waves of the Gulf of Mexico fell listlessly on the shore. He passed Mississippi City and approached Biloxi, by now keenly anticipating a cool shower and an ice-cold beer. His hotel was on the beachfront. He checked in under an assumed name, showered and went down to the poolside bar for the rewarding drink. The harbour was crammed with small craft, pleasure boats and shrimp trawlers. A mouth-watering aroma of grilling seafood filled the late afternoon air. He was getting hungry, but he'd have to wait. At 6pm he left the hotel and made his way to a quayside bar, the one specified by Huey when he'd last seen him at Bethany Beach a couple of weeks before. Huey had described his contact as a small, worried looking Latino man with dark-rimmed spectacles.

He walked in at exactly 6.30, on schedule. He waved to him and invited him into the vacant seat beside him.

"I'm Donald. Huey sends his regards," he said.

"Carlos," the worried man said, extending a damp hand briefly, "I can't stay long."

"OK. Would you like a drink, Carlos?"

"A mojito, please. It reminds me of home."

He asked the bartender for two mojitos and watched as he crushed mint leaves and squeezed lime-juice into frosted glasses, topping them up with rum, ice and soda. It seemed unnecessarily complicated. The drinks were served. He toasted Carlos and took a sip of the acidic drink. He suppressed a grimace.

"I'll stick to beer, I think," he said to Carlos.

Carlos drained his mojito, accepted the offer of his barely touched one and gestured to the bartender for another.

"So, Carlos, how long have you worked at Stennis?"

"Long enough, I don't want to discuss it. Huey asked me to get something for you; I don't want to know why. It's too big to carry with me, so I sent it to your hotel with UPS. It's addressed to the name Huey gave me for you. What you do with it is up to you. When you get back tell Huey we're even now, quits. Tell him not to contact me again."

With that Carlos drained his third mojito, wiped his sweaty hands on a napkin and scuttled off, not saying goodbye. He watched him go, wondering what Huey had done to persuade the man to steal sensitive classified documents for him. After a decent interval he too left the bar and made his way slowly back to his hotel. He stopped at a crab shack on the way and ordered grilled shrimp and salad, with another beer. All the while he scanned the restaurant and the street outside. He was sure that no one was watching him. Nevertheless, he was on edge when he returned to the hotel. He asked the check-in clerk if anything had come for him.

"Sure, Mr Anson. This package arrived just after 6. I signed for it for you."

The clerk handed him a bulky package and got a two-dollar tip in return. The clerk smiled happily. He carried the package to his room but didn't open it. He sat tensely, waiting for a knock on the door, or worse for the door to be smashed in. Neither happened.

After a night of fitful sleep, he woke and showered. He checked out, settling his bill in cash. He drove to a UPS store in Mississippi City, re-addressed the package and dispatched it to the guesthouse he and the family had taken to using at Bethany Beach. He then called the guesthouse owner from a pay phone and said that a package would be arriving for him. Could the owner keep it for him to collect the following weekend? Of course, it was no problem.

He was back on Highway 10 by mid-morning. Just after he crossed the Old Pearl River he took Highway 12 round the north side of the lake. It was mid-afternoon when he turned south again on the 61 and dropped down towards Gonzales. Gonzales was a small town whose claim to fame was its self-appointed title of 'Jambalaya Capital of the World'. He had no idea what this meant.

His hotel was in Gonzales itself, and neither it nor the city was particularly inspiring. He dined alone, choosing chicken instead of fish for a change. That night sleep came more easily, and he woke refreshed on Friday morning. He was looking forward to being back in Alexandria that night.

It took longer than he thought to find the crab and crawfish place, and he'd had to ask a stranger for directions. Eventually he pulled up at a tidy-looking bar / restaurant beside a muddy canal. The morning was still and relatively cool. A tall, lean black man in jeans and a chef's jacket was lounging in a chair on the veranda. He was probably in his late thirties.

"Good morning," he called, "a friend of mine back in Washington said this place was the best for Cajun seafood in the whole state. His name's Huey. I don't suppose you know him?"

"Indeed I do. Huey is a friend, and if you're a friend of his you're welcome here. I'm Jerome, this is my place."

Jerome went inside and returned a few moments later with a glass of chilled cloudy lemonade.

"So, what brings you to Louisiana?" he asked.

"The name's Viktor. I told Huey I had to come down here on business and he suggested I look you up. I like fish and fishing; he said you did too."

"He's right. I knew him when I was up in DC. We used to have a beer together sometimes, and we kind of kept in touch when I moved back here."

"You're from here, then?"

"Born and bred. I only went to Washington when I worked for the government. I'm glad to be back. Look, it's quiet. Laverne can manage on her own for a while, and I need some fresh fish. Shall we take a ride on my boat and see what we can find?"

"I'd be delighted," he said, meaning it.

Jerome led them down to the quay and a respectable looking river cruiser. It had an enclosed cabin and a spacious open rear deck. Jerome started up the inboard motor and they puttered off.

"The canal joins Blind River a few hundred yards up. Blind River runs into Lake Maurepas, which is tidal and quite brackish, but it attracts some decent fish. The typical swamp fish you get round here all taste of mud, so I go a bit further down to catch the ones I like to cook."

Jerome was busy baiting a few lines and steering at the same time; he set about helping.

"I see you know your way around a fishing line, Viktor," Jerome said.

"I've been doing it since I was a boy. My dad had me fishing almost as soon as I could walk. It's been second nature ever since. I've always been around the sea, navy first, then a marine scientist."

Jerome went into the cabin and emerged with two bottles of beer. He passed one over.

"So, how did you end up in Washington, Jerome?"

"Well, like I said I'm from these parts. Born and bred in Gonzales. I'm not looking for sympathy, but my folks were poor, they've both passed now. We lived hand to mouth, catching fish for extra food. Making jambalaya and selling it to tourists from a stall by the road for a few extra cents."

"What *is* jambalaya?" he asked, sipping his beer with his feet on the gunwale.

"Jambalaya?" said Jerome. "It's a marketing triumph, that's what it is. It's typical poor folk's food, a one-pot dish. You stick some rice in and throw in any protein you can find. To stop it tasting like a garbage can you put in a whole bunch of spice and chilli, cook it forever, and that's jambalaya. It's based on the West African food that the slaves ate. They still eat the same stuff in Ghana and Nigeria, but they call it jollof rice. Anywhere there's poor people you get a jambalaya equivalent. The clever guys here in the deep south have turned it into a tourist attraction. Imagine that?"

"They write songs about it too," he commented.

"Anyhow," Jerome continued, "back when the war was going strong, Vietnam, I'd read about the veterans' programmes. It was a way I could get to go to college, so I enlisted. I landed in Saigon on my eighteenth birthday and had my first firefight six days later. I did three tours, that's one more than most people, but it was usual for us black soldiers. The white boys did two mostly, sometimes just one. My third tour was cut short because I got hit. A sniper killed my buddy, and the round went straight through him into my shoulder. Smashed it up pretty bad, but at least I wasn't dead. I reckon my buddy saved my life, not that he meant to.

"So, I had a few weeks in the field hospital until they figured out I wasn't going to be able to use a rifle again any time soon. They gave me a Purple Heart and a ticket home. I was in a VA hospital for another month for some surgery and therapy. It was great, almost worth getting shot for, then I got discharged. The VA people were good. They told me about the veterans' college programme and gave me a counsellor to help me work out what I wanted to do. I'd seen how screwed up Vietnam was after all the years of fighting, so I got interested in how places like that could ever get back to being normal. I spoke about it to my counsellor, and she told me about disaster management and recovery and said there were degree courses I could do to get qualified to do that sort of thing.

"That's what I did. Four years at college, courtesy of Uncle Sam, two years in the field with USAID, then I got married to Laverne. I needed work at home so we could start a family and I got into city regeneration, got hired by the government in the Department of Housing and Urban Development. Life was good. We had two kids and a nice apartment in Maryland. Not bad for a black kid from the swamps of Louisiana."

"How come you're back here?" he asked.

"Three years ago President Carter set up FEMA, the Federal Emergency Management Agency, which rolled a whole bunch of other departments and agencies into one. I thought it was a good idea at the time, but it turned out to be a disaster. Sustained and sustainable development to prevent things breaking down when the going got tough was pushed to the back of the line. Civil defence and domestic emergency response were all that mattered. Civil defence is a joke anyway, and with all the hurricanes and ice storms we get hit by every year but still can't manage, we're not doing so good at emergencies either.

"I was going places in Urban Development, helping to make good strategic plans to regenerate neighbourhoods and reverse inner-city decay. I put forward some proposals, just suggestions really, about how FEMA could get smarter and better by having coordinated programmes and sharing resources and information. It really upset my boss, who was from Civil Defence. He made sure I was in line for any shit that was coming down, and the first chance he had he got me fired. He said it was 'rationalisation and headcount realignment', but I know when I've been canned.

"I was out. Broke again - you don't get to save much on civil service pay with a wife and two kids to support. Laverne was being strong about it. I just got angry. I vented to Huey over a beer one night. He suggested I get out of town and do something I wanted to do. When I mentioned opening a seafood place down here, he lent me the money to set it up, no questions asked. He had faith in me. And here I am, here we are. Doing OK. I keep in touch with Huey. He comes down every once in a while and we tell each other stories. He's still interested in the people I knew at FEMA, and I like having someone I can talk to and can grouse about some of the assholes this government employs. That's how I'm here, now let's fish."

Over the next hour or so he gently probed Jerome about the US's capabilities to withstand a major natural disaster. Everything that Jerome told him supported his own observations that anything much worse than a seasonal hurricane or two would be devastating and could disable the US for a considerable time. In short, for all their military might and economic power the United States would be as helpless as a kitten if nature hit hard enough, either of its own accord or with a little help from Moscow.

They caught a few plump bass and were back at the restaurant in time for the late lunchers and early afternoon snackers. He bid Jerome a fond farewell and promised to look in again next time he was passing.

"You'll always be welcome, Viktor. Any friend of Huey's is. Take my number and give me a call if there's ever anything I can help you with."

He was in a thoughtful mood as he drove back to New Orleans for the early evening flight back to National Airport in Washington. He still needed a few more pieces for the plan he was working through, but he was nearly there. He was home by ten in the evening, just in time to get a full and lively account of Sasha's week while he watched Natasha smiling contentedly.

Chapter 20 - Wintergreen, VA, October 1981

The Blue Ridge Mountains rise a hundred miles or so inland, west, of Washington. It's a relatively easy drive from the capital, so many of the DC residents who can afford it buy holiday homes in the various ski and hiking resorts. In the autumn the colours of the trees are easily as spectacular as those in New England. Since his return from the trip south to Mississippi and Louisiana, he had been closeted alone in his office in the embassy, or equally alone in the reading room of the Library of Congress.

The material he had obtained from the nervous and unhappy Carlos was astounding. The bulky package, which he had retrieved from the Bethany Beach guest house and transported back to Washington in a canvas diplomatic mail sack in the trunk of the Lincoln, contained a complete set of classified charts and tables which precisely mapped the eastern seaboard of the USA. Most were marked 'Secret', and a few 'Top Secret'. They were intended for naval planners and submarine navigators, and they showed the exact topography of the seabed. The documents also contained detailed seismic survey data which charted the sub-surface geological structure, indicating the most accessible entry points to the tectonic fault lines that so interested him.

He was worried, however. The documents seemed to be a complete set, and they were marked with a serial number. This meant that sooner or later they would be missed, and an investigation into what had happened to them would be mounted. If this happened it would not be good for Carlos, he suspected, and possibly not for Huey either. He was fairly certain that his own role in obtaining the documents wouldn't be immediately apparent; he had taken care to disguise his identity and his travel route, and there would be no image or record of him in possession of anything that could possibly resemble the bundle of secret documents. He had already warned Huey and had discussed the implications with Leonid.

Natasha had been accommodating and tolerant of his long working hours and absent nature, but enough was enough. It was time for some family social life. The mother of one of Sasha's school friends, a vivacious divorcée called Carol, had clung on to ownership of her ex-husband's vacation house in the Blue Ridge Mountain resort of Wintergreen. Carol had invited Sasha and her parents up for a 'fall weekend' to make the most of the autumn leaves in the forests. Without consulting him, Natasha had readily accepted the invitation and on the appointed day off they went.

The vacation house was spacious and comfortable. Each of the three guest rooms had its own bathroom and terrace or balcony. He was a little surprised to find that they weren't the only guests. In addition to the two of them and Sasha, Sasha's school friend Stacey - Carol's daughter - was there, as were two young men. One was Steven Rourke, the other was Stacey's current beau. On the face of it, Sasha and Stacey were to share one room, the boys another, and he and Natasha the third. Carol had her own suite at the rear of the house. Just after six pm the youngsters all went out into the village. He didn't doubt that they would each have their own fake ID to get served alcohol. It was part of the everyday law-breaking that seemed *de rigueur* among American high-school and college students. He couldn't understand why in some US states you could get married at 15, drive a car at 16, join the army and go to war at 17, vote at 18 and still not be allowed to buy a beer until you were 21.

He and Natasha ate with Carol. After their relaxed dinner Carol flicked on the TV for the evening news. The set flickered to life and in an instant there were images of riot police firing tear gas and beating people with clubs. At first he thought it must be some uprising in a distant land, but Carol told him that it was actually in an eastern suburb of Washington. She explained that a rumour had started that the water supply had been contaminated and the entire population had descended on stores and food markets to buy up as much bottled water as they could. Inevitably, Carol explained, this leads to people grabbing for each other's purchases, which then leads on to fistfights, which in turn leads to stores pulling down their shutters, which leads to people breaking down the shutters to get at whatever it is they want, which leads to the riot police and the National Guard being turned out to quell the 'looting'. Carol reckoned that the rumour would turn out to be false, and that everything would be back to normal in a few days.

"Are you saying, Carol," he asked her, "that people react like this often?"

"All the time. The slightest rumour of shortages, even of things no one usually wants, generates panic buying. It's some sort of insecurity or anxiety mechanism, I suppose. It's worse if whatever is supposedly in short supply is one of the essentials, water, gasoline, bread or meat, that sort of thing.

People will kill each other for a gallon of gas or a hunk of beef; it's astonishing!"

"So, there isn't going to be a water shortage? The supply isn't contaminated?"

"I don't know," Carol said, "but I doubt it. People just don't have any faith in the water company or the government to make sure that there's enough clean, safe water for everyone. There always is, but people fret about it. I kind of dread what would happen if there really was a serious disruption to food, fuel or water supplies. It'd be like the civil war all over again!"

Carol turned off the TV. He poured more wine for them all. They spoke for ages about art and politics and travel, and they turned in long before the four youngsters got home.

He and Natasha were in a deep sleep. Around 2am he was awoken by a scratching sound at their balcony door. He was alert immediately, and he flicked the bedside light on in time to see a shadowy figure dart across the small terrace. He yelled out, leapt from the bed in his nightclothes and ran to the balcony door. As he did so the bedroom door burst open and there was Carol, wearing a skimpy nightdress and holding a small pistol.

"What is it? Is there somebody out there?" she said.

"I think I saw someone on the balcony," he replied.

By now he had the door open and the outside light was on. A flowerpot was on its side, and there were muddy paw prints on the tiles.

"Raccoons!" Carol said, uncocking her pistol. "You never know if it's one of those pesky creatures, a bear or a burglar prowling around. We've had all three up here. That's why I keep a gun in my bedside drawer, just in case. Especially if it's just me and Stacey up here."

"You keep a gun in the house? Is that legal?" Natasha asked nervously.

"Sure, it's legal. Second Amendment. Just about everyone has a gun in this country. Well maybe not just about everyone, but everyone here in Wintergreen will have one. The police department is small with a lot of homes to protect. They encourage us to keep a weapon in the house."

"What's a second amendment?" Natasha asked.

"The American constitution has an amendment which says that every citizen has the right to bear arms. It's from seventeen-ninety something. It was initially put in to make sure we had enough armed farmers to fight off the British if they decided to come back, and they kept it in when people started to think that the new federal government might need to be kept at a distance too. The amendment says that an effective militia is essential to our democracy, which is why we're allowed to have guns. Of course, some of the crazy people have taken it to extremes and keep enough guns to fight a war, but most people just have one or two, like I do. Don't people have guns in Russia?"

"No," Natasha answered, "only the police and military, and some people who live in the middle of nowhere and are worried about wolves, or who need to hunt their own food. Our government wouldn't allow people to have their own guns at home, I expect for the same reason that the people who wrote the Second Amendment said they can!"

Carol laughed.

"I must admit, it worries me sometimes. When you see people screaming at each other over a bottle of water and you don't know who's got a gun and could start shooting! But let's get back to sleep. I heard the kids come home a while back, I'll just make sure everything's locked up."

Natasha cuddled into his chest and was asleep again in moments. He found that sleep had abandoned him, and he lay in the darkness, thinking about what Carol had said about the American psyche, the way of life, and how he could adjust his plans to take advantage of the volatility and insecurity of everyday folk.

The following day started slowly. He was up early, as usual, and he went for a walk along a nearby forest trail. When he got back the four youngsters were seated round the kitchen table sipping coffee and orange juice. Steven and Sasha sat close together and looked at each other shyly. He guessed something had changed. Stacey and her young man (Todd, was it?) were more at ease with each other and were clearly used to having breakfast together. Carol emerged around 10 in the morning, still in her dressing gown. After a while she suggested that the grown-ups went off for lunch before saying something had come up and she needed to get back to the city on Saturday evening. Viktor and Natasha were welcome to stay if they wanted, if not Stacey could drive Sasha and the rest of them back to Washington on Sunday as planned.

The two of them were back in Alexandria that evening, enjoying some rare time alone without their little girl, who now needed her own time alone with her man just as much as her mother did.

Chapter 21 - Boston, MA, November 1981

As the year rolled on he decided to spend more time getting to know Steven Rourke. It seemed likely that the personable young man was going to be part of their life in the USA, if not beyond. Sasha was *extremely* fond of him. He had made a couple of business trips back to Boston to meet up with the Harvard professor, on one occasion taking Sasha with him. Steven met them at Logan airport, and with Viktor's blessing promptly disappeared with Sasha, who he persisted in calling 'Lexa'. The following day Sasha and Steven joined him for lunch in a café near the aquarium on the waterfront. It was a beautiful autumn day. He liked the young man and was happy for Sasha.

"How is your course going, Steven?" he asked.

"It's great, really interesting. I'm always amazed at how complex the marine environment is. I suppose you get used to looking at what you can see around you and forget that most of the world we live in is underwater. This semester we're looking at seabed topography and tidal dynamics. We are so lucky! There's a visiting professor from Kaiyodai, that's the Japanese Maritime University in Tokyo, teaching us until the New Year."

"I've heard of Kaiyodai," he said, "it's supposed to be the best for studying ocean dynamics, especially big dramatic events. I suppose Japan is quite sensitive to that sort of thing."

"They have a vested interest in understanding them, that's for sure. Professor Saito will be doing some public talks in November. Why don't you come along?"

So it was that he and Sasha made a return trip to Boston in November. He planned to attend the talk by Professor Saito, and Steven had arranged for them to meet privately afterwards over dinner. Saito's talk was about currents and climate change, with a focus on the oceanological effects of the *El Niño* and *La Niña* oscillating air streams. He was fascinated and made lots of notes. Afterwards Steven introduced him to the diminutive Japanese academic, whose spoken English was excellent.

"Professor Saito," Steven said, "this is Viktor Gumnov, he's my girlfriend's father. He's a diplomat based in the US, but a marine scientist like us by training and inclination."

Saito bowed. He returned the compliment and invited Saito to dine with him. Steven and Sasha took their leave.

"Mr Rourke said you are a scientist, Mr Gumnov," Saito started once they were seated and had ordered.

"I was at the Shirshov Institute in Moscow before I was seconded to the Foreign Ministry. My discipline was, and still is, currents and dynamics, but I've been asked to look at recent studies on massive water movement, like tsunamis, and their impact on land-based communities."

"I know of the Shirshov Institute, of course. I would love to visit one day."

"I'd be very happy to help with the arrangements, Professor Saito."

"So, what interests you in respect of tsunamis, Mr Gumnov?" Saito had not made any attempt to drop the formality of address.

"We haven't had much direct experience of them, certainly not in populated areas, unlike Japan and other countries in Asia. Can I ask what typifies a problematic tsunami for you?"

"That's a big question. To answer you I'm going to have to start at a basic level, so forgive me if I sound condescending. As you know, there is tectonic movement occurring nearly all the time. Mostly it has no discernible effect, but sometimes the movement is severe enough to cause a seismic event, an earthquake. When these occur in the oceans, water is displaced causing waves. Usually these waves have no significance; if they happen in deep water they generally go unnoticed, and the vast majority of them do no damage whatsoever. You will understand the word tsunami. It is Japanese, and it means literally 'harbour wave', so called because a tsunami that gets noticed usually manifests itself by causing a flood surge in a sheltered spot which would normally be protected from a normal ocean wave, such as a harbour. In the past, a tsunami was erroneously referred to as a 'tidal wave'.

"A tsunami caused by a sub-sea seismic event is the displacement of a body of water by the movement of a tectonic plate, which acts like a plunger. It pushes or pulls the water, causing it to start a surge motion which can move at very high speeds. In deep water the energy of such motion can be quickly absorbed, but where it meets shallower water the wave velocity decreases quite suddenly and the mass of water in the surge causes its height to increase rapidly and significantly. In open sea, a tsunami would rarely generate a surge of more than a few metres. But a ten-metre surge wave, say, arriving in shallow water will grow in magnitude, sometimes to two or three times its height. Often the surge wave of a tsunami will become a series of waves arriving one after the other; the second and subsequent ones tend to be more harmful because they can carry debris and contamination from the preceding one. The waves can present themselves more as a succession of very powerful flood surges rather than more familiar surf waves which tend to break on the shore. Such a sequence is a problematic tsunami if it affects a populated or developed area. It can be devastating, but generally within a limited coastal area. From time to time a tsunami can affect different shorelines over a very wide area, such as the rim of an entire ocean, but this is uncommon and would need a very major event to trigger it.

"There is another type of problematic tsunami, though. You may recall the tale of Noah's Ark. According to the story, the prophet Noah built a boat, an ark, to enable some humans and most species of animal to survive a catastrophic world-wide flood. The idea of such a global flood, scientifically speaking, is fanciful. However, there is a body of archaeological evidence to suggest that a catastrophic flood event did affect the Mediterranean area - which at the time was the known world - and it caused widespread loss of flora and fauna and, of course, human life. It happened around 1600 BC. The evidence I mentioned includes finds of organic and mineral materials further inland and at greater altitudes than is normally possible, even after the largest known conventional tsunami.

"The event was caused by a volcanic eruption on the island of Santorini, which was followed by the collapse of its caldera. This meant that an enormous mass of rock and solid matter fell into the sea in a very short space of time. This type of incident causes what is termed a mega-tsunami, although I have no idea why someone felt the need to use a Greek prefix - we have any number of Japanese ones which are equally suitable."

"So the bible story has some basis in fact. What exactly is a mega-tsunami?" he asked the professor.

"As well as massive water displacement underneath the surface," Professor Saito continued, "a mega-tsunami caused by millions or billions of tonnes of solid matter falling into the sea creates a surface wave of gigantic proportions; one which moves extremely fast. The force of a huge fluid mass travelling at high velocity, in excess of seven or eight hundred kilometres an hour, is hard to imagine. While a normal tsunami would dissipate its energy in the ocean, a mega-tsunami is moving through air just as much, if not more, than through water, thus losing less of its energy. When a mega-tsunami hits land it can be incredibly 'problematic' over a very large area. A mega-tsunami can impact a very long coastline and penetrate a long way inland, much more than an ordinary tsunami usually can.

"Historically there have been several mega-tsunamis, but none in recent times. The last one recorded was Krakatoa in Indonesia in 1883. When it erupted, an estimated 25 cubic kilometres of matter was expelled and dumped in the sea. The event released the energy equivalent of 13,000 of the nuclear bombs that the United States dropped on my country in 1945. It caused mega-tsunamis that travelled around the world. The human death toll, mostly from those mega-tsunamis, was anything between 40,000 and 100,000. Bearing in mind this happened very nearly 100 years ago, a century in which the global population and population density has grown exponentially. Were a similar event to happen today, it would be a global catastrophe with many millions of casualties. That is what I would define as a problematic tsunami."

He was momentarily speechless. He replenished their wine glasses and paused while the waiter served their food.

"You say 'were a similar event to happen'. Is it possible?" he asked.

"It is not only possible, in my opinion it is also probable," said Professor Saito. "Krakatoa was not a large island, and it was a long way from the densely packed continents of Europe and America. Do you know of an island called La Palma?"

He shook his head.

"It is one of the Canary Islands, off the west coast of Africa on roughly the same latitude as Florida, and about 2,000 miles from the US coastline. The Canary Islands are Spanish territory, and all are volcanic. La Palma is occasionally active, and it is unstable. It is a little larger than Krakatoa was. I will admit that scientific opinion is divided on what would happen if or when La Palma either erupts again or breaks in half. My view is that in the most benign incident, a collapse without a volcanic eruption, the probability of which happening within the next century is in my view greater than 40%, a mega-tsunami would ensue. It would travel westwards at about the speed of a jet airliner as a surge wave in excess of 50 metres high at sea. It would impact the eastern seaboard of North America from Newfoundland to Florida, and according to my theoretical modelling the first surge wave would penetrate inland to a distance of 50 to 80 kilometres, or until it hit land above say 150 metres above sea level. We would not be sitting where we are, Mr Gumnov. Boston would be destroyed, as would everything low-lying between here and Miami, including Washington and New York. In addition, the wave would emanate in a circular pattern, as all waves do. It would affect the western seaboard of Europe, Britain and Ireland, the whole west coast of Africa and most of the east coast of South America as far as Buenos Aires. The further from La Palma one gets, the more energy is dissipated. Even so, many hundreds of millions of people would be displaced, injured or killed. If the event were triggered by a volcanic eruption the impact would be worse."

"You said opinion is divided. Why?" he asked.

"Some of my colleagues argue that the Atlantic Ocean could and would absorb a lot of the energy, and that the Mid-Atlantic ridge would act as a barrier, a kind of breakwater. In the case of a regular tsunami I would tend to agree, but not a mega-tsunami."

"Would there be any warning, any indication that the event was going to happen?" he asked.

"If it was volcanic, possibly, but a sudden massive landslip could be triggered by an earthquake or even simple weather erosion without any prior indication. There are studies, of course, and ongoing monitoring, but there is rarely any advance warning of an earthquake. Erosion might be easier to spot, but not to prevent. My best estimate is that there might be a few days warning, but probably none at all. If there was any advance warning, the first difficulty would be to get every government likely to be affected to acknowledge the fact, and then do something about it. To the best of my knowledge there are no plans in the areas concerned to carry out a mass emergency evacuation on the scale and at the speed required. Can you imagine what the east coast of the USA would be like?"

"I can't, professor, it is beyond comprehension. You have my sympathy for having to contemplate such things."

"If it happens, Mr Gumnov, I only hope that you and your lovely daughter are safely back in Moscow, with dry feet. Even then, I have no idea what sort of world you, or I, would be living in after such a catastrophe."

Viktor and Professor Saito finished their wine. Neither felt like ordering dessert.

Chapter 22 - Washington DC, December 1981

The snow had started. Already the traffic bulletins were over-excited with hyperventilating presenters repeating over and over that 'conditions were becoming difficult'. He was with Leonid, closeted in their secret dungeon, wondering how Americans would ever cope with the sort of snow they had in Russia. Leonid was preparing for a visit to Moscow for end-of-year discussions at Head Office, followed by a period of leave with Katya. He thought maybe a skiing trip to Sochi, or perhaps a week or two in Crimea, away from the biting cold.

They had booked the dungeon for the whole day. He sipped his green tea.

"OK, Viktor," said Leonid, "what have you come up with? What devious scheme do you have to help us beat the Americans?"

"I've been thinking about it day and night for months," he replied. "It won't be easy, and there are no guarantees, but I think there is a way for us to disable America long enough for the balance between our nations to be reset."

"So not an outright defeat? No killer blow?" Leonid asked.

"It's not possible, not now. It would need an all-out nuclear assault, throwing everything we have at the US all at once. We know that within a few minutes of us launching the first missile Moscow would be a smoking pile of ash. Even if we were able to take out the US nuclear strike capability there's still NATO to contend with. Whatever we do must not look like an act of aggression. We will need to use the most powerful weapon at our disposal to disable America, but no one can know it is us using it."

"What weapon is that, Viktor?" Leonid asked.

"The American people," he replied.

"I don't understand," Leonid said.

"I'll explain. I've been doing a lot of thinking about what motivates Americans. They profess patriotism, but what matters most to them is their family and their home. The United States has never had to endure a war with a foreign enemy on home soil, it hasn't had an invasion, and since the civil war it hasn't had to contend with any large-scale social upheavals, unlike Europe or the Soviet Union. They aren't equipped as a nation to deal with such things. My conclusion is that when a massive, unexpected crisis strikes the US at home it will be every man for himself. They'll pull up their drawbridges and protect themselves and their families. They'll turn on each other if they feel threatened. This is what we can exploit.

"I've come up with a staged plan to cause disruption and panic, enough to cripple this country socially and economically, and therefore militarily, for years. It starts with setting the scene for unease, followed by initiating mass panic, and then causing something significant to happen, in this case a possible earthquake affecting a major urban centre - coupled with multiple and severe coastal inundations.

"We start with media manipulation, which we know we can do well. There is a volcanic island called La Palma off the west coast of Africa. Some scientists are predicting that this island will break in two at some stage, possibly quite soon, and half of it will fall into the sea. Reasonable worst-case predictions are that the collapse will trigger something called a mega-tsunami. If this happens it is probable that the entire eastern seaboard of the United States will be hit by a massive wave travelling at up to 500 miles per hour. This wave will effectively disable and possibly destroy every major city within 30 to 50 miles of the coast, including New York, Boston, and of course Washington DC. Obviously, we cannot make this event happen without launching a suicidal nuclear attack on a defenceless Spanish island, but we are able to make sure that the possibility of it happening, with a graphic description of what the consequences would be, starts to circulate in the western media. The US government will inevitably deny it, but that is of no concern. My bet is that the American people will not believe what their government tells them anyway. Our desired outcome will be anxiety, panic and confusion among the millions of people who would be directly affected if it did happen.

"The second stage will be escalation of the anxiety into mass terror. Using our influence with western media, we let it be known that the collapse of La Palma is imminent, within hours or a few days at most. We emphasise the speed of the mega-tsunami and tell people that once it starts, they will have no more than four hours to save themselves.

"We will tell them that a wall of water more than 300 feet high will hit their cities at the speed of a runaway train. The wave will not just be sea water, but it will carry debris; ships, automobiles, trucks, buildings, you name it. Whole skyscrapers will collapse, electricity will be cut, all transportation will stop. There will be no food, fuel, water or medicines, all

177

within four hours. Tens of millions of people will jam roads and airports trying to flee the cities. People already in the safer areas where they're headed will fight them off with guns. The government will be forced to declare a state of emergency and deploy the National Guard and the military to try to restore calm.

"The purpose is to cause chaos, to make it very difficult to establish any sort of order, to destroy the ability of government to govern. Then we deploy the last stage. Underneath New York State there is a geological feature called the Ramapo fault. It is a crack in the earth's crust, specifically in the North American tectonic plate. It's around 600 miles long, and it lies beneath New York City, extending out into the Atlantic Ocean. I've seen on US Navy seismic geological surveys exactly where the fault lies, and how deep it is. I estimate that one large nuclear device positioned in just the right place will be sufficient to initiate a significant movement of the fault, in short cause an earthquake. Probably, but I can't be certain - no one can. The best opinions I have been able to get tend to support my theory, but of course it is neither possible nor wise to go around asking people directly. *If* such an earthquake can be generated, and *if* it is of sufficient magnitude, it will seal the fate of the US as a super-power. New York City will disappear, along with much of New Jersey.

"A tsunami would be created, but a conventional one. The tsunami would be going the wrong way to cause widespread devastation, but nevertheless it will cause some significant damage up and down the coast. But we would need some additional insurance.

"All along the continental shelf, that's the sloping seabed that rises up to the shoreline, there are a series of perpendicular canyons which are a thousand metres or so deep at the widest end, furthest away, and rise to 50 metres or less near the shore. Perfect funnels with the right pressure profiles. I've selected several of these, five in fact, as being suitable for our purposes. If a large nuclear device is detonated in the deep ocean, it is most likely that it will be ineffectual. The mass of water would absorb the energy released, and all you'd get is a few boiled fish. When I met with Baranov in Jacksonville, he suggested setting off nuclear devices at sea to cause tsunamis. I've looked into this, and I know it wouldn't work.

"It would, however, provoke a nuclear response against us from the US and NATO. But if we were to detonate smaller devices in selected canyons they would serve to actually amplify the explosive effect due to their pressure profiles. In my opinion, significant tsunamis, similar in character to mega-tsunamis, on a smaller but still considerable scale, would be caused. The main target of two of these will be Washington DC, which must be disabled rapidly. If the timing coincides with the Ramapo seismic event the initial thinking will be that the mega-tsunamis hitting the coast between New York and the Carolinas are associated with the earthquake. There should be no immediate credible suspicion that the Soviet Union has caused the disaster.

"If the US government is already struggling with a civil emergency when its nerve centres in Washington are inundated, the entire leadership could be crippled in one fell swoop. A United States in turmoil, with most of its economic might - which is largely centred on New York - disabled, and without leadership or military commanders empowered to take offensive action becomes completely harmless as far as the Soviet Union is concerned. And we can say it had nothing to do with us.

"That's the plan in a nutshell. For obvious reasons I haven't written it down as a report. All the notes I made during my research have been incinerated, and there are no copies. I've committed the details to memory, and I suggest you and I go over it a few times now so that you can do the same and deliver it to Baranov, or even Andropov himself, when you are back home."

Leonid was speechless. He stared at Viktor for a long time, then a smile appeared. Slowly at first, but then he beamed.

"Viktor, that is genius! I have many questions, but I like your proposal. I like the different stages, and the way we can use our proven capabilities to make this happen. Congratulations! Before we go through it and I ask questions, and before I forget, how would you and the family feel about spending Christmas in New York? It is quite something. Most of our people at the UN mission are going home next week; I can arrange for you to have one of their apartments on the East River for a week or so. Show Natasha and Sasha the town. It could be their last chance to see it."

"I know they would like that, Leonid," he answered, "I will try to empty my head and enjoy the experience too. Now, let's go through the details."

******

He arrived back in Alexandria late that evening. He was exhausted. He'd left the car at the embassy and had walked most of the way home, not minding the snow on his shoes or the chill on his face. He had stopped off at a few bars along the way. He wasn't drunk but he wasn't sober either. A cab dropped him at the apartment building. He opened the door of the apartment and called out to Natasha.

"I was getting worried," she said, "I called Leonid and he said you'd left work at 6."

"I'm sorry, Nata, I needed some air and a walk. I should have called you. I'm here now, and I have news. We are going to spend Christmas in New York, like you wanted to!"

Natasha squealed with delight and ran immediately to tell Sasha, who squealed even louder.

"New York! For Christmas! Can we go to a Broadway show? To Bloomingdales and Macy's and Tiffany's? And eat hot dogs in the street?"

"Whatever you want, Sasha, whatever you want. Now, let's eat."

Chapter 23 - New York City, December 1981

They had travelled by car. He said it would give Natasha and Sasha a chance to see a bit more of the countryside and they had happily agreed. Before they set off Sasha asked shyly if they could make a detour to a town called York in southern Pennsylvania. She had a present for Steven, and if it was OK with them she'd call him and arrange for them to meet somewhere convenient, just for a few minutes. Viktor and Natasha looked at each other, each trying to suppress a smile.

"We can do that, darling," said Natasha, "we can see where he lives."

He was pleased, and relieved. In truth he had been dreading travelling by train or even on a plane. Now that his plan had been made flesh by telling it to Leonid, and by Leonid's enthusiastic exploration and questioning, it was as if something troubling was haunting him. While it was still something only in his head, as yet unborn, he could tell himself that it wasn't real. Now it was out, even if known to just one other person, it had life and breath of its own. His sleep had been troubled. He hadn't wanted to sit on a train or in an airport looking at the faces of innocent Americans, cheerfully excited at the thought of spending the holidays with loved ones and families. In the car he would be insulated from them, safe from their benign happy smiles.

The conjoined sprawl of Washington and Baltimore fell away as the family progressed up Highway 83 towards Pennsylvania and the town of York. Following Steven's instructions, as read out by Sasha, they followed the freeway through York to the interchange with Highway 30. Steven was in the car park of a small mall waiting next to a neat pickup truck emblazoned with the words 'Rourke Heat and Air Conditioning' and a local phone number. Steven's grin was dazzling. He hugged Sasha and shook hands with Natasha and Viktor.

"It's good of you to stop by. If you weren't in a hurry to get to New York I'd ask you back to the house. Mom's really keen to meet you. Maybe you can come by on your way back?" Steven hadn't let go of Sasha for an instant.

"We'd like that. We're just going into the store for a few minutes," Natasha said, "come along Viktor."

They left Sasha and Steven to their own devices for twenty minutes. By the time they came back Sasha had handed Steven a gift, a small box which held a Russian-made steel military-style watch.

"It's so cool, Lexa," he said, "this Soviet stuff is really in. The kids at college will be green with envy."

Sasha blushed with delight. She'd bought the watch at the commissary in the embassy. It had only been $13 and no one could understand why she would want such a thing when for just a few dollars more she could get one of the latest colourful American timepieces. Steven had given her a delicate gold chain with a single pearl pendant. It was already around her neck.

"My folks also wanted you to have these, Mr and Mrs Gumnov," Steven said, handing over two parcels wrapped in Christmas paper. "Happy holidays."

Back in the big Lincoln Sasha sat in the back dreamily gazing out of the window as they followed Highway 30 eastwards. Soon they would join the turnpike and head north towards the Big Apple. Inside the car the radio played calmly and softly, apart from the hysteria-laden traffic reports every fifteen minutes or so.

There is no way in which you can prepare for your first sight of the Manhattan skyline. Whichever way you approach New York there will be a point at which its jagged majesty hits you. Sasha and Natasha gasped in unison; he smiled at their surprise. The winter sunshine backlit the outline of the buildings, towers and canyons of this unique island. Sasha had glimpsed it from above once before from the window of a plane the day they arrived in the United States; for Natasha it was brand new. But New York teases. The spectacular view disappeared as suddenly as it had materialised, obscured by the railyards and warehouses and factories and tank farms of Jersey City and Union City. There was noise and clamour everywhere. They stopped at the tollbooth and as he lowered his window to present his ticket his women were assailed by the loud crude voices of truckers and labourers shouting and cursing each other.

Eventually they set off again along the bewildering confusion of roadways, tunnels and overpasses towards the mythical city. The noise level increased; darkness and gloom surrounded them as they descended into the Lincoln Tunnel, probably the least inviting and least attractive of all the approaches to New York City. After a few seemingly long minutes they emerged, not into light and air but into the grime and pollution of the Lower West Side. The road surface was potholed, steam belched up from manhole covers, ragged people lay in doorways under piles of cardboard. As they drove further into the centre of

Manhattan the sights changed. Sasha and Natasha sat in shocked silence as various tableaux played out on the sidewalks. A street preacher yelling damnation; a garish prostitute of indeterminate gender hawked on a street corner; women in dungarees and men in dresses walked with each other hand in hand; dealers popped out of doorways to accost potential buyers; buskers played - some quite well. Natasha remained stunned, but Sasha was starting to come alive, invigorated by the strange sights and sounds. He was silent, measuring the relative reactions of his wife and daughter.

After just a few wrong turns he found the apartment which had been lent to them for the short holiday. It was on the East Side in the mid-fifties, conveniently situated midway between the UN complex on the bank of the East River and the USSR's Permanent Mission to the UN on East 67th Street. The apartment block had its own basement car park - a luxury in Manhattan - with an allocated space for the apartment the family was using. He dealt with the suitcases while Natasha explored the kitchen and two bedrooms. Satisfied, she made tea. Meanwhile, Sasha was studying a notebook in which her school friends had written down everything she *really had to do* in New York. After the shortest possible time she skipped out of the apartment with a map in one hand and the notebook in the other.

"I'll be back in a couple of hours; I'm just going to get my bearings," she called.

"Be careful Sasha!" Natasha shouted at her daughter's retreating back. Sasha waved a hand and was gone.

The apartment was warm and comfortable. They had tea and some time to themselves. Two hours passed very quickly and Sasha reappeared, glowing pink from cold air and excitement. She took a deep breath and started talking, telling her parents about everything she had seen.

"....and there was a young black guy by a phone booth. He said if I gave him $2 I could call anywhere in the world for fifteen minutes! That's really cheap! You know how much a five- minute call to Anya in Moscow normally is? If you can ever get through! So, I paid him the $2 and placed the call. I tried asking for the USSR, but the operator had no idea where that was. In the end I said Russia and she said why hadn't I said that in the first place. Really! I talked to Anya, even though it's really late in Moscow. She says it's very cold and everyone's worried about Brezhnev. She's so jealous I'm in New York! I said I was going to get a hamburger and go to Bloomingdales!" Sasha paused.

"First," he said, "you shouldn't talk about Brezhnev on the phone; you never know who's listening. Second, that call to Moscow will end up on some poor person's phone bill. The boy at the phone booth will have found a way to have it charged to somebody, so please don't do it again."

Sasha completely ignored him. "So, I found Bloomingdales - it's huge! And I went into a café, only they call them delis here, and ordered a burger and a soda. I mean a Coke of course. The burger was enormous! I've brought half of it home. It seems you're not allowed to leave food behind if you've bought it. They insist on putting it in a bag for you to take with you. They said it's for the dog. I said we haven't got a dog and they looked at me in a funny way."

Sasha plonked the lumps of bread and cold congealed meat, onions and coleslaw on a plate. Natasha picked it up and threw it in the bin.

"We are going to have a proper dinner, Sasha. If you keep eating all this American stuff you'll get fat and have spots. I thought we could do some visits tomorrow. There's the Metropolitan Museum and the Guggenheim. They're quite close together and we could go tomorrow morning. Then we can find somewhere nice for lunch and maybe see some shops in the afternoon."

"Can we go to a show on Broadway?" Sasha asked.

"I'll ask at the mission about tickets," he said.

As they were about to go out to find a restaurant the apartment phone rang. He answered it.

"Comrade Gumnov? This is Irena from the management office. I'm sorry to call you at this time, but I'm afraid you didn't sign off the departmental expenses before you left. I need to get them submitted before the end of the month for the annual accounts. I've sent the forms to the Mission in New York. Could you go there tomorrow and sign them? Then they can be sent back to me in time."

"My apologies, Irena. I'll do it first thing tomorrow," he said.

Across the city the FBI monitors made a note of the call. It didn't seem significant. The following morning other FBI agents in their observation post in the NYPD 19th Precinct House took photographs of Viktor Gumnov as he went into the Permanent Mission of the USSR to the United Nations. They noted that he showed a pass to the security guard and was admitted. They didn't hear him use that month's codeword which would identify him as a KGB officer and allow him to get into the KGB section of the building, but the security guard would tell his FBI handler sooner or later.

Inside the mission he was handed an envelope by the KGB duty officer. The call from Irena had been a coded notification that an urgent communication had arrived for him. He opened the envelope, which was from Leonid. All really sensitive messages that aren't extremely urgent are sent by hand in diplomatic bags rather than in electronic signals. This message was sensitive and had arrived in the hand luggage of a senior member of the Mission who had returned from Moscow the day before.

'*Comrade Lt Colonel,*' the short message began formally, '*your plan has been extremely well received by Comrade General Baranov, who has taken it personally to the Chairman. I hope to meet with the Chairman in the New Year as I am told he has many questions. For now, the Chairman has expressed his thanks and appreciation for your ingenuity in approaching this task. In recognition, you have been assigned a new apartment in Moscow, fully furnished and equipped, for your exclusive use on your return. The keys and the address will be sent to you in the routine despatch. Congratulations on your excellent work, Comrade! Enjoy the rest of your holiday!*'

He held the note and re-read it. Andropov had been told of his plan and had approved. This meant that by now Brezhnev would know of it too. And he had been rewarded with a new apartment, one of the special KGB ones with spare rooms and big refrigerators. He should be excited and happy, but he couldn't shake his feelings of unease. For now, it was time to get back to his family and pretend to be enjoying himself. He fed the note into a shredder and it was gone.

The FBI watchers took more photographs and logged his exit. They thought the Russian looked worried. They wrote everything down and put it in the pile for typing and filing. Someone might read it one day.

Chapter 24 - New York City, December 1981

Christmas Day in New York. The family slept in and rose late. Sasha had been out with a couple of her school friends whose families had homes on Long Island and had come to the city for Christmas Eve. He and Natasha had been asleep when Sasha had stumbled in at whatever time it had been. He had heard her, and once she'd settled in her room he looked in on her. She was curled up, sleeping soundly and innocently. He was amazed, as always, at the way his little girl could be so confident, grown-up and outgoing, so adventurous, and at the same time look like the child she still was in his eyes. He kissed her sleeping head and let her be.

Being Russian, the family had never paid much attention to Christmas. Looking at the sparkling lights and false cheeriness of Manhattan didn't inspire a religious sentiment in any of them, but it did look like fun - something Moscow tended to be short of. All the shops were shut but restaurants and hotels were open. He had asked someone at the mission to book a table for them for a leisurely Christmas meal, and the chosen venue was a traditional steak and seafood place near Central Park.

The family walked together in the chilly air, getting there around 1pm. Their table had a view of the park; the waiters and waitresses were cheerful and bright; the food was good. All of them had chosen steaks, *filets mignons*, with baked potatoes and vegetables. They had smoked salmon and salad to start, and elaborate ice cream desserts to follow. Rich red Californian cabernet sauvignon complemented the meat. Afterwards he treated himself to cognac, a French one, not Armenian. When the bill came it was eye-watering, but he pulled out a wad of bills and paid it without question, adding a generous seasonal tip.

Throughout the meal his women chatted about their experiences in the city over the past few days. He listened contentedly but distractedly, asking occasional questions. They'd had a good time, but even Sasha was tiring of the frenetic pace of Manhattan. They would rest tomorrow and head back to Washington on the 27th. The three of them strolled arm in arm across Central Park towards their borrowed apartment. As they walked a light snow started falling and the temperature dropped.

"We must find something for Steven's parents," Natasha said to Sasha, "they sent us those gifts. Chocolates and mittens for me, a bottle of bourbon whiskey for your father. Any ideas?" Sasha hadn't.

"I know," he said, "there are some Russian shops in Brooklyn, near Coney Island. I think it's called Brighton Beach. The embassy and the mission here get some proper Russian things from there. I'll look up the name of the place and we can go down there tomorrow."

"That sounds perfect," Natasha said, holding his arm more tightly.

The *Gastronome Odessa* was on Brighton Beach on the corner of 14th Street. The current owner, Moishe Israelovitch, had been a Moscow dentist until a few years ago when he had decided his best interests lay elsewhere. He'd bought the deli and made his peace with the current regime, mostly by offering spectacular discounts to USSR staffers and by providing a good range of food and drink that were hard to get hold of in America. Moishe greeted them effusively.

"Seasonal gifts, you say, for Americans? Of course." Moishe gushed.

Natasha chose a large *medovik,* the multi-layered Russian honey cake popular for celebrations. He chose a spiced vodka and some tins of smoked fish, pickled vegetables and caviar, all better than anything he could get through the commissary. The gifts bought, they browsed a little longer and used more of his supply of KGB dollars to buy a few things for themselves. Moishe refused to let his new customers carry the goods themselves, especially on the subway. They would be delivered at 6 that evening to their borrowed apartment, the address of which Moishe was familiar with.

Back in the apartment he and Natasha rested while Sasha went out one last time. She was curious about Greenwich Village and the bohemian arty lifestyle of areas like Hell's Kitchen and the wiggly streets between orderly upper Manhattan and the financial district of Wall Street and the World Trade Center.

They had done all the usual tourist things, except it had been too cold for the Circle Line. They nearly froze on the observation deck of the Empire State Building, took the Staten Island ferry to get a close-up view of the Statue of Liberty. They went up the twin towers to look back at the city and across New Jersey in one direction and Long Island in the other. From their vantage point they looked down on little ships and watched tiny airliners take off and land at JFK, La Guardia and Newark. While Natasha and Sasha gasped with wonder and tried to see places they had been, he felt his knees tremble. Then he realised it wasn't just him. People were murmuring about an earthquake. A small earthquake was happening beneath their feet, under the foundations of the World Trade Center.

"Is this usual?" he asked an attendant, "this shaking?"

"Yeah, small earthquakes happen a lot, I hardly notice them anymore. I suppose a big one will happen one day. I might notice that one," the attendant grinned.

Yes, you might, he thought.

On Sunday 27th they left New York, starting the Lincoln for the first time in almost a week. The family was tired and happy, and almost relieved to be leaving New York behind them. Sasha had called ahead to Steven to say they were coming. To her delight he said he would meet them at the same place and take them all back to his home to meet the family. She was thrilled. Even though she'd already met Steven's parents several times, this would be the first time for him and Natasha.

Steven was waiting expectantly beside the pickup. He offered to ride with the family in the Lincoln and on the short drive to the Rourke house he kept up a steady commentary on the town and the district. He was particularly animated about the Amish, descendants of German Christian fundamentalists, many of whom had settled in the neighbouring Lancaster County. Steven said the Amish were often seen in York and its environs riding in their black horse-drawn buggies and wearing dark clothing that hadn't changed much since the seventeen-hundreds. Steven admired them for their resilience, and their refusal to bow to new unnecessary technology and trends. They lived, he said, self-sufficiently and with great respect for the environment and each other. They had endured civil war, persecution, hardship and hunger; they were true survivors. He listened with interest, thinking he could be hearing the description of an American future.

The Rourke house was spacious and comfortable, built on two storeys with a broad porch for shade in the warm weather. Steven's parents were waiting, smiling and open.

"Viktor!" said the father, "Brendan Rourke. Great to meet you at last. Lexa's told us a lot about you. And you must be Natasha!"

Brendan Rourke, a lean and ruddy fifty- or sixty-year-old, shook his hand vigorously and threw his arms around Natasha. "This is my better half, Hazel. She's put up with me for longer than I can remember." Hazel Rourke was younger than her husband, short and dark-haired with pink cheeks, warm from the kitchen and her slight embarrassment at her husband's enthusiasm.

They exchanged greetings. Natasha thanked them for their kind gifts, which had been most unexpected.

"I've brought you some Russian cake," Natasha said, "it's called *medovik*. It's delicious but very fattening, full of cream and honey. We have it for special occasions and it lasts quite a long time. Viktor also has some special vodka for you, Brendan, and some things that men like to eat while they're drinking it."

They went inside the warm and welcoming house. In all their months in America neither he nor Natasha had been in many private homes. Natasha looked around curiously. What she saw was a family home that had been assembled by people who knew about value. The Rourkes had become successful, obviously, but they were not ostentatiously rich. They had worked hard and wasted little, and now they had everything they needed and wanted nothing more. Natasha liked them immediately.

"Stevie says you're headed back to DC," Brendan said to him, "how was your break in Gotham City?"

"Interesting, to say the least," he replied.

"It's a crazy place - I lived there for a while. I'll tell you about it when you've more time. Lexa's a great girl - you're a lucky dad, Viktor."

"We've got to get back to Washington, Brendan, but I'd really like to talk with you further. Can we do that?"

"Any time, Viktor. Lexa's almost like family, so I guess you are too." Brendan smiled.

"We call her Sasha. She's adopted the name Lexa all by herself."

"Kids, hey?"

A little while later Steven guided them back to his pickup truck. He kissed Sasha shyly and shook his hand. Natasha avoided Steven's outstretched hand and gave him a hug instead. He blushed. All the way back to Washington he and Natasha interrogated Sasha about Steven and his family. Had she met them often? Had she visited the house before? What did Brendan do? Did Hazel have a job? What about brothers and sisters? Sasha hid nothing, Natasha was satisfied. He listened and absorbed all the details and information. He hoped the Rourkes were genuine, as genuine as they seemed. But in his secret world of spies and agents, one never knew. It was possible that Steven had been sent to target him and his family by the Americans. The Rourkes would need to be checked out, thoroughly but discreetly too. He knew that his position could be compromised if Head Office found out he and his family were developing a personal relationship with real Americans. He felt a rare moment of real fear. If he had to prohibit Sasha from seeing Steven, she would probably never speak to him ever again. It would break his heart.

Chapter 25 - Washington DC, January 1982

As always, the Soviet Embassy held an annual drinks party for friends, and sometimes enemies, as soon as possible after New Year's Day. It wasn't as grand as the November 7th Gala Reception, which commemorated the October Revolution, but it was an event that was acceptable to people who normally wouldn't want to be seen celebrating a violent socialist uprising. This year it was to be on Tuesday 5th January, which was when people would be back from their holidays and would have had a day or two to clear the garbage that had landed in their in-trays while they were away. He was obliged to go along, and like most embassy wives Natasha would be equally obliged to help prepare the food and drink and be on hand to be decorative. Some of the younger wives were made to dress and behave as waitresses, as were some daughters when there were any. Sasha had refused point-blank, saying she would rather put needles in her eyes than die of boredom pouring vodka down the throats of old lechers with wandering hands.

"Don't be so harsh, Sasha," her mother had said, "some of them aren't that old!"

In the embassy ballroom tables were laid with canapés and trays of glasses of *Sovetskoye Shampanskoye,* the surprisingly palatable Soviet version of champagne. He moved among the guests, and although he disliked drinks receptions he managed to engage several people in conversation. Craig Durov from the State Department was there, of course, as were members of various US / Russia friendship societies. He was seeking out people whose opinions about the thinking and sentiments of the Reagan administration might be more realistic than idealistic; not regime insiders as such, but people who talked freely with them. These were the people spies liked, people who could help make sense of the partial pictures and snippets that could be so misleading if misinterpreted. He wasn't disappointed. He made the acquaintance of a lady who worked in the international NGO sector whose husband was a White House staffer; he met a businessman from New Orleans seeking to trade with Warsaw Pact states whose cousin was a Republican senator said to be close to the president; he met an elderly actress, now married to a banker, who had been at Smith College and had become close friends with Nancy Davis, another actress, who went on to marry a film star and who was now the First Lady of the United States. The two of them were still friends and every now and then they had cosy lunches together. He chatted amiably and uncontroversially with his new contacts and made tentative lunch dates with several of them. A good evening's work.

The following week Leonid was back. They met in the dungeon. Leonid looked tired and hung-over.

"Congratulations on your promotion, Comrade Major General. It's well deserved," he said.

"It's bullshit, Viktor, that's what it is. It means that when I leave here I can say goodbye to my field days. I'll be driving a desk in Moscow until the end of time."

"You're in a good mood today."

"They say, Viktor," Leonid said, "that alcohol has greater effect when consumed at altitude. I think those bastards at Aeroflot have done something to their drink. The pleasant effects are less but the hangover is a killer!"

He passed Leonid a glass of tea with added sugar, and some Alka Seltzer in water.

"Maybe you should have stopped after the first bottle, certainly after the second," he said, "you look terrible. How is Katya?"

"Katya is fine," Leonid said, "but she's getting anxious. She knows something's going on and she doesn't want us, me or her, caught up in it. She knows nothing about VRYaN, but she's a smart woman. The interrogation she gave me after my meetings with Baranov were worse than anything they do to us at the training school. I didn't get to see Andropov after all, which I'm quite glad about."

Leonid downed the fizzing Alka Seltzer and sipped at his tea.

"He was impressed - Baranov, I mean. He's given you a codename, *Chapai,* after Vasily Chapaev. It means he thinks you're a hero. It also means that he can keep your real name away from the people at the top and make sure he gets the credit for your thinking. He said he's spoken to Andropov about you and your plan to defeat the Americans; he says Andropov likes it and has taken it to Brezhnev. Baranov even said that Brezhnev himself sends you his personal appreciation, and he asks that you now occupy yourself with another task. I'm sure you can guess what it is." Leonid paused for more tea.

"I would imagine," he said, "that the Kremlin now really needs to know what Reagan and his inner circle are thinking. Are they really planning a pre-emptive strike on us? Am I right?"

"Unerringly so, Viktor," Leonid said. "Even the craziest people in the Kremlin don't want to take on the US and all their allies unless they really need to, at least not yet. Not until the odds are well and truly in our favour. The Politburo is privately divided on the matter. Some of the older ones who still believe their own propaganda think we should be prepared and willing to fight. The more pragmatic ones, those who read the reports and listen to other views, think that a balance of power is best for everyone. They want to keep talking with Washington about arms limitation, but they also want to have a big stick to hit the Americans with if it looks like they're double-dealing.

"Moscow is uneasy, Viktor. Brezhnev is getting older and slower and sicker. The others are mostly old and slow and sick already. People have been saying for years that the only viable successor to Brezhnev is Mikhail Suslov, and he's already eighty! They're now saying Suslov isn't at all well. If he goes first, who knows who'll replace Brezhnev? If it's a hawk, we're in trouble. If it's a dove, we're in more trouble. That is why our mission here is so important. Everyone in Moscow who matters is busy saying what they think Reagan is going to do, but no one really knows. Everyone has an opinion, the Foreign Service, the GRU, in the KGB we have at least six different opinions. Then there are the academics, the economists, the finance ministry, the military. They all have an opinion to suit their own priorities. You know what Baranov said? He said: 'opinions are like arseholes; everyone has one and they are usually full of shit!'. Is it too early for a drink?"

"It is only 9.30 in the morning, Leonid. It's too early for a drink, but maybe just late enough for a final nightcap. Why don't we go to my office and have one? Then you should go home. Come back tomorrow when you're more rested."

"Good idea, Viktor. By the way, what do you think about your new apartment?"

"It's very generous, I appreciate it. I won't miss the journey to and from Chekhov, but I'll miss the forests and the water."

"Then you must have a better *dacha* deep in the forest! I'll try to fix it for you so you can commune with nature, or whatever it is you get up to in the woods. Let's go."

Two large bourbon whiskeys later Leonid started to look better and almost wanted to stay, but he persuaded him to go home and rest. Privately, he was concerned for Leonid, who had become a friend. He knew he had a duty to report his concerns, but there was no way he was going to do that. Not unless he really needed to, later. Throughout the day he reflected on Leonid's comments about Baranov and the stirrings in Moscow. These were dangerous times, dangerous for everyone. It was vital that Moscow, the right people in Moscow, knew and understood what the Americans were thinking. If they didn't know, or worse didn't understand, the consequences were unimaginable. None of this lifted his spirits or eased his sense of impending doom. He drained his whiskey and poured another. Then he opened the cabinet in his room and started to read through the plans for SSOD in the year ahead. He still had his day job to do.

Chapter 26 - Washington DC, 13th January 1982

It took him several days of discussions with his SSOD team to map out a plan for the year ahead. On the schedule were visits by various Soviet institutions, including his own former employer, the Shirshov Institute of Oceanology. They were coming late in the summer to show off their flagship research vessel, the *R/V Akademik Mstislav Keldysh*. It was brand new, in service for less than a year, and it was state of the art. He was keen to see it, along with the new submersible craft it carried, which would be needed to execute the plan. He needed to speak to some people from Head Office who would be on board too. In the meantime, he had to ensure that appropriate invitations to American naval and academic dignitaries were sent out and accepted, and that the right number of flags and speeches would be in evidence during the visit.

As well as this, the Bolshoi Ballet was coming to tour the western outposts of the United States in the spring. A visit by the Bolshoi was never a simple thing. It would cost a vast amount of money, and it was almost certain that at least a few of the dancers would attempt to slip the leash and stay behind in the free world. It was rumoured that many Russian ballet dancers, of whatever gender, ended up partly naked on the stages of seedy nightclubs in Las Vegas and Los Angeles as a living backdrop for better paid, fully naked, strippers. Very few who jumped ship achieved the same degree of success and acclaim as Baryshnikov or Nureyev, and many eventually went home with their tail between their legs. The plan was for the tour to culminate in a gala performance of Swan Lake in Las

Vegas, an event which would require both him and Natasha to be present. He had never been to Las Vegas but had heard a lot about it. He wasn't looking forward to the trip but couldn't avoid it.

In between his SSOD commitments, now that the initial planning for VRYaN had been accomplished, he took on other highly sensitive work for Head Office. He and Leonid were, they hoped, under the CIA / FBI radar, unlike the other KGB staff at the embassy and other missions. As such, they were charged with covert sensitive contacts with bodies and individuals in the US who could mobilise American sentiments in a way that suited Moscow. Many of the contacts were high-profile, and all meetings with them were risky. Careful planning was required to protect both the American and Soviet participants. Good, well-placed friendly contacts were very rare and valuable, deep-cover covert KGB officers even more so.

On top of this, he still maintained links with 'Jim', aka Huey, the also rare and valuable field agent employed by the KGB as an intermediary between them and the many knowing and unknowing sources they had in almost every significant area of American commerce, industry, science or the military. It was going to be a busy year. Normally he would relish the challenges, but the ever-present sense of oppressive doom weighed heavily on him.

He looked at the clock, it was nearly 3pm. Outside it was snowing heavily, and the temperature had fallen. He decided it was time to go home. He called Natasha in the library and said they should leave soon as it was likely that the roads would be bad because of the blizzard. She agreed and told him that Sasha had phoned. She'd been sent home when the school closed at lunchtime and was at the apartment. He and Natasha left in the Lincoln. As he had predicted, the traffic was appalling and their normal route towards the Arlington bridge was completely jammed with immobile buses and trucks. He decided to go further east, across the Williams Memorial Bridge close to National Airport. Usually he avoided this route; there are three parallel bridges across the Potomac all close to each other, attracting heavy traffic most of the time. Arlington was quieter, and although a bit longer it was mostly quicker. They sat in the Lincoln and inched forward. The traffic thinned a little as drivers parted ways to take different bridges, and soon they were moving a little more freely. The snow was even heavier now, freezing on the windshield and the road surface.

Halfway over the bridge the car radio was drowned out by a screaming roar. They looked to their left and were blinded by bright lights, behind which was a massive dark shape. The noise was incredible. A jet aircraft, a passenger plane, passed just a few feet above their heads. The car was rocked by the wake of the jet and the blast of the engine exhaust. The tail passed less than ten feet above them. Everything on the bridge slewed as drivers panicked. They watched the stricken aircraft as it plunged downward to their right, heading straight for the 14th Street Bridge crowded with traffic. The tail of the aircraft struck the bridge and sheared off, showering aviation fuel and sparks onto the vehicles below. The front of the plane plummeted into the freezing waters of the Potomac as cars on the 14th Street Bridge burst into flames.

They both sat shaking; Natasha was as white as a sheet, trembling. Instinctively they hugged and held each other. Everything was still for what seemed like an age. Then the red flashing lights started to appear, the eery silence after the screaming jet engines was broken by sirens and the sound of whirling helicopter blades. Still the snow fell. In the distance there were sounds of faint screams from beyond the shattered 14th Street Bridge as bystanders yelled and rescuers called out to survivors in the freezing river. There was nothing they could do. As soon as the traffic in front of them began to move they started the car and inched off the Williams Memorial Bridge. It was almost 7 by the time they entered the apartment. Sasha ran to them, her face tear streaked.

"Thank God you're both OK. I was so scared! Have you heard about the plane crash? They said cars had been hit on a bridge and people have died. I called the office but they said you'd both left by car and were going home! I turned on the news and it's all over the TV."

The family hugged and held each other close.

"The plane went right over us," Natasha said, "I thought it was going to hit us. We must have been lucky. Those poor people on the plane, and in the cars that were burned!"

What they had witnessed, and so nearly been part of, was the destruction of Air Florida flight 90 from Washington to Fort Lauderdale. It crashed a few moments after taking off in the freezing blizzard without de-icing properly. In all, 78 people died. It was the closest he had ever come to a real disaster, real death and destruction. His professional self was watching the TV news dispassionately and observing the emergency response, noting its inadequacy in the face of this sudden incident involving one aircraft, a few motor cars and a damaged road bridge. His personal self was tearing its heart out watching the fear and anguish of ordinary people caught up in a disaster not of their making.

For the first time in very many years he drank himself to sleep.

Chapter 27 - Washington DC, January 1982

While Washington picked up the pieces from Florida Airways flight 90, life continued as normal further up the Potomac at Langley. The CIA counterintelligence (Soviet - East Europe) analysts with their embedded FBI colleagues sifted through reports, phone intercepts, signal intelligence and agent reports looking for clues to the identity of Soviet secret agents. One report crossing their desks originated with the Naval Criminal Investigative Service a few miles downstream in Quantico.

The report concerned the probable theft of classified documents from the Naval Meteorological and Oceanographic Command in Mississippi a few months earlier. The documents included detailed seismographic charts of the eastern seaboard, and a complete set had gone missing. After a slow but painstaking investigation suspicion had fallen on a clerk, one Carlos Gomez, but nothing conclusive had been found. During a routine interview with NCIS investigators at the Stennis Space Center, Carlos Gomez started to admit stealing the documents on behalf of a foreign agent before suffering a massive fatal heart attack. The enquiry moved up a gear and the late Carlos Gomez's life, sad and lonely as it was, was subjected to extreme scrutiny. Again, nothing conclusive was found, but the names of anyone who had ever been in contact with Gomez were sent as a matter of course to the CIA and FBI for researching. It was standard practice.

The counterintelligence (Soviet - East Europe) analysts crunched their way through the lists. One snippet that fell out was a possible trace on an Ewald Koenig who had been reported to the FBI by an employee of the Boeing Corporation in Seattle who thought he was about to be coerced into passing information. Unfortunately, the Boeing employee always thought he was about to be coerced into passing information and was well known for it. The FBI felt at the time they had no grounds to pursue Koenig. Now Koenig's name appeared in the contact lists for the late Carlos Gomez, the lowly navy clerk from a backwater in Mississippi who had been about to confess to a crime of espionage. The embedded FBI agents at Langley sent a report to their field office in Wilmington, Delaware asking them to find out more about this Ewald Koenig. That was where he lived.

The same counterintelligence (Soviet - East Europe) analysts also read a report from an FBI informant, a Russian with a severe illicit gambling habit who was employed as a security guard at the USSR's Permanent Mission to the UN in New York. That report was brief and factual. A Soviet diplomat named Viktor Gumnov had presented himself at the Permanent Mission and had given the current password to be allowed access to the KGB communications suite. Gumnov, ostensibly some sort of cultural attaché, had to be a KGB officer.

The embedded FBI agents sent another report to FBI headquarters asking for a comprehensive profile of Gumnov, while the CIA sent a request to all friendly intelligence services asking for any traces on him.

******

On 25th January he received an early call from Leonid. They needed to talk. In the dungeon Leonid poured tea; he didn't look well.

"Suslov is dead," Leonid announced. "He died last night. It seems he had a heart attack a few days ago and never recovered. It may not mean much to you, Viktor, but this is a real crisis. Suslov carried a lot of weight, a lot of influence, in the Kremlin. He was a Russian first and foremost, and a communist second - even though he was the Party's chief idealogue. He was a steadying influence who stopped a lot of potentially disastrous adventures that the hotheads wanted to embark on, military interventions in Hungary, Czechoslovakia, Poland, places like that. He kept things in order. Now he's gone. But the next bit is startling. The new Second Secretary of the Party, which means Brezhnev's probable successor, is going to be none other than our own Yuri Vladimirovich."

"Andropov?" he said, surprised.

"Yes, but not immediately. Chernenko will stand in for a few months while the transition pantomime plays out. Chernenko won't have any power, though."

"So, who's going to take over at Head Office?" he asked. "Not Fedorchuk, I hope."

"You hope wrong. My information is they're bringing Vitaly Vasileyevich back from Kyiv to take over as Chairman of the KGB for the whole USSR. He's a bastard, a hard-liner, and he hates Andropov. I don't know where all this leaves VRYaN. The whole power balance in Moscow has changed; instability now will cost us time and possibly bring the unthinkable closer. It will also encourage our Warsaw Pact allies to start flexing their muscles. The GDR has been pushing for

On 25th January he received an early call from Leonid. They needed to talk. In the dungeon Leonid poured tea; he didn't look well.

more autonomy - they want to demolish the Berlin Wall and have closer relations with the West! The Czechs never liked us anyway. The Solidarity thing in Poland is getting out of hand, and Lenin only knows why Jaruzelski allowed that interfering Polish Pope into the country! Hundreds of thousands of Catholics on the streets cheering for him! As for the Huns, the Bulgarians and the Romanians - who knows?"

Leonid paused.

"It affects us too, Viktor, you in particular."

"How so?" he asked, stirring his tea.

"It's opened up a second intelligence front. Until last night our priority was to get inside Reagan's head, to work out his intentions. Now we also have to get inside the heads of all our Warsaw Pact allies - thank God the Albanians and the Yugoslavians are out of it - to work out what their intentions are too. They may start to try to do deals with the Americans, and if they do we need to know about it. The Americans, if they have any sense at all, will want to divide and conquer, do what they can to weaken the Pact. And if the Pact is weakened, the Iron Curtain, as Churchill called it, will be eaten by moths and will be left full of holes. That will worry the hard-liners and even the moderates in Moscow. It will threaten our very existence just as much as Reagan's missiles.

"So, Viktor, and this is just between you and me, get yourself into the Warsaw Pact meeting circuit. Ambassador Brevnov meets all the other WP ambassadors on a regular basis. I want you there too, talking to the hangers-on. I want to know what they are thinking, what they're whispering to each other over the *samovar*. I want you to see the looks they give each other; hear the questions they ask and the questions they don't answer. Do you understand what I'm asking?"

"I do, but I have a question too," he said, "why are you doing this? Why are you saying it's just between you and me?"

Leonid sighed.

"I've been here before, Viktor. I've lived through Stalin and Khrushchev; I've seen the power plays during transitions. Our great experiment needs to survive all that, Russia needs to survive. Whoever comes out on top, whether it's one man again or another collective leadership, they will need to know the reality. We will tell them when the time is right. If we're too open with Head Office now, whatever we say could be used to promote or defeat one faction or another. Our goal is more important than that. Is this heresy to you, Viktor?"

"Heresy is not a word I use, Leonid," he said. "What you're doing is dangerous, and not just for you…but I agree with you. The country and the revolution are what we need to protect."

The two men looked at each other for a long time. Then they stood and quietly left the room.

Chapter 28 – Washington DC, late June 1982

It was happening as Leonid had predicted. Yuri Andropov had become the Second Secretary of the Communist Party, *de facto* successor to the aging and increasingly unwell Leonid Brezhnev. Vitaly Fedorchuk had also become Chairman of the KGB, and already there were feelings of disquiet in the lumbering department. He was reflecting on this, and all the other events that had happened so far in a packed 1982. He and Leonid had been busy pulling strings, paying agents, talking to influencers, all in support of their quest for knowledge about the intentions of the Reagan administration. In parallel they were keeping tabs on their Warsaw Pact allies. As always, Leonid was grounded in the embassy while he went out and performed in the field. It was a fruitful partnership.

There was a passing frisson of excitement on the international front when, in late February, the Argentinians decided to invade the Falkland Islands. While neither he nor Leonid, or indeed anyone at Head Office, cared who owned the tiny archipelago of windswept warts in the South Atlantic, their interest was piqued when the British went to take them back and asked their closest allies, the Americans, for help. Reagan said no.

Reagan's refusal led to some acrimony, and for a moment it looked like the two stalwarts of NATO could be heading for a serious falling out. America held firm and the Brits had to get their refuelling and resupplying done elsewhere. But having beaten off the invaders and reclaimed her god-forsaken territory, Margaret Thatcher seemed to be in the mood to kiss and make up. Rather than witnessing the longed-for fragmentation of NATO, he and Leonid saw an invitation extended to Ronald Reagan to pay a State Visit to Britain and address both houses of Parliament! Reagan used the opportunity to tell the British that Marxism / Leninism was soon to be dead and buried, 'confined to the ash heap of history' as he put it in his speech.

In the summer Natasha and Sasha had been perplexed more than once by his insistence that they go on trips as a family, trips to places he normally wouldn't want to be seen dead in. Apart from the trip with Natasha to Las Vegas to see a mediocre performance of Swan Lake by an off-colour Bolshoi Ballet company, he had dragged his reluctant women to Memphis, Tennessee, to visit Graceland, the former home of and shrine to the late Elvis Presley which had just been opened to the public as a museum, and to Disney World in Florida.

"But Papa, I'm nearly eighteen years old," Sasha protested, "why are you making me go to a kids' playground to see a giant talking rat? It's gross!"

"Mickey is a mouse, not a rat," he had said, "I'm sure we will all enjoy it, if only because it will make us feel culturally superior."

In truth, the trip to Memphis and Graceland was to make a brush-contact with a long-standing 'friend' of the Soviet Union, a senior figure in the Labor Movement - an Elvis fan - who was actively pushing the anti-nuclear agenda in the US. Using the family visit as cover, he had located the contact and fell in behind him in the long line to file past the grave of the late superstar. They had exchanged identical backpacks without Natasha or Sasha noticing. In the backpack he swapped with the 'friend' were bundles of used banknotes totalling 800,000 US dollars; in the one he received were detailed plans for an imminent mass rally demanding nuclear disarmament. The plans laid out how many people would attend, who the celebrity cheerleaders were going to be, and an account of expenditure to date. The rally happened a few days later on 12th June in New York and it was on TV all around the world. Three quarters of a million people attended, the largest protest in US history at the time, and that was the official figure. The musical star-turns performing on the day included Bruce Springsteen, James Taylor and Linda Ronstadt. He and Leonid had celebrated their achievement by the pool at the *dacha*.

The trip to Orlando was to inflate the already significant ego of a Russian émigré in the Jewish community of Florida who was still a closet friend of the Kremlin and a powerful agent of influence. He left the quietly fuming Natasha and Sasha in their nauseating hotel while he went through the pretence of a secret award ceremony with the émigré, presenting him with a medal celebrating his 'outstanding contribution to peace'. In return he got a detailed briefing on the progress of developments for a new missile guidance system for the US government which one of the émigré's golf buddies was participating in.

The visits to three of the glittering pleasure-domes of the United States, Las Vegas, Disney World and Graceland, had done little to boost the family's opinion of popular American culture. Even Sasha found the enforced jollity wearing and irritating, and she couldn't wait to get back to Bethany Beach and the love of her life.

Sasha had spent a lot of time at the beach, often going on her own by bus or train, or with Steven in his borrowed pickup. She often spent weekends there, and longer if she wasn't in school. He and Natasha discussed their daughter's relationship, and at his insistence Natasha agreed to have 'the conversation' with her.

With more than a little trepidation she sat Sasha down at the table the balcony and poured them both a glass of wine.

"Sasha, we know you're serious about Steven. We just want to make sure you know what you're doing, and that he's serious about you too. We don't want you to end up with the consequences of a teenage crush and a boy's desire to experiment with sex. Mostly we want you to be happy."

Sasha reached out and took her mother's hand.

"I know what I'm doing, Mama, and I do know how to not get pregnant if that's what you mean. We do take precautions. I love Stepan, and he loves me. It isn't a crush or a sexual experiment. It's real, like you and Papa. We want to get married."

Natasha let out a cry and for a moment thought she was going to faint. She called for him.

"You can't get married," he told Sasha, "you're much too young!"

"I'm the same age Mama was when she married you," Sasha said.

"That's different!" he protested.

"No, it isn't!" Sasha and Natasha cried in unison.

"So, you're happy for her to do this?" he asked his wife.

"If she really wants to, and he does too, then yes. I am happy for Sasha to be happy."

Inwardly he groaned. He wanted happiness for his daughter too, and for all he knew this Steven might be the man to do it for her. But he was an American, and Viktor was a KGB officer spying on Americans. The thought of the paperwork and the approvals from Moscow and the visa and immigration issues made his palms sweat.

"Very well," he said, "but I want to talk to Steven and his parents first. You'll need my permission, whether you like it or not, because of the paperwork if nothing else."

"Thank you, Papa," Sasha said, "I do want your permission, and I want you to be happy for us. We've thought about the official issues with immigration and our embassy and everything. Stepan's dad's lawyer is looking into it, and he says that as long as you and Mama say yes, he thinks he can get my immigration status changed and eventually get citizenship. I can have dual nationality, apparently, so I'll still be Russian as well as American. He said you'd have to help with the Russian government side, seeing as I only have a diplomatic passport. I'll need an ordinary USSR one at first."

"So, you've been planning this?" he asked.

"Of course we have; we're not stupid! If we couldn't get married because of all the nationality and immigration rules we were going to wait, but now it looks like we can overcome the difficulties and we won't have to. We want to get married next spring.

Then we plan to get an apartment in Boston while Stepan finishes college."

"What will you do for money?" Natasha asked.

"We've thought about that too. Stepan's fixed it for me to help out in the Slavic languages department at Boston, nothing very complicated, just doing some conversation with Russian language students, some translations, making some audio tapes for the language laboratory, that sort of thing. With the money he makes in the summer we'll have enough to keep us through the winter. When he graduates next year, he'll get a good job and then I'll go to college. Then we'll have some babies. It's all worked out."

All this was going through his tired mind as he drove slowly down an unmade dirt track. He'd found a place a few miles upstream on the Potomac where there were some rapids. He'd taken to early morning fly-fishing and had left the apartment before dawn to drive up there. The track led down to a wooded area on the riverbank; there were forests on both sides, and even with his headlights on there were patches of deep shadow. He wasn't driving fast. He rounded a bend and suddenly a dark shape darted across the track, too small for a bear, too large for a raccoon. He stood on the brake and the Lincoln's tyres skidded on the loose surface. The car drifted and wallowed like a boat in a current. A larger dark shape appeared in front of the car. He couldn't control it, and with a startled cry the larger figure disappeared in front of the hood. The car came to a halt. He leapt out and ran to the front. A man was lying crumpled in the dirt, covered in dust. He had rolled himself into a ball and he was half-covered by the front fender.

"Oh my god!" he exclaimed, "are you alright?"

"That damn dog!" the figure on the ground muttered.

With this, a large black Labrador came trotting out of the woods, its tail wagging. The Labrador started licking the fallen figure before turning his friendly attention to him.

"Are you hurt, sir?" he asked.

"I don't think so - just shaken up, and I think my dignity is bruised. Help me up, will you?"

He did so, supporting the man until he was able to lean on the car.

"I think the stupid dog must have seen a squirrel or something and just took off. My wife would kill me if anything happened to it, so I went after him. We come down here a lot and I've never seen a car on this track before. I wasn't thinking. My fault."

The man stood upright, and in the pale dawn light he looked at him. The man was in his fifties, with a distinctive pointed nose and a high forehead with a widow's peak, his hair turning from dark brown to grey. His heart skipped a beat as he realised the man he had just run down, the man he could easily have killed, was none other than Zbigniew Brzezinski - until January 1981 President Carter's highly esteemed National Security Advisor. It was said that Reagan wanted him to stay on but he had politely declined.

"I'm so sorry, Mr Brzezinski, I didn't see you. You're sure you're not hurt?"

"You pronounced it right. You're not from round here, are you?" Brzezinski said, a smile flitting across his face.

He looked at the car and noticed its diplomatic licence plate.

"You're Russian, Soviet rather. That could have been awkward, couldn't it, if you'd killed me? Especially if you're KGB or something. And let's face it, everyone at 1125 16th Street is 'something'."

"Viktor Gumnov, First Secretary. I'm head of the Union of Soviet Societies for Friendship and Cultural Contacts. I'm a keen angler and I've taken to fly-fishing in the rapids just down there. It's best this time of day."

"Ah! The SSOD. Less of a mouthful. I know what it is, and I know what it does too. Well, Mr Gumnov, thank you for not killing me. I'm not ready for that yet; these are interesting times and I've things to do. I hope I haven't ruined your fishing."

"Well, the moment has gone. You need to be tranquil and focussed to succeed with a fly rod. Your trousers have a rip in them, can I give you a ride home or something?"

"Thank you, yes. It wouldn't do for me to be stopped by the cops looking like a bum who's been out on the town all night, would it? You don't mind the dog in the car? He's been rummaging in the bushes, so who knows what he's covered in."

"I'll have someone clean it out later."

"Some are still more equal than others, eh?"

He drove the slightly battered statesman a couple of miles to his Virginia home. Brzezinski gave him a card with his office number on it, he reciprocated.

"It would be good to meet and talk, Mr Gumnov, Viktor. There are things happening here and in Moscow that are worrying. I'd like to try to understand it all from another viewpoint. Nothing sinister, I assure you, I'm not asking you to be a spy - not for me, anyway. Let's have lunch next week."

"I'd like that. Mr Brzezinski. I'll call your office."

"Call me Zbig, it's easier." He held out his hand and they shook. Zbigniew Brzezinski dragged the very comfortable Labrador out of the back seat, where he'd left a muddy trail on the leather. He attached a leash and walked the dog up a path to a neat, welcoming looking house, waving at him over his shoulder as he opened the door.

He sat for a moment in the car, trying to ignore the smell of wet dog. Leonid would not believe him.

He poured tea for them both. In the dungeon they sat and talked.

"Moscow was very pleased with the anti-war demonstration in New York," Leonid started. "At first they complained about the money we'd spent, but I told them where else can you get Springsteen and Ronstadt and the other famous musicians and movie stars, not to mention three quarters of a million people shouting your message to the world, all for around a dollar a head? Head Office is happy now. They told me that Brezhnev invited a select audience to his state *dacha* to watch a video of the demonstration over and over again. He's still not well, you know."

"Who, Brezhnev?" he asked.

"Yes, after the accident in March in Tashkent. The platform he was standing on collapsed and he injured himself quite badly. Fedorchuk sent a few people to the *gulag* to encourage the others, even though he himself withdrew the order for a full KGB advance team to check everything out. Andropov and Fedorchuk are at each other's throats over it. Andropov wants Fedorchuk punished for his negligence, but Brezhnev won't hear of it. So, Andropov and Fedorchuk are throwing verbal rocks at each other every chance they get. It doesn't bode well.

"Meanwhile, we need to get on with the real work. They like that you had lunch with Brzezinski, but they don't believe the report you sent back. They say it's just the Washington message."

"I just repeated what Brzezinski told me," he said, "it may be Washington messaging, but I believe him.

He said that the US isn't going to start a war, but it is ready and willing to defend itself if someone else does. My reading of it is that by 'start a war' he meant against us, the USSR. I asked him about America's position in respect of NATO and the commitment to mutual defence. He just smiled and said NATO isn't going to be allowed to start a war either."

"So why the new Pershing missiles then?" Leonid asked rhetorically. "Why does the US need to place nuclear missiles so close to our borders? Our sources close to Martin Marietta who make them are saying the new missiles will be ready for deployment in a few months. The Americans are messing with the SALT treaty, cheating so that they can deploy the new missiles with converted existing launch systems so they can say they're just replacements, not additional new weapons. The Pershing IIs are more adaptable than the original Pershings, and between them and the Cruise missiles in Germany they can take us any time they want. Our Pioneer missiles can wipe out Europe, but they won't touch the US. Only our ICBM's can do that, and we wouldn't get a chance to use them.

"It's getting tense, Viktor. Even though Fedorchuk and Andropov hate each other, they're more or less in agreement and are telling Brezhnev the same thing. Fedorchuk is the more outspoken; he says the Americans will strike first. Andropov is trying to be more rational, but the fact is he doesn't trust Reagan or the people around him. He thinks they're all liars and homicidal maniacs."

"So, we just have to keep digging, Leonid," he said, "try to find out what the Americans are really thinking. I've used Brzezinski's name to get to meet some other people close to the White House. Also, that old actress I met at the embassy reception mentioned me to the First Lady and I've got to know her Chief of Staff. They call her that, but she's more a social secretary; she arranges Nancy's appointments and parties. I've been to a couple of drinks receptions now, and although I've not met Nancy Reagan herself to speak to yet, I've seen her. Strange colour. Anyway, everyone knows I'm Russian but they're still friendly and curious. I'm pretty sure if any of them had a feeling that the president was planning to annihilate us they might give it away by the way they treat me, or rather avoid me."

"Good point, Viktor, but I'm not sure Vitaly Vasilyevich is going to change his mind based on how Nancy Reagan looks at you over the rim of her champagne glass. Keep it up though. We've got work to do on your plan, too. That research ship is coming in soon - you need to fix your schedule to spend a day or two with them. They need to know exactly what they might need to do, and more importantly exactly where to do it to make the plan work. You haven't changed your mind about it, have you?"

"About the plan? No, but I really hope we never have to use it. I'll go and visit the research ship when it's in Alexandria and brief the captain in detail, and the Head Office man on board."

"Careful what you say, Viktor. It will get back to Fedorchuk."

"Understood. Anything else?"

"Yes. There's a cargo plane coming into Chicago O'Hare with art works for that exhibition."

"The Roerich one? My SSOD team's organising it."

"That's it. You'll need to go and check the artworks before they're offloaded - get Craig Durov to fix you an airside pass at the airport. One of Baranov's guys is going to be on the plane and it's important you see him. He won't be getting off, just using the plane as a convenient and secure meeting place."

"As long as I don't have to do anything technical with the paintings. Nicholas Roerich is a bit modern for me."

"Don't worry. There'll be a proper art expert nearby who will really check that they're the right paintings and none have gone missing or been switched on the way, and to make sure they hang them the right way up in the exhibition."

"I'll head up there after the Independence Day weekend. By the way, did anything come back on the checks I asked for on the Rourke family? I've had 'Jim' checking them out with his sources and so far, they seem genuine."

"Clean sheet from Moscow. I slipped it in with the routine stuff for searching across all the Warsaw Pact and non-aligned allies. As far as anyone knows, no one in the family is associated with any friendly or hostile intelligence or security agency. They're good honest working folks. Are you sure it's a good idea to let Sasha do this? Marry an American, I mean?"

"Steven Rourke's a good kid - bright, decent. He loves her, she loves him. I don't really have a say in it. They're going to do it sooner or later, no matter what I think or say. Natasha is excited and pleased. I've explained the bureaucratic nightmare it's going to cause but she doesn't care."

"Nightmare? You're not kidding. You could get a recall to Moscow to explain yourself when they hear about it. Good job you've got plenty of credit in the bank. And anyway, if Fedorchuk is right about what the Americans are planning, why not let her be happy while she can."

He glared at his friend and boss as the meaning of what he had just said sank in.

******

On 3rd July the family left Washington for York, Pennsylvania. They had been invited by the Rourkes for the holiday weekend, the first 'proper' meeting of the two families soon to become one. It was a warm and pleasant day, and the traffic was light. The mood in the car, however, was somewhat tense. Natasha was in the back, Sasha alongside her father in the front. Neither felt much like talking. He concentrated on driving, grateful for the distraction.

When they got to the Rourke's, Steven was outside pretending to be doing something to the pickup, but in reality just waiting nervously. His face lit up when he saw the Lincoln turn into the driveway. He restrained himself and helped Natasha out first before reaching for Sasha.

"Glad you could make it, Viktor, Mrs Gumnova," Steven said, holding Sasha's hand proudly. "Mom and Dad are on the back porch with a cool drink for you all. I'll take you through and come back for your bags."

Steven led them through a cool shady house to the shady porch. Brendan and Hazel Rourke were standing together, smiling."

"Welcome, all," said Hazel, "it's so good of you to join us for the weekend. We've been looking forward to it so much. Will you have some lemonade? I made it myself this morning."

After a while Hazel took Natasha off for a tour of the house and a discussion about wedding plans. Sasha and Steven had disappeared somewhere together. He and Brendan sat on rocking chairs watching swallows swoop balletically.

"Are you happy about all this Viktor?" Brendan asked, having replaced his lemonade with a beer.

"I'm not unhappy, Brendan. Frankly though, I think they're too young and I don't know how Sasha's going to manage in the US, so far from her friends and family."

"We were all young once and she'll have friends and family here too. It's a big move, I'll grant you, but the US can be a good place for immigrants. The world will get smaller one day soon, and it'll get easier for people to mix."

"Let me turn it around, Brendan. Are you happy that your son is marrying a Russian?"

"He's marrying Lexa - Sasha. It doesn't matter to me or Hazel where she's from or what her first language is. I'm happy he's marrying your daughter. They're meant for each other, the same as you and Natasha, the same as me and Hazel."

"*Na Zdorovie,* Brendan."

"*Slàinte Mhòr!* That's Irish for good health. Welcome to the family, Viktor. We'll take care of Lexa for you, and one day we'll all come to your home in Russia. That's going to be the hardest, I guess, it being so difficult for us to see each other when your time here is up. I suppose you'll have to go back, and it won't be easy for us or Steven to come and see you, or for you to come here. Lexa will be able to - she'll be keeping her Russian nationality, or so the lawyer says. She'll be able to come and go, every now and then."

"I'm sure we'll adjust. The whole concept of migration and resettling in another country is new for me and Natasha. We're both Russian, we've only ever lived in Russia before coming here. We can't imagine just going to live in another country."

"America is full of people living in another country, Viktor. Like I said, it's a country of migrants. I'm a migrant, so is Hazel. I came here in the fifties with my brother. We're from County Kildare, just near Dublin, from farming people. After the Second World War Ireland was broke, even though it wasn't involved in the fighting. Times were hard. Me and my brother, Liam, we went to England for work. We'd heard there was plenty of it, but if there was we didn't get any. We couldn't even get a place to stay. Every time we went for a room there were these signs in the windows: 'no blacks, no dogs, no Irish.' Not exactly welcoming. I thought it must be because we'd stayed neutral in the war, but it turned out the English just don't like foreigners that much. After best part of a year Liam and I gave up and went home.

"Then someone said go to America. Irish people could back then, for just a few quid. Third class on a steamer. I wouldn't fancy it these days, but back then it was fine. Cramped, noisy, lots of drinking and a bit of fighting, just like home really. We landed in New York, and guess what? The streets weren't paved with gold.

There was no one waiting with open arms and an open cheque book giving out jobs and houses.

"Liam and I eventually got through the immigration and were directed to the Lower West Side. It was where they sent the Irish immigrants. Jewish ones were sent to Brooklyn, the Italians to New Jersey or the Lower East Side. We got Hell's Kitchen. Lexa said you'd been there. It's better now than it was then. Anyhow, in the fifties you had few choices as a young Irish immigrant. You could be a criminal; you could be a cop - which was sort of the same thing but with worse pay - or you could go into whatever construction work the Italians didn't want. Liam and I went on the buildings for a couple of years, then decided enough was enough.

"We went south, to get away from the icy wind and the gangsters and the Teamsters. We'd learned enough to start our own business, heating, ventilation, air conditioning, it's a great climate for that - freezing in the winter, roasting in the summer. We worked hard, and the business was good, still is. We have a reputation for being reliable and honest, and for good craftsmanship. Sadly, Liam took a heart attack a few years back and died. His family is just a few doors down. You'll get to meet them, I'm sure.

"So, what I'm getting at, Viktor, is that this is a land for migrants, as long as they work hard and give good value. I've done OK for a potless Irish farm boy. I'm an American now, but most Americans hang on to their roots and I'm still thought of as Irish. So is Steven, even if he's only ever been there twice. There are opportunities here in the States if you're prepared to see them and take them. Sure, there's poverty and injustice and discrimination, but you get as much of that in London or Paris or even Moscow, I'd guess. Now, how did you like the bourbon I gave you? No matter, I've some proper Irish whiskey for you to try. I'm dry with talking."

Chapter 30 - Chicago, IL, July 1982

He waited at the cargo terminal at O'Hare airport while the Aeroflot Ilyushin IL-76 cargo plane taxied slowly along the tarmac. A small squadron of customs officials clustered around the aircraft steps when it had stopped, shadowed by anxious representatives of the shipping company who had been paid handsomely to ensure the safe and timely arrival of the precious artworks on board. When they had done what they needed to do the customs officials and handling agents drifted off, leaving him alone with a team of porters borrowed from The Hermitage in Leningrad. The real art expert busied herself checking the packaging's security seals before ordering each piece to be removed from the cargo hold to the waiting vans.

He climbed the steps to the aircraft galley where an attendant was hovering. She pointed wordlessly to the small passenger cabin where a thin man with cropped grey hair sat alone. He had never seen him before.

"Comrade Lieutenant Colonel," the man said, "I am from the Chairman's office."

The man didn't introduce himself further.

"Comrade," he said cautiously.

"I have come a long way to talk to you. I would have preferred that you had made the journey to see me, but it seems that Comrade General Baranov still holds you in some esteem. He insisted that you be left here for now. The Chairman reluctantly agreed."

He was concerned and perplexed by the anonymous man's tone and apparent contempt for him. He said nothing. The man had not invited him to sit.

"The previous Chairman was impressed by your rambling commentaries about the Reagan regime's intentions towards the Soviet Union. He was persuaded by your assessment that the Americans are unlikely to strike a first blow without some clear warning, or in response to some visible, if fabricated, international threat. Comrade Chairman Fedorchuk is not so gullible. He knows that the Americans are preparing to strike us! Your so-called intelligence merely confuses our political masters and makes them deaf to the correct message. The Chairman directs you to stop reporting these falsehoods and submit to us only clear intelligence that the Americans are planning to attack. That is an order!

"Next, you are to proceed with preparations to implement the plan you have devised to disable the enemy and disrupt their unprovoked aggression. The research vessel from the Shirshov Institute arrives in Alexandria in the next few weeks. You are to arrange to visit it and make yourself known to Colonel Lebedev. He also represents the Chairman's office. You will brief him fully and in detail about when and where the devices must be placed. The devices are to be prepared with ultra-low frequency receivers so they can be activated locally by remote control. You will need to plan to have agents in the near vicinity to detonate the devices when instructed to do so. We cannot afford to have detonation signals traced back to one of our vessels or establishments. Do I make myself clear?"

"Yes, comrade. You do realise that those agents, who we do not yet have, will almost certainly be killed, don't you?" His question was rhetorical, but the man answered anyway.

"That is of no consequence to us, or to you. The survival of the Soviet Union is all that matters. You will be here to ensure that it happens, and we will be taking measures to ensure that you do not fail in your duty. People very dear to you will suffer badly if you waver."

"Do you realise how stupid that threat sounds, Comrade? If you are correct about the Americans, all of us will suffer badly regardless of what I do or don't do."

"You are impertinent, Gumnov!" the man spat. "Don't you dare imply that the Chairman is stupid!"

"Maybe it's just his messenger boy, then!" He was fighting to control his anger. "You have delivered your message, whatever your name is, and I have heard it. I know my duty, and now I wish to get on with my job."

With that he turned on his heel and left without a further word. He had no doubt that his response would get back to Fedorchuk, and that his time in the USA and the KGB would probably end quite soon, and with some ignominy. Despite his anger, his blood was chilled at the prospect of what he had been ordered to do. He wondered how he would feel if he had the same view as Fedorchuk about the Americans. He had met some who would indeed be happy to strike a first fatal blow and start the war that really would end all wars, and probably all civilisations too. But these people had only a small voice and next to no influence over the Commander in Chief.

Most of the people he had come to know were patriotic Americans, of course, but they had a world view rather than a narrow nationalistic one. They wouldn't initiate, or even allow, a course of action that would result in the USA going back to the pre-industrial age. What good would superpower status be then? The Americans would only attack in the face of extreme provocation. The real risk of a sudden cataclysmic holocaust lay in accidents and misunderstandings. Such was the level of fear and distrust on both sides it would only take a small spark to light the final fuse.

He walked back to his car in the cargo terminal parking lot. He wanted more than anything to drive back to Washington, to Natasha, for her warmth and comfort but he knew he must stay in Chicago until the exhibition opened. He would call her tonight, just to hear her voice. By the time he got back to Washington Leonid would probably have received a nuclear telegram from the Chairman's Office, maybe demanding his head on a silver platter.

******

As he was meeting with the curators at the Chicago art gallery and helping to interpret for the Hermitage experts, all the while trying to put his encounter with the unnamed messenger of doom out of his mind, the secret joint intelligence and security committee was having its weekly meeting at FBI Headquarters in Washington. This week the CIA had brought more people, and the FBI had Senior Special Agents from both their counterintelligence and counter-espionage units. Something was happening for a change.

"What we're seeing," said one of the CIA analysts, "is a marked increase in the frequency of attempted agent recruitment and hostile surveillance at our military bases in Europe. Apart from the Russian services, the East Germans and the Czechoslovakians are prominent players. Our colleagues in Defense are doing OK at fending off the attacks and thus far we're not aware of any successful recruitment of our people as agents, but the intensity of activity is highly unusual."

"We're seeing the same in the signals area," said a representative from the NSA, "concerted interception efforts directed at our traffic, mostly aimed at the military and with special focus on our activities in Europe. Again, it's mainly the Russians and the East Germans who are doing it."

"So, what's behind it?" asked the FBI Special Agent in Charge, the SAC, who was chairing the meeting.

"They could just be worried about the annual joint exercise," said the CIA analyst, "given all the hostile comments from both sides. The Able Archer war games take place every November and we always see a surge in the preceding months. It's activity we've seen before, but not on this scale."

"Is there any agent intelligence from inside the Russian camp to enlighten us?" the SAC asked. "Anybody?"

"None of our existing sources can give us anything," the CIA analyst said, "I checked with the Ops Directorate before this meeting. They're working on it, but so far nothing. The British have told us that one of their assets said there have been some strange personnel postings over the last year or so, unusual in the type of people being moved and in the level of activity. The Soviet agencies like to work in a methodical way, they plan ahead. A sudden flurry isn't their style. The Brits can't or won't elaborate, and they won't say anything about their asset. That in itself must mean the asset is very valuable. Do you have anything in the US?" This last part was aimed at the FBI.

"Not in the Soviet Embassy," said the Senior Special Agent (SSA) from counterespionage, "at least not yet. The Russians only ever let other Russians from back home work in the embassy. They fly in everyone from janitors to drivers, chambermaids to cooks. They don't employ anyone local at all, not even to fix the plumbing, so we don't get many opportunities to get anyone inside. We've got a low-level asset at the Soviet Mission in New York, and we did have a guy in the East German Embassy, but he's been moved now. Before he went he told us that new people were arriving every week. Not all Stasi intelligence people, at least not acknowledged as such, but mostly being put in jobs they're not qualified for, in place of professional diplomats. The ambassador wasn't happy about it but was told to shut up by Berlin."

"You said 'not yet' about the Soviet Embassy?" the SAC queried.

"I can't promise anything, but there's a prospect we're working on - someone at the embassy here in Washington." The SSA said.

"Tell us more," the SAC invited, "this is a cleared meeting."

"OK," said the SSA, "there's a guy called Gennady Vlasov. He's an ex-quartermaster and he served in the same outfit as the current ambassador when he was in the army. Anyway, Ambassador Brevnov brought Vlasov to Washington with him to work on supply chain and procurement. Technically he's in the

Management Department under Leonid Grachev - more on him later - but it seems that Grachev doesn't direct what Vlasov does, or maybe he doesn't want to. Anyways, Vlasov goes up to New York every week or so in an embassy panel van. He takes diplomatic mail up and stocks up on things that people in the embassy want. He has his own sources of supply up there, some legit, some not. We've tailed him quite a few times now. Most of his trips are two, maybe three, days. He stays in the staff quarters of the Permanent Representative on the Upper East side.

"When he's dropped the mail, he dismisses the van and heads for his quarters, but he doesn't stay long. He's got a taste for the ladies, if you get my meaning, and he heads off to the girly bars and peep shows on 42nd Street and south. He's got a few regulars he goes to, and a few regular companions too. So, that doesn't make him a bad person, but it's interesting. When he's finished being 'entertained' our guy Vlasov heads off to see some other suppliers. Electronic goods, small items that cost a lot, knocked off US brand-name stuff, things like that. He buys cheap, often from Russian exiles who might not really want to be doing business with the Soviets but may have no choice, and we think he sells stuff on to other staff at the embassy. A lot of the stuff is defective or stolen.

"We've got a few levers on him now, and we're just about ready to pitch him. Now for the best bit! We have first rate information that he's been buying guns, Remington hunting rifles mostly but handguns too. As a foreigner he's not allowed to do that, and the Russians take an extremely dim view of privately owned firearms. With that and all the other stuff we've got on him so far, with photographs and statements from some of the folks he's been 'entertained' by or dealt with, we've got enough to get him sent home for criminal activity. We've also got enough to get him to work for us if he doesn't want his bosses to know what he's up to."

"What else do we know about Vlasov?" asked the SAC.

"We've pulled his passport from Immigration. He's fifty-one, married and accompanied by his wife. They live in an embassy apartment near Dupont Circle, it's tiny and a rat-hole. The wife doesn't work and never goes out. He's out nearly all the time. We know he's a heavy drinker from the bottles in his garbage, or maybe it's her who does the boozing. He's also a gambler, does some big bets on horses at the tracks, more than he could afford on his embassy pay. He's been here since Brevnov arrived - so longer than most staff at his level. The Russians rotate the lower grades every six to twelve months, their drivers every couple of years; it stops them getting too used to the good life. Vlasov's been here much longer than that, longer than most of the diplomats come to that. He's a classic for us."

"Sounds good. We need to get inside the embassy, find out what's going on in there. Let us know how the pitch goes. Anything else?"

"Yes," said the SSA, "you remember the project we had running to identify hostiles? We invited snippets from the Brits and West Germans, even the French. We got what we asked for, thousands and thousands of bits of gossip and hot air. In amongst it all were names, a lot of names, of possible KGB agents and officers. We've been cross-referencing and analysing it all. I mentioned Leonid Grachev a while ago. He's the Second Secretary in charge of the Management Section at the Soviet Embassy here, so not senior and not glamorous. Also, it's not one of the known or suspected KGB roles. We already know the identity of the *rezident* and a handful of KGB officers. However, in amongst all the crap there was a mention of Grachev from the West Germans. They had him marked as a KGB Major in Warsaw and a Lieutenant Colonel in Budapest. He showed up here in the US a few years ago as a Second Secretary in the consulate in San Francisco, now he's back - still a Second Secretary - at the Embassy in Washington. We think that Grachev heads up an ultra-covert KGB team here in the US. We've tried surveillance and phone taps and got absolutely nowhere. One interesting thing is that his wife is very friendly with another embassy wife, Natasha Gumnova. Gumnova's husband is Viktor Gumnov. He's been here a little over a year as head of the friendship and cultural outreach office, the SSOD.

"Two interesting things about Viktor Gumnov: first he's come out of nowhere to a plum overseas position. Our research says he's a marine scientist and a former naval officer. He's been to the US a couple of times as a delegate to scientific conferences; he's got a good reputation as an academic. So how come he's now in charge of friendship and outreach, which mostly entails having lunch with crazy American socialists? Second, Gumnov's name was on a list we got from the Brits as a suspected KGB officer, rank of Major. They won't tell us any more than that.

"We've looked at Gumnov and he doesn't seem to do anything he shouldn't. Craig Durov at State knows him, says he's an OK guy. Durov gets all Gumnov's travel plans and clears them, so we know everywhere Gumnov's been, at least officially. We've spoken to the people he's met with, and they all say he seems a genuine guy, everyone except some dumb asshole professor at Columbia in New York who refused to speak to anyone from the Fascist Bureau of Intimidation. He's one of those guys who inherited a fortune and can afford to be a commie.

"Gumnov's a fisherman and spends hours on the beach with his lines. Bethany Beach mostly, it's a couple of hours from here. He rented a room for his wife and daughter in the summer and he's been down there most weekends. When he doesn't spend the weekend on the beach he and the wife go to the Soviet R and R place at Pioneer Point. They have a daughter who's loved up with an American kid and she spends weekends with him. I'm nearly done. Just one more thing.

"In among all this other stuff I mentioned, something else from the West Germans. Deep in their old files are a few mentions of a teenage black-market dealer in Berlin just after the war. Seems he fell in with the Russians - it was either that or getting shot by gangsters or the Brits or us for looting and racketeering. They gave us a list of his known aliases. Routine searches show that a guy using one of his names ended up here in the USA. He's an engineer working for DuPont in Delaware. The name he's using is Ewald Koenig, but he's known as Huey. Huey's name appeared as a contact of a US Navy clerk who died of a heart attack after he'd been arrested by the NCIS for stealing secret documents. Huey was also named by a guy at Boeing in Seattle who thought he was being pitched by a Russian spy. Nothing came of it. So, we've been following Huey around, and guess what? He goes to the beach most weekends. Not just any beach, but Bethany Beach, Delaware, the one that Viktor Gumnov likes. How about that?"

"You should've been a detective," the SAC said. "Keep going on Grachev, Gumnov and Koenig, give them the works, and keep me informed. Could you guys at Langley and NSA run them through your systems? We'll catch up again next week. Good work, everybody."

Chapter 31 - Pioneer Point, MD, August 1982

He and Leonid sat in the shade near the pool. He sipped his tea and batted away an inquisitive fly while Leonid drank strong black coffee. It was late on Sunday afternoon and soon they would both head back to the city, Leonid with Katya and him alone. Natasha and Sasha were in the beachfront room, or rather Natasha was. Sasha, as usual, had disappeared with Steven, her Stepan, as soon as she decently could after arriving in Bethany Beach earlier in the week.

"Tell me again," Leonid said.

"I saw the chalk mark yesterday and went on to Bethany in the afternoon. This morning I took my rod to one of the regular places and set it all up. Jim didn't show for a while, but I was enjoying myself anyway. After an hour I saw him, or rather his shirt, coming down the beach. He was stopping to talk to just about everybody. There was a guy about a hundred yards from me also fishing. Jim stopped and spoke to him for five minutes and then wandered up to me."

"Tell me what he said, exactly what he said." Leonid demanded.

"He said hi, how're you doing? Like we'd never met before. He asked if I'd caught anything, and what was I using for bait. Then he said the feds are everywhere, all over Bethany and at his place too. They're looking at Natasha's room, they've set up across the street in a Ford panel van. His words. He told me not to move or speak to him, just to stay there for another hour or so and go back to Natasha later. He said it looked bad, and he was going to try to find out what was going on.

He said we'd do a fallback meeting in Washington on Wednesday morning."

"What do you make of it?" Leonid asked.

"After he spoke to me I did become aware of surveillance. They followed me back here. If they're on to Jim as well as me, it looks like there's been a serious compromise."

"The thing is, Viktor, they're on me too," said Leonid, "they have been for a while now. I thought it was just routine, and if it was only you too I'd still think it was just routine. But Jim? They'd have no routine reason to look at him. When you see him on Wednesday, if it's safe, tell him to put his work for us on hold, just do his day job as usual. You and I need to do that too. They, the FBI and the CIA, can't keep up this sort of surveillance forever if there's nothing to see. If we act normal for a couple of weeks, it should blow over."

"I hope you're right, but it's not good timing. The last I heard from Jim was that the Americans are getting ready to ship the new Cruise missiles to England, to that airbase at Greenham Common. The Cruise missiles are a danger to us; they fly low and slow, not like conventional nuclear missiles, so they're harder to detect. The missiles going to Greenham have a range of up to 2500 kilometres. They can reach well into our territory, Ukraine and Belarus, Leningrad even. The missiles carry nuclear warheads. The first we'd know about it was when they hit; we'd get no warning from our defence systems. Jim's got a guy inside the logistics chain for the Cruise missile project - they'll be deploying further east in Europe too by the end of 1983. Moscow is getting very jittery and hungry for intelligence. Putting Jim on hold now isn't good."

"There's never a good time to put people like Jim on hold, but we need to play a long game, Viktor. We Russians are chess players, are we not? Americans prefer checkers, it's quicker and simpler. We'll outplay them if we're patient."

"I hope so, Leonid, I do hope so," he said. Despite his expressionless face he was deeply worried. Not for himself, not even for Natasha. They would be fine, even if he was expelled as a KGB spy. He was worried for Sasha, whose happiness was so important to him. She would be distraught if she could never see Steven again because of what her father did for a job, spying for his country. But most of all, he was worried for Russia.

******

Weeks rolled on. He hadn't been able to meet Jim, Huey. He hadn't shown up on that Wednesday at all, so he'd waited a week before placing an advert in the newspaper. In response to that he did see him, but he didn't enter the Franklin Square Park as planned. He just kept walking fast along K Street towards the subway station. The meeting was being aborted. Three weeks after he'd last seen Jim, he could no longer see the surveillance operatives following him as he took his usual route to the embassy. Traffic was heavy, so he tried a few turns that would expose a tail if there was one. If there was, he didn't see it. He hoped that Leonid's prediction had been right.

Seven blocks south and five blocks east from where he sat in his office, the weekly meeting of the joint intelligence and security committee went into session at FBI HQ. The meeting had been larger than usual since the developments a few weeks before. The Special Agent in Charge called the meeting to order.

"Ok, folks, let's get an update from counterespionage first," the SAC started.

"As you all know," the Senior Special Agent from counterespionage said, "we've had two lines to follow. The first, recruitment of an agent inside the Soviet Embassy, has been successful."

The SSA paused as a ripple of excitement fluttered around the table.

"Gennady Ilyich Vlasov, codename 'Schooner', eventually agreed that his best interests are served if he cooperates with us. We're paying him a sizeable amount of money and have hinted at an offer of asylum and a new identity in the US as and when the time comes. We'll discuss this further in due course, but for now Schooner is sailing for us. So far, he's installed listening devices in the offices of the Ambassador and the Deputy Head of Mission, as well as in the office and meeting room used by Nikolai Semyanov, the KGB *rezident*. The devices are wireless recorders and transmitters that can be downloaded on demand by a listening post across the street out of hours. That way we minimise the risk of transmissions being detected."

"What about Grachev and Gumnov's offices?" the SAC asked.

"Schooner says that Grachev only does his management stuff in his office, nothing of any interest.

He never takes calls or has meetings in his office, so we don't think it's worth the risk. Same with Gumnov. He has a secretary in his office, and he spends a lot of time outside anyway. Schooner says that there's a secure meeting room in the basement, sound-proof, electronically shielded, no windows, self-contained lighting and ventilation, so no contact with the outside world at all. We have the same set up in our embassies too. It seems that Grachev and Gumnov get together in the secure room, which they call the 'dungeon', quite often. Schooner has access to the dungeon booking system and he's responsible for making sure it's stocked with tea, coffee, water and so on. We've given him a miniature recording device with one of these new-fangled memory chips in it. It is voice activated and the battery lasts a week at least. It has no moving parts and doesn't transmit or emit anything, so unless it's physically found it's undetectable. Schooner put the first one in a couple of weeks ago and changed it after a week. We've got it; it works."

"What did it tell us?" the SAC asked.

"It told us that the embassy is pretty well empty in August and that the dungeon wasn't used for much. It also told us that a married female Second Secretary is getting it on with a married male Third Secretary, and she's a screamer. Which is why they meet in the sound-proof dungeon. The point is the device works. The next time Grachev and Gumnov have one of their cosy chats we'll get every word no more than a week later."

"Great. What about the surveillance on those two and Koenig?" the SAC asked.

"We couldn't keep the authority open for Grachev and Gumnov, not without further intelligence. The tip we had from our low-level source in New York that Gumnov went to the mission last Christmas and used a KGB codeword to get in isn't considered enough, apparently, even if it does point a finger at Gumnov as a KGB agent. State and the Department of Justice are worried about infringing diplomatic treaties and inviting retaliation. We've kept it open on Koenig, though. He's cute; he knows surveillance and I don't doubt he knows that we're there. He's been behaving normally - he goes to work, he travels on business according to plans we know about, he goes home, he goes to the beach at weekends. He lives on his own in a two-room apartment in Wilmington. We've had a look-see and it's like a hotel room. Nothing personal in there at all, no books, no papers, no spy-stuff, just a few loud shirts and pairs of pants, two work suits and five white shirts. Socks and underwear. Some tinned food. He eats at a local diner when he's at home."

"What's your assessment?" the SAC asked.

"It's a classic cover base, and I'd guess he has somewhere else to call home. It's not a crime to have a tidy apartment, but I have no doubt at all that Koenig is an agent, deep-cover, but if he knows we're looking at him we're not going to find it easy to prove it."

"What's his immigration status?" one of the CIA people asked.

"He's West German, he has a Green Card and his work visa is in order. DuPont are sponsoring him for naturalisation. He's been in the US long enough and has no criminal convictions; isn't bankrupt or a drug user, so unless something happens, he could be an American in a couple of months."

"Can we stop it?" the CIA analyst asked.

"Not without probable cause," the SAC said. "We need evidence that he's committing a crime or acting against the interests of the United States, and we just don't have that yet. Anyway, it's hard to rescind naturalisation but not impossible. We'll keep on him."

******

In the Soviet Embassy Gennady Vlasov was doing the rounds of the few people who remained at their posts during the long, hot weeks of August and early September. The air-conditioning was broken again, and Gennady's shirt was soaked with sweat. His sparse hair stuck to his scalp. An aroma of stale garlic and rancid animal fat followed him. He was taking orders for his next shopping trip to New York the following week. Vlasov knocked on Leonid's door.

"Good afternoon, Comrade Second Secretary. Is there anything you need from New York? The commissary here is a bit short of supplies, but I can get anything you need while I'm up there."

Leonid looked up.

"No, thank you, Comrade Gennady Ilyich. I'm not a rich man and I can't afford your prices! For a communist you make a very good capitalist." Leonid said this with a smile, beneath which was nothing but contempt for this slimy black-marketeer.

"Very well, Comrade. While I'm here, will you be needing the secure meeting room while I'm away? If so, I will arrange for it to be restocked."

"Yes, I'll be using it later this afternoon. Please put fresh tea and water in there and be sure to put the air-conditioning on."

"Of course, Comrade Grachev."

Gennady slunk off and set about his task. The tiny device the Americans had given him was already secreted under the conference table, stuck on with a thin adhesive pad.

Leonid accosted him in the corridor. He told him to come to the dungeon at 5pm. Bring some vodka, he'd said.

Leonid was glad to see that Vlasov had restocked the room and had turned the air conditioning on. The room was pleasantly cold. He arrived on time and opened a bottle of ice-cold Stolichnaya. He poured two shots.

"A Red Flag over the White House, comrade," he said to Leonid.

Leonid chuckled.

"I said that to an FBI man once when I was in San Francisco. He was a good guy. I said it was a toast we said a lot, he said they have one too. Theirs is to a White Flag over Red Square. It's funny. Now, how are you doing?"

"OK. I haven't seen a tail in a couple of weeks. It's like you said it would be. I've been going about my SSOD business as planned and cleared with Craig Durov at the State Department. The only risk I've taken is the visit to the research vessel, the *Mstislav Keldysh*, when it came to Alexandria. That creepy guy in Chicago told me to meet with a Colonel Lebedev."

"You really upset him, Viktor. I had to call in a few favours with General Baranov to stop Fedorchuk from getting you recalled. I've heard that Andropov is determined to get rid of him and replace him with Chebrikov - he's called Viktor too, by the way, so you should get along. It's going to happen in the next couple of months and when it does the creepy guy from Chicago will be toast, or at least checking sailors' identity cards in Arkhangelsk, I've seen to that. So, you got to see Lebedev?"

"Yes, he seems OK. I told him about the locations for the devices. The big one on the Ramapo fault line near Long Island, five smaller ones at the head of the canyons I've identified between New York and Cape Hatteras. We discussed the coordinates, depths, and the detonation mechanism. Lebedev dismissed having individual agents initiate the devices with close-range low-frequency radio transmitters - he said it was a silly idea. He's going to get the scientific branch to develop receivers for the detonators that can be activated using the Inmarsat satellite network. It will be more reliable and much less risky than relying on six people committing simultaneous suicide to order. I just hope we never have to use them."

"Are you still getting the same messaging from your contacts?"

"Yes, even though the facts are tending to make it hard to believe. I'm still convinced that the Americans won't launch an attack without provocation but pushing on with their new Pershing II missiles and BGM-109 Cruise missile programmes - not to mention the Strategic Defence Initiative that Reagan's been talking about - all point to preparations for war. All it would take is an error or a misunderstanding at the wrong time."

"I agree. That's why we need the back-up plan you've come up with. It'll reassure Moscow that we're not helpless, and that will make them more confident."

"I hope you're right, Leonid. More vodka?"

"Why not?" Leonid said, draining his glass and banging it down on the table.

They both heard it. A light tap as something hit the carpeted floor. They peered under the table at a tiny plastic box with the remnants of an adhesive pad still attached.

"That bastard Vlasov!" Leonid exclaimed.

Chapter 32 - Washington DC, September 1982

After the discovery of the listening device in the dungeon Leonid arranged a discreet meeting with KGB *rezident* Semyanov at Pioneer Point. He handed the device to Semyanov, who studied it closely.

"You think Vlasov placed this?" he asked Leonid.

"Almost certainly, Nikolai," Leonid said, "only a few people have access to the dungeon alone, and he was the only one in the embassy, apart from me and Viktor, in the whole of August. I suggest you have your technical team sweep the embassy and the ambassador's residence. In the meantime, I want to know all about this device, how long it works for, what it records, how it is downloaded. I'm guessing it's not a transmitter. We might be able to use this to our advantage for a while, just until we decide how to deal with the traitor Vlasov."

"What if we can't do that in time?" Semyanov asked.

"Then we'll have to make sure it is completely cleared of anything it's recorded, or it must be destroyed. It can't go back to the Americans as it is. Vlasov is in New York for two days. I suspect he'll need to return this device to wherever he got it from soon after his return, so we, or rather you, don't have much time."

"Leave it to me. I'll see you in the dungeon tomorrow afternoon to update you."

Semyanov stood. He bowed his head slightly, after all Leonid Grachev was his senior and, technically speaking, his boss.

"Thank you, Nikolai. Can you also get me anything you have on Vlasov? I believe he is, or was, a friend of Ambassador Brevnov from his army days."

"Not so much a friend, Leonid," Semyanov said, "more of a useful loyal servant. He made life comfortable for Comrade Brevnov. As a quartermaster Vlasov was able to obtain goods and services that an officer like Brevnov would miss while on field duty. I'm not suggesting that Brevnov is disloyal, but as we all know he does like his comforts."

"Will Brevnov take our 'advice' on how to deal with Vlasov?" Leonid asked.

"I'm sure of it. He will understand the implications if he doesn't. His mentor is Brezhnev, and by all accounts Comrade Leonid Ilyich will soon be joining Stalin and Suslov and the rest of them in the Kremlin Wall. He's been out of action in all but name for months. Gromyko, Ustinov and Andropov are the ones in charge right now. None of them have much time for Brezhnev's old favourites."

"You're well informed, Nikolai. It pays to spend time in Moscow. As you know, my position makes it difficult to make frequent journeys. How long do you think Brezhnev has?"

"A few weeks, two months at most."

"I will have my black tie pressed and get some dark ribbon for the picture frames. I'll see you tomorrow."

******

Ambassador Brevnov was furious. He looked at the dossier which had just been handed to him by Nikolai Semyanov, his KGB chief.

"Explain, please," he demanded abruptly.

"Of course, Comrade Ambassador," Nikolai said, "in our security routines inside the embassy we discovered certain items, specifically radio-transmitting listening devices secreted in your office, my office, and that of your deputy. It is an outrage, of course. Furthermore, we found a concealed non-transmitting device in the confidential conference room. The conclusion we came to was that a member of embassy staff must have placed the devices, we presume on behalf of the Americans.

"We have deactivated the transmitting devices and will need to speak to you and Comrade Kvartetov to ascertain what information may have been inadvertently divulged and transmitted to someone outside. We think that the devices have been in place for around a month. The device in the confidential conference room is one we haven't encountered before. Our technical experts have examined it closely and concluded that it is a self-contained recording device with a battery life of up to one week and a storage capacity for around three hours of speech recordings. They were able to construct a similar device and test it. It will re-record over anything already recorded once it reaches the limit of its storage capacity, but it can't be wiped without leaving a clear trail. We don't want the Americans to know we've discovered this device just yet, not until we have effectively removed the traitor who planted it.

"I have therefore replaced the device in the conference room and have deployed two members of staff to read aloud articles from the Washington Post, translated into Russian, for several hours. I have placed a concealed camera in the room, and we will have photographic evidence of the traitor when he retrieves it."

"He?" asked the ambassador. "You know who it is?"

"I believe I do, Comrade Ambassador, but if I may I will wait until we have final proof of his guilt before I disclose his identity."

"If you insist, Nikolai, but tell me as soon as you have your proof."

"One more thing," Nikolai said, "we do not want the Americans to be alerted to the fact that we have detected the traitor until he is safely in custody. This will require some subterfuge and I would ask you to cooperate fully."

Brevnov glared at the chief spy but said nothing.

"You may go, Comrade Semyanov. Keep me apprised. Good day."

Two days later Nikolai showed Leonid clear photographs showing Vlasov reaching under the conference table to remove the device.

"We followed him, naturally. At the end of the day he went to a bar near his apartment. There he met briefly with a man, the one in this photograph, and the two of them exchanged newspapers. The other man, who we think is an FBI agent, then left. Our team followed him but lost him near the FBI building. Vlasov went home. The next day he went directly to the dungeon, and you will see him replacing the device with a new one. It is compelling. Vlasov is definitely our traitor."

"Excellent, Nikolai. Has Brevnov agreed to the plan?" Leonid asked.

"Yes, after some bluster. He will speak to Vlasov later today and ask him to get a special present in New York for Tatyana Filippovna, Andropov's wife, a discreetly expensive item of jewellery that she can wear at the October Revolution Politburo dinner. When he gets back Brevnov will pretend to be delighted and will ask Vlasov to take it personally to Moscow. Head Office will be waiting for him at Sheremetyevo, but it will be weeks before the Americans know their asset has been taken. In the meantime, we will reactivate and use the transmitting devices to feed disinformation to the Americans. The device currently in the dungeon will be removed; I'll send it to Moscow. I'm sure the technical branch will be interested."

"Good," said Leonid, "I'd like to know how the Americans got their claws into Vlasov. I doubt it will surprise me, though. Whether Vlasov is shot or spends the rest of his life in Siberia will depend on who his friends are in Moscow. I expect his wife will be pleased to get home and get rid of him at the same time, the poor woman."

******

The autumn evening had a chill to it. He and Leonid sat beside the barbecue fire pit at Pioneer Point while Natasha and Katya were indoors chatting. There had been more *shashlik* tonight, with heavy Georgian red wine.

"Do you ever get homesick, Viktor?" Leonid asked.

"Not often," he replied, "as long as Natasha and Sasha are with me, I'm at home. After nearly a year and a half here I'm used to it. At one time I used to find the language tiring and the food unbearable, but these days it's OK. What about you?"

"I'm getting weary, Viktor. That makes me long for home, for familiar simple things. Not that there's anything simple about the country or profession we inhabit. Did you hear what happened to Vlasov?"

"No, I was waiting for you to tell me."

"Apparently he arrived at Sheremetyevo completely hammered and grinning like a fool. He was delighted to be met in an official car, not quite so delighted when it took him to the Lubyanka. He got one of the special Head Office welcomes, and when he'd stopped crying he started talking.

"It seems he was up to all sorts in New York. The FBI had been made aware and were monitoring what he was doing. Sex, alcohol, gambling, some drugs, weapons, talk of underage girls. They gave him a choice. Work for the FBI or they'd get the State Department to make an official complaint about his criminal conduct. Between a rock and a hard place, as the saying goes. Vlasov wasn't a very good traitor. He didn't think about the adhesive on the bug in the dungeon. With wildly varying heat and humidity in there it became less sticky, and when we were talking the air conditioning was so efficient the glue stopped working altogether and it fell off. It was the second bug Vlasov had placed in there, so week two of his treacherous career. The other devices had only been in place for a week longer, and not much damage has been done.

"We will be making an official complaint to the Americans next week. Vlasov said that the FBI were less than excited by the first intelligence product they got from the dungeon. It was mostly a recording of Ludmilla and Kolya from the Economic Section going at it like enraged rabbits on the conference table. I doubt they would have been any more pleased with the second recording either. The Washington Post is hardly riveting in English, but when it's read out loud in Russian by two people with the most boring voices in the world it's like a sleeping pill."

"What will happen to Vlasov?" he asked.

"Once upon a time he would have been shot in the courtyard at the Lubyanka. Now he'll have a secret trial and get sent to a labour camp or one of the nastier jails. I think I'd rather be shot, but these days they prefer not to execute people. Under Stalin they'd shoot you for doing nothing; under Khrushchev they'd shoot you for doing something; these days they don't want to shoot you at all for doing anything."

"I suppose that's progress for you," he said, reaching for the wine bottle.

"I think we can get back to proper work now. Try to arrange another meeting with Jim. I want to know how it's going, see if he thinks he's still under scrutiny. I checked the mailbox and there's no mark, so try another advert in the paper next week. What else is on your horizon?"

"I'm meeting a few people for lunches, nothing special, but arrangements were made while we were being watched so I chose innocuous contacts. Thanksgiving is coming up in November. There are a lot of receptions being planned, and I'm going to go to a few. Brzezinski is on the First Lady's guest list, and so am I now; I want to squeeze more out of him. Gently, of course. Natasha and I are spending Thanksgiving with the Rourkes. I think Sasha and Steven are going to announce their wedding plans. Thanks for smoothing that with Head Office, by the way."

"They weren't happy about it I can tell you. Luckily, it didn't get as far as Fedorchuk. Baranov OK'd it in the end, once I'd assured him that there was nothing compromising about the Rourke family and there would be no impact on your VRYaN work. I hope I'm right in saying that Viktor, about no impact on your VRYaN work?"

"The preparation and planning are done. The only VRYaN work I have now is reporting my observations on the Americans' ability to withstand what we're planning and working out how long it would take them to recover. Knowing that my Sasha will be in the middle of it doesn't make it sit easily. I just hope that if it ever happens they'll be safely with his family at home in York and not in Boston or New York City."

"What does Natasha think?"

"About VRYaN? She doesn't know anything about it. About Sasha staying here and living in America? It's a rollercoaster. Sometimes she's hysterically happy for Sasha, other times she cries buckets about losing her only daughter. But it would be the same if Sasha married at home and moved to Azerbaijan or Kyrgyzstan or somewhere."

"Except you wouldn't be planning to destroy where they lived."

He glared at Leonid, briefly angered by his friend. Then it passed.

"There is that, yes. Let's drink," he put down his wine glass and reached for the vodka chilling in an ice bucket, a wan smile flitting across his face. "VRYaN! May it never come to pass!"

"*Na zdorovie!*" said Leonid.

Chapter 33 - Washington DC, November 1982

On 10th November Brezhnev's death was announced. He had suffered a heart attack, seemingly brought on by the effort of attending the annual military parade in Red Square three days earlier. Although officially in a period of national mourning, he had decided to attend the pre-Thanksgiving reception being held by Nancy Reagan's Chief of Staff a week later. He walked down to the Hyatt Hotel on K Street and announced himself to the Secret Service door keeper. FBI watchers took pictures of him and all the other foreign guests in the twilight.

In the smaller ballroom around fifty people were gathered, holding glasses of wine or sparkling water. He knew a few of them and circulated towards the hostess to make his presence known. In a far corner he saw Zbigniew Brzezinski, pinned down by the aging actress he had previously encountered at the embassy function. Brzezinski looked like he needed some help. He went over and politely interrupted the conversation. The actress took the hint and drifted away.

"You rescued me again, Mr Gumnov," Brzezinski said, "I'm glad you didn't have to run me down this time. Condolences on the loss of Leonid Ilyich, by the way. I heard he'd been pretty sick for a while."

"That's true, sir," he said, "he never fully recovered after the accident last March."

"How do you think he'll be remembered?" Brzezinski asked.

"I think the Soviet people will see him as the leader who kept the revolution going, or rather put it back on track after Khrushchev. Khrushchev was a bit too liberal, too keen to ease up and let things slide. Brezhnev reasserted the principles of the revolution."

"Good official answer, Viktor. Now what do you really think?"

He smiled and nodded slowly, thinking. Then he answered Brzezinski's question.

"Brezhnev was a bureaucrat with a massive ego. He let his friends get away with anything they wanted. He's driven the Soviet Union towards the brink of ruin while he's been luxuriating in privilege and titles. But he will be remembered as a Soviet hero and honoured accordingly, I don't doubt."

"A fair assessment. Will Andropov do any better?"

"I don't know. If you consider that Brezhnev was effectively incapacitated for most of the last year and Andropov's been running things with Gromyko and Ustinov, I'd imagine that not much will change. Do you know Andropov?"

"I've met him a few times; I've met Brezhnev too. Did you know I saw Stalin once, when I was a kid? My dad was a Polish diplomat, and we were in Moscow for a while. I saw him at the November Red Square military parade, I must have been eight or nine years old. He looked small, but still scary, with black staring eyes and that dirty moustache. Before Moscow we were in Berlin when the Nazis were in power. I never saw Hitler, or if I did I don't remember it, but I saw the Blackshirts and more military parades in Unter den Linden. As I said, I was only a kid, but Berlin with the Nazis and Moscow with Stalin looked pretty similar to me. Khrushchev must have been a breath of fresh air after Stalin."

"I hardly knew anything about Stalin. I was only six when he died, and we were at the other end of the country, nine thousand kilometres from Moscow. I barely noticed Malenkov and Bulganin; their pictures went up in our school and then they came down again. The first leader I became aware of was Khrushchev. From what I could see as a student in the naval academy and then as an officer it was party time for the liberal elite in Moscow, but in the military we were lurching from crisis to crisis - Berlin, Cuba, Hungary. Then in '64 Brezhnev threw him out. So, for eighteen years he's been in charge - he's all I really know."

"Bill Clark's concerned about Andropov," Brzezinski said.

"William Clark? The National Security Adviser?"

"Yes, we talk. Bill's unusual like that; he actually speaks to former NSAs, former presidents too. Bill's one of the few people, apart from the First Lady, who can walk into the Oval Office without knocking and call the president Ron. Up at Camp David him and Reagan sit around the campfire and act like old cowboys or ranch hands singing 'Home on the Range'. They go way back. Bill's worried that Andropov doesn't understand the US position."

"You have to admit the rhetoric makes it quite hard to misunderstand it, at least as far as the president is concerned. He's made it clear that he dislikes the Soviet Union intensely, and he's aiming more and more missiles at us," he said.

"Fair point, but it *is* just rhetoric. Reagan doesn't hate the Soviet Union - he hates communism. Americans need to have something to hate, it pulls them together. For now, it's communism, in a few years it'll be something else. Reagan sees it as a threat to the American dream. The truth is that Bill Clark has persuaded Reagan that the Soviet system is doomed anyway. It's going broke. He never would have persuaded Haig, but George Schultz is more pragmatic. The policy is going to be to apply economic pressure to hasten the collapse of the Soviet system. Economic pressure, not military force. The arms race is crippling us both, but it's crippling your side more, Viktor. Clark's giving the Soviet system five years, ten at most, before it implodes. Reagan would like to be in the chair when that happens, so the pressure will increase. If the Soviet Union can adapt enough to survive as a system, who knows where we're going. If not, whatever the future holds it won't be nuclear devastation. America doesn't want nuclear devastation, not for anyone. It's bad for business.

"But we need to be very careful, Viktor. When I was President Carter's NSA I got a phone call one night at 3am. It was three or four years ago. The call was from the duty officer at the early warning control centre. He told me that the system had detected 250 incoming missiles from the Soviet Union. My golden rule in that sort of situation has always been to count to ten before doing anything. I told him to call me back. Two minutes later he did. He said that there were now 2,000 incoming missiles showing up on the detection screens. I was momentarily confused. This couldn't be happening out of the blue with no warning or build up at all, could it? I got up and went to the bathroom. By the time I got back and was just about to call the president to initiate a retaliatory strike the guy was on the phone again. It was a false alarm. Someone had forgotten to take a training scenario tape out of the computer and it was running as if there was an exercise. If I'd called the president, he would have initiated a counterattack. Once the button is pressed it's not so easy to un-press it. We were a minute away from it, because of a mistake.

"Now, if you'll excuse me, Viktor, I have to go," Brzezinski said. "Good talking to you. Give my best to Yuri Vladimirovich."

He stood quietly for a few moments before he too left the reception. There was no disguising the message he'd just heard. He needed to talk to Leonid.

******

"Phew!" Leonid said, "that's exactly what he said to you?"

"Word for word," he said. "Now, what do we do with it?" They were in the dungeon, having carefully searched it first.

"One of us needs to speak to Baranov. If it goes through channels before Fedorchuk moves on, it'll be buried. He won't want to hear that the US isn't planning to strike first. He also won't want to hear that they want to bankrupt us instead. Baranov still has Andropov's ear. We'll have to trust it to him. The thing is, if either of us leaves the US after the FBI and CIA attention on us over the last few months we probably won't get back in. I don't want to send this by telegram. I could write a letter to Baranov, but we can't guarantee he'd get it before anyone else has had a look. I expect Fedorchuk will be trying to rein him in and will be monitoring his communications."

"How long until Chebrikov takes over from him?" Viktor asked.

"If we're lucky, a few weeks. If not, a few months. If Brezhnev was still around I'd wait, but Andropov may be under pressure from the hawks. What Brzezinski said about a mistake being enough to start it troubles me, mostly because he's right. That's why it's crucial that Andropov gets to know what he told you - if he knows he'll count to ten, like Brzezinski did. If he doesn't, well, let's not even think about that. We'll come up with something. Changing the subject, have you seen or heard from Jim lately?"

"Not for months. He's not responding to the ads, so I've stopped placing them. There hasn't been a chalk mark since he told us that we were being watched. Is there no other fall-back communication with him? No crash call we can make?"

"Not with him. He's totally deniable, and he knows that. If he's cut the strings, they're cut."

"I suppose it's a long shot, but I'm going to go to Bethany this weekend and sit there on the beach on Saturday and Sunday just in case he shows. If he doesn't, I'll try again next weekend."

"You want to sit on an Atlantic beach for two days in November?"

"It clears the mind," he said, "you should try it."

"I prefer to clear my mind with Stolichnaya, nice and cold, but in a warm dry room. Good luck."

******

The following Saturday was wet and cold and windy. Bethany Beach was deserted, apart from the odd dog-walker trying to make their charges get a move on so they could go back indoors. The plus side was that he could be certain there was nobody following him. The only place that was open was a diner set back from the beach. It served the few locals who lived in Bethany all year round and came along for their breakfasts or coffees or Danish pastries. He ordered a black coffee and a plain croissant. He smiled as he recalled that Sasha always mocked the American pronunciation of 'cross ant' by calling the pastries angry termites.

"You fishin' today?" the waitress asked him.

"I thought I'd give it a try," he replied.

"They say snow's coming; it's mighty cold enough. You won't have much competition for the fish, though."

He had seen the waitress on and off over the months and they were on nodding terms.

"Has that guy Huey been in?" he asked her. "He mentioned that a friend of his was selling some fishing gear and I'm looking for another sea rod. I thought I might take a few boat trips next season and do some deep sea."

"He was around a couple of weeks ago. Shall I tell him you're looking for him if I see him?"

"Could you? I'm planning to be down here for the next couple of weekends. My wife's away so there's no chores to keep me busy. If you see him tell him Vic's looking for him."

"Sure thing. More coffee?"

******

The following Saturday the weather was colder and wetter. He sat alone behind a canvass windbreak that did little to keep him warm or dry. He was well wrapped, though, and quite content with his reflections. As before, Bethany Beach was deserted, and he could be sure there were no hostile eyes following him. If Huey were to show up it would mean that he too felt sure that he didn't have a tail.

"Long time no see," Huey said, appearing from the dunes further down the beach. "You must be nuts fishing on a day like this."

"How've you been, Huey?" he asked.

"I've slept better," Huey said. "I think they're bored with me, but they're cramping my style. I think my time here is nearly done."

"You're leaving?"

"I'm thinking about it. I'm going back to Europe for a while. I'll speak to Head Office; maybe they want me to go back to Germany or something. Things are going to get interesting there in the next few years. I'll give you a couple of names before I go though. We need a better way to talk, we look weird sitting on a beach in winter. I've still got my apartment in Wilmington but there's another place I can use. It's in Newark on the Delaware / Maryland state line, just off Highway 95." Huey passed him a folded envelope. "Here's the address and a key. If you want to communicate anything let yourself in on a Tuesday or Thursday; I won't be there. Leave a note in a pack of frozen pizza you'll find in the kitchen freezer. There'll always be two or three in there. Put the note in the Margherita. If I've got something for you it'll be in a plastic canister in the coffee pot. There'll be coffee in there too, so don't spill it everywhere. I'll maybe see you round, Viktor, it's been a blast. You take care now, of yourself, and Natasha and Sasha."

With that Huey / Jim stood up and left without saying another word. He wasn't whistling or wearing a loud shirt.

They got married on the Saturday after Easter. The night before the wedding the Gumnov family stayed in a hotel in the centre of the city. It was called The Yorktowne, and it was pure old-fashioned opulence. Brendan Rourke picked up the bill, saying that it was the tradition that a bride and groom never spent the eve of their wedding under the same roof, and Lexa couldn't stay somewhere on her own. He hadn't argued.

Sasha, Natasha and Hazel had gone off to the beauty parlour for something or other, so he went down to the bar and found a quiet corner on his own. He sipped a beer and reflected on the last few months, a mix of highs and lows.

He had almost panicked when he got the news that his father was seriously ill, but it had allowed him a fortuitous opportunity to travel back to Russia with his message from Brzezinski. He and Natasha were granted compassionate leave with valid return visas and were given flights back to Moscow. He had arranged immediate onward flights to Vladivostok with Aeroflot, which made it impossible for him to complain about American domestic air travel ever again.

His father had made a good recovery, and seeing his parents and Natasha's mother, and their collective extended family, went a long way towards reassuring him about his reasons for doing what he was doing. These were his people, and if the Americans did decide to obliterate the Soviet Union these were the people, and millions like them, who would perish. That could not be allowed to happen.

After a fleeting week in the far east of Russia it was time to go back to Moscow and prepare for their return to Washington. He was tempted to try to persuade Natasha to stay behind, but he knew that with Sasha's wedding coming up there was no way she would agree. In Moscow they found their new accommodation, a spacious third-floor apartment with two bedrooms, a sitting room, kitchen and bathroom, overlooking the river and with distant views of the Kremlin. He had no doubt that he was the most junior ranking officer in the neighbourhood, let alone the building. Natasha was impressed but not overawed. Their apartment in Alexandria was more than twice the size and much better equipped, but for Moscow it was a good place to live.

On their second day in Moscow he went to Head Office. He found Baranov's staff officer and made an appointment to see the General the next day. Baranov was courteous and he listened intently to his account of the conversation with Brzezinski several weeks earlier.

"So, Viktor," Baranov had said, "you are saying that, on the basis of this one conversation with a former official in the previous administration, you do not believe the Americans have any intention of launching an attack on the Soviet Union. Are you asking me to take this message to the new Chairman, or even to the old Chairman who is now the General Secretary and leader of the Union?"

"Brzezinski is still very well connected, Comrade General," he had said, "and what he said to me was a message for the Kremlin from the White House - I'm certain of it. I expect the Americans will be using any channel they can to convey this message, but they cannot be seen or heard to say it specifically in public. I believe that what Brzezinski told me is the American position: they will not launch a pre-emptive strike, but they will respond militarily to provocation or an attack from our side. As I told you, the Americans, or at least the most influential ones, believe that our socialist system will collapse in a few years, and they are prepared to wait it out."

"Do you believe our socialist system will collapse?" Baranov asked.

"I would like to think it won't, but frankly I think that unless a large part of the western world starts to believe in socialism, and to practice it, free-market economics will prevail."

"A few years ago a comment like that would have changed your life, and not for the better. Under Stalin it would have cost you your life," Baranov said sternly. "Be careful who you say such things to Comrade Lieutenant Colonel. Just between us, I agree with you. I also think that you are right about the message from Brzezinski. We heard a similar but less well-sourced message from our station in London just last week. I will speak to the Chairman, Comrade Chebrikov, when we meet later in the week. He is a close friend of Andropov, as am I, so your message will be heard if not believed. When do you return to Washington?"

"We leave on Saturday, Comrade General."

"If there is a response to be communicated I will contact you before you depart. I take it you don't plan to leave Moscow before then?"

"No, Comrade General. Natasha is getting the new apartment organised and she has things for me to do. Thank you, by the way, for the apartment. It is very spacious and convenient, and we do appreciate it."

"It's nothing, Viktor Vladimirovich, but remember what the Party giveth the Party can also take away. What you said about the risk posed by a misunderstanding or an accident is sobering. I will need to do a lot of persuading to build some tolerance here in Moscow. I hope I don't burn my boats in doing so."

"I hope so too," he had said as he prepared to leave.

"No, stay for a few moments. We must drink to your daughter's future happiness," Baranov extracted his habitual Armenian *konjac* from a drawer and poured two large glasses. "Tell me about this American family she is marrying into...."

He had finished his beer and was brought abruptly back to the present by a hovering waiter.

"Another beer, Mr Gumnov?"

"Thank you, no. I think I'll have an Irish whiskey, a double with some branch water."

"We have Powers or Jameson's."

"I'll start with the Powers, thank you."

The whiskey was good, and he started to feel a little bit more hopeful for the future.

******

The wedding took place at City Hall. Steven's older brother was one witness, his sister the other. The sister looked after Sasha, while the brother calmed Steven's nerves and made sure the rings didn't get lost. The ceremony was simple and short, but nevertheless both Natasha and Hazel wept copious floods while smiling broadly, as only mothers at their children's weddings can. Viktor and Brendan exchanged sympathetic fraternal glances. Sasha was radiant in a cream-coloured dress, not a traditional wedding dress but something elegantly understated. Her hair and make-up were perfect, and he looked at this exquisite, poised young woman with admiration and adoration. He remembered her as a child, with grubby hands and grazed knees, her rare occasional temper tantrums, her listening intently to stories he read to her as she went to sleep. His daughter was still his daughter; now she was also Steven's wife - but she would always be her own person.

The dinner was a family affair in The Yorktowne Hotel. Both he and Brendan made short speeches full of hope and happiness. Steven's brother told some embarrassing stories about his younger brother, and once all protocols had been observed the happy couple piled into Steven's preferred pickup truck and headed off to Bethany Beach, where it had all started, to begin their married life in Sasha / Lexa's favourite boarding house on the beach, right next to the boardwalk.

Afterwards, he and Natasha lay side by side in their large comfortable bed in an old-fashioned luxurious American hotel.

"We could always have another," Natasha said.

"Another what?"

"Another Sasha. Maybe a boy one this time."

"Have you gone mad?"

"Possibly, but in America it's quite common for women to have babies well into their forties. We have some time on our side, and we have the space in the new apartment in Moscow. Anyway, trying is fun."

He looked at her and reached for the light switch.

"No, leave the light on," his wife said, "I want to look at you."

Chapter 35 - Washington DC, July 1983

The joint intelligence group was meeting at FBI Headquarters. The Special Agent in Charge was not happy at all.

"Are you telling me that after nearly a year on these goons we have precisely diddly-squat? That the combined efforts of the FBI, the CIA, the NSA, and who knows who else, can't prove or disprove that we're looking at a couple of deep cover KGB officers? That we can't find any trace of this Koenig guy who's vanished off the face of the earth? Jesus H Christ!"

"They're being cute with us," the Senior Special Agent said defensively, "I think State would approve their expulsion on a balance of probabilities, even if the Russians retaliated. I spoke to Craig Durov who agrees. Durov also said that there's a lot of sensitivity about Soviet intentions down there at the moment."

"Which means," said the SAC, "that they're not going to do anything to upset any apple carts. We need more! Let's go through the highlights, if you can call them that, of the last few months."

"We maintained a tail on Koenig as long as we could. We have a contact in DuPont security who fed us his travel plans and kept an eye on his work communications. He didn't deviate at all. He travelled all over the US visiting DuPont clients, including several government departments here in DC and other places. We've spoken to every federal employee who met with Koenig while we were on him and every one of them says it was just a regular business meeting about ongoing projects. Out of hours Koenig went to his local diner and to one or two bars in Wilmington. We didn't see any suspicious meetings or contacts.

"We lost him a few times, always in the Wilmington area. He went off the radar for two or three hours, once or twice for a whole day and a night, but he always popped up again at his apartment or at work. We put a tracker on the car he uses, it's provided by DuPont and they gave us permission, but it didn't give us anything. He didn't use the car when he went missing, and we never saw him with another one. Our team is going through every scrap of anything looking for traces of Koenig in and around Wilmington while he was adrift. We have one or two sightings of him at or near the Amtrak station - he lives quite near there anyway - but there's nothing on the station cameras that shows him getting on a train. He hasn't made or received any personal phone calls at his apartment, and all the numbers he called from work are legit."

"Like I said, diddly-squat!" the SAC said. "So where was he when he disappeared?"

"He was on a regular visit to Boeing in Seattle. We had a local team follow him from the airport. He went to the plant, had his meetings, and went back to the airport. Only he never got on the plane. The team went with him to the boarding gate but pulled back because there was no one else around. It seems he just changed his mind and walked out of the airport."

"He waited until the surveillance had been withdrawn? He knew they were there?" the SAC said.

"Looks like it. We haven't seen or heard of him since. We checked every border post west of the Rockies and no one using his name or looking like him crossed over into Canada in the weeks after he went missing. He's gone, chief."

"Great! And what about Grachev and Gumnov?" the SAC asked.

"We haven't been able to do round-the-clock surveillance on them, but we've kept the phone coverage on. NSA at Fort Meade has been looking for anything concerning them on embassy traffic. Nothing out of the ordinary at all. Nothing in unusual codes, no secret contacts, nothing. When we've had teams out, they just go about their normal business. Grachev goes to work, goes home, at weekends he goes to Pioneer Point. His wife does the same.

"Gumnov is more active. He went back to the USSR once with his wife. According to Durov, there was a family health emergency so Gumnov and his wife went home on compassionate leave for a couple of weeks. Now he's back here he travels like before. He drives himself; we've thought about putting a tracker on his car but we figure all embassy cars get searched at least once a week for bugs and trackers. One time our surveillance thought they saw a Soviet counter-surveillance operation around Gumnov, but they can't be sure. One strange thing happened. Gumnov disappeared for three days. He wasn't in his apartment - we have the janitor on the payroll - but his car was there. He didn't go to the embassy; he wasn't at Pioneer Point or Bethany Beach. Three days later he shows up again like he'd never been away. Craig Durov doesn't know where he went, and there's nothing on any flight manifests out of DC. He didn't get the train, and as far as we can tell he didn't rent a car."

"When was this?" the SAC asked.

"It was about a week after Koenig disappeared," the SSA said.

"Why the hell didn't you say that before?" the SAC yelled. "I want every airport and airfield, every train station, every car rental depot, every seaport, every bus station checked. Send out pictures of Gumnov and Koenig to all field offices, top priority! I want to know where they went. We've got nothing on Grachev, but I want a report through the Director for State making sure that Gumnov is on the list next time we're doing any expelling. Get me enough to put Grachev on that list too, unless you like tacos and want to spend a very long time in the El Paso field office. Jesus! OK, Langley, what have you got?"

The CIA delegation had been sitting quietly while the FBI SAC was yelling at the hapless Senior Special Agent.

"We asked the British for any more on Gumnov. They say they think - no more than that - that he might have been deployed to Washington as part of a major intelligence operation involving the Russians and the East Germans. They've heard a codename for the operation; it's Ryan or Rayon or something like that. They don't know what it means or what it's about yet, but they say they're confident that they'll get to know soon.

"Globally, we're seeing more and more intelligence activity and military movements. We've reported it, obviously, and are waiting for a steer from the National Security Advisor. His office's initial assessment is that the situation is quote 'worrying', unquote."

"No shit," said the SAC.

******

They were in the dungeon. They hadn't had an opportunity to speak for a few weeks due to his SSOD work schedule, which he was sticking to meticulously. He had come to recognise signs of the FBI's surveillance, and with the help of some of Semyanov's team had confirmed his suspicions that he was still under periodic observation. He'd managed almost two years without raising their concerns, so he wasn't too surprised.

"I saw Jim before he left," he said. "He'd left a message at the safe house in Newark, Delaware. He said he was going for some salmon."

"Salmon?" asked Leonid.

"It meant he was heading to see his friend Mike up in Washington State."

"Oh. First, tell me about this safe house."

"It belongs to a lady friend of Huey's, sorry, Jim's. He's got quite a lot of charm and he's collected a few, apparently. She works for an airline and is away from Monday to Friday, which is why I could have a key and go there on Tuesdays and Thursdays. I never saw him there, and I don't think I was ever followed when I visited. I left him things he asked for: some cash, I got him one of the fake driving licences, keys to a car that I'd obtained for him through one of his 'friends'. In return he gave me lists of useful contacts, people he'd used over the years, together with details of what access they had and what their relationship with him was. It was clear that he was planning to leave, as he'd already indicated. When he left the message about salmon, I had an idea of what he intended to do.

"So, I went up to Seattle. It was a risk, but I had to do it. I made sure there wasn't a tail on me. I used an assumed name and paid cash for an air ticket. I rented a car and drove up to Anacortes and I found Huey in Mike's apartment. Mike was on his boat with clients, and he let Huey use his place. We had a long talk. His plan was to hitch a ride on Mike's boat across to a place called Gabriola Island, it's just off the south-east shore of Vancouver Island and there are lots of small craft in and out of there. He could land unnoticed. From the landing place there was a bit of a hike, but he could get to the ferry port and across to Vancouver Island at Nanaimo.

"From there he got the regular ferry to Vancouver on the mainland. He said he'd already made arrangements for this sort of thing; he didn't tell me the details but said he could get back to Europe with no difficulty, so he must have had an identity and a passport waiting for him. He wanted to see me one last time to hand over his contact book. It's quite something; it's in code, of course, but he told me how to read it. The book lists *all* his people and says whether they are knowing or unknowing sources, what area of access they have, any points of leverage, the works.

"He also wanted to tell me that the Americans and the British are going crazy trying to find out what we're up to, I mean the Soviet Union, not just you and me. He said that one of his friends, a communications clerk who has access to secret telegrams at the State Department, says the British have a well-placed asset in Soviet Intelligence, possibly in London but certainly in Europe. Huey said he thought we'd like to know. He said the British source has mentioned the codename Ryan or Rayon but doesn't know what it means. What do you make of that?"

Leonid sat silently for several minutes.

"I think this is a very serious situation. I need to see Baranov, and soon. I will be having a medical emergency in the next few days and will need to be sent home urgently with Katya. I doubt we'll be back. I'll have to hand some things over to you to look after until someone arrives to replace me, but you must be ultra-cautious. Jim has done well, he is, was, a marvellous asset. We will need to try to replace him too, which is one of the things I must speak to Baranov about.

"The main thing, though, is that someone who knows the operation codename is leaking it to the British. Most of the people involved in VRYaN do not know that they are, and very few of us are aware of the operation name. I suspect the British are not being entirely honest with the Americans. If they have a source who knows what the codename sounds like, that source will know what the codename really is, and what it means. The British may know too. If VRYaN is blown, the Soviet Union could be in big trouble. I think that this weekend we will need to go to Pioneer Point and get heroically drunk for the first and last time before my heart attack at 3pm on Monday. I will be on the Wednesday flight to Moscow. Comrade Viktor Vladimirovich, you are a good friend, a good patriot, and a good officer."

Chapter 36 - Washington DC, September 1983

September started badly. In mid-August Natasha had gone with Hazel Rourke to Boston to help Sasha, Mrs Lexa Rourke, settle into their new, very small, apartment. Steven had taken an extended break from college to amass funds to see them through the winter. Sasha had even been waitressing at Bethany Beach so she could contribute. The newlyweds set out from York in Steven's preferred pickup truck towing a U-Haul trailer packed with bits of furniture and household items, most of which had been 'recycled' from the Rourke home. Natasha and Hazel followed in Hazel's station wagon.

He had been planning to go along too and had submitted the travel authorisation request to Craig Durov at the State Department as normal. It had been refused.

"What's this about, Craig?" he asked on the phone. "I've just had a formal letter from you declining my travel request. Why not just call me?"

"I'm sorry, Mr Gumnov," Durov had said, adopting a formal tone, "the decision has been made that this journey would not be compatible with your role or function, so the Department has declined authority."

"Are you telling me, Craig, that I can't go and visit my daughter?"

"I'm not saying you can't go, Mr Gumnov, just that the State Department will not approve it. If you choose to go it's up to you, but I would imagine that the probability of your journey being interrupted for checks and searches by officials and law enforcement officers is quite high. I also have to tell you, Mr

Gumnov, that your existing standing authorisation to visit the Maryland and Delaware shore as and when you want has been rescinded with immediate effect. From now on you are only authorised to travel within 20 miles of Washington DC, and to Pioneer Point. Any other travel authorisation requests will be considered, of course, but you should be aware that such requests will take much longer to process and will possibly be declined. I'm sorry to have to tell you this."

"Why are you doing this, Craig?"

"It's not me, Mr Gumnov, it's the United States government and your own. We're just pawns in this game."

******

Natasha got home on Wednesday afternoon, August 31st. While she and Viktor were drinking tea on the balcony in the autumn sunshine, the world was about to enter a new and perilous state.

In Moscow, the new KGB Chairman Viktor Chebrikov had taken to his bed for an early night. It was barely 10pm. His bedside phone rang, and he answered grumpily. It was Ustinov, the Defence Minister.

"Comrade Dmitriy Fyodorovich, how can I be of assistance?" Chebrikov asked.

"We have a situation, Comrade; I just need to check your position. An unidentified aircraft has entered prohibited airspace in Kamchatka, near Sakhalin. I suspect it is the Americans on one of their spy missions. I intend to order that the aircraft be challenged, identified and if needs be destroyed. Do you have any information or intelligence that I should be aware of?"

"No, Comrade Marshal."

"Good. I will have it shot down if it is an American spy plane."

"I concur, Comrade Marshal."

Chebrikov hung up, turned over and went back to sleep.

On the far side of the empire, some 9,000 kilometres away, a flight of MiG and Sukhoi warplanes took to the air. Their orders, having been transmitted through a chain of command, were no longer the same as those issued by Marshal Ustinov. They were to find and destroy the intruder. Communications were poor, it was a very dark night, the interceptors were operating at the extremes of their range and endurance. Shortly before 7am local time the lead pilot saw blinking lights. There was a large, slow-moving aircraft above him at an altitude of over 11,000 metres. As the pilot climbed to get a better look his much faster jet overshot the target and had to turn around. The fighter behind him fired warning shots in the darkness, but they were ordinary cannon shells rather than incendiary tracers and were invisible, and at that altitude and speed totally inaudible.

The target aircraft did not change course or speed. A third interceptor, a Sukhoi-15, fired one proximity-fused air-to-air missile. It detonated just behind the target aircraft, which the fighter pilot could see was painted in the livery of a civilian airliner belonging to Korean Airlines. The detonation was close enough to tear holes in the airliner's pressurised fuselage and suck the air out of the lungs of everyone inside it in the subsequent instant decompression. Destruction was rapid and complete.

Apart from the pilots on the flight deck and the cabin crew, almost everyone on board Korean Airlines flight 007 from New York to Seoul via Anchorage was asleep. A total of 269 people - men, women, children - were on board. Only the pilots had any idea of what was happening to them as the Boeing 747 was ripped apart and everyone and everything in the plane plunged in total darkness and freezing howling winds into the icy waters of the Sea of Japan.

Chebrikov was awoken once again by the Marshal of the Soviet Union.

"General Tretyak, in charge of the Far Eastern Military Command, has reported back," Ustinov stated. "The good news is that the intruder has been destroyed. The bad news is that the intruder seems to have been a Korean airliner flying off-course. We will start a search immediately."

Chebrikov was now wide awake.

"A civilian airliner? Didn't they see it was an airliner?" he spluttered.

"An inquiry will be held, of course, but it seems that the pilots had been instructed to destroy whatever aircraft it was - it is prohibited airspace. They are trained to do what they are ordered to do."

"How many aircraft were scrambled, and how many missiles fired?" Chebrikov asked.

"At one time there were five or six interceptors in the air, but not all could stay aloft for the entire mission. I believe that one, possibly two, missiles were fired."

"It's likely that the Japanese air defences will have seen the incident. They will be telling the Americans as we speak. We must agree a holding statement. I suggest we say nothing until asked, and then deny any involvement at all," Chebrikov stated.

"I agree, Comrade Chairman," Ustinov said, "I will call Andropov immediately. I am sure he will order the armed forces to raise the alert status - given the recent tensions and that naval exercise, this could be the only reason Reagan needs. Stand by to initiate the VRYaN plan. Have your propaganda people ready to start the rumour that La Palma is about to collapse. Oh, and Chebrikov, don't communicate this to any of your stations abroad, especially Washington."

"Of course, Comrade Marshal. I have appointed Major General Grachev to coordinate the VRYaN implementation - he is as familiar with the plan as anyone. He will do a good job."

Chebrikov slumped back on his pillow. He groped on the bedside table for his spectacles, and wearily got out of bed. His wife hadn't stirred.

******

On 1st September the morning news in Washington was all about the missing Korean airliner, which was believed to have crashed over the North Pacific. He sat watching the misery unfold on the TV screen as he sipped his tea. He knew the area, knew it well. He knew about the military establishments, the missile testing grounds, the prohibited airspace. He knew about the fragility of communications and the unreliability of navigation beacons for aircraft. He knew about the naval exercise that the Americans had recently completed, and he knew about the febrile state of mind among his country's leaders. In all, he didn't buy any theory about an aircraft accidentally crashing. It was most likely, he thought, that his countrymen had shot down an unarmed civilian airliner, seemingly with 269 souls on board. If the Americans came to the same conclusion and if they responded, VRYaN could be about to happen. He thought of Sasha.

The Korean government made a statement a few hours after the incident saying that the aircraft had been forced to land by Soviet aircraft, and that all passengers and crew were alive and well on the ground in Sakhalin. Not true, said the Americans a few days later, as they released transcripts of intercepted Soviet Air Force communications detailing the shooting down of the airliner. Over the coming days the world's media started to point fingers at the Russians over KAL-007, as the flight was known. The Japanese government released details of radar and radio tracking indicating that the airliner had been shot down. The silent Soviet Union eventually issued a statement denying all knowledge of, or involvement in, the regrettable tragedy. Nobody believed them. Behind the scenes the military alert levels on both sides of the Iron Curtain were ramping up.

Eventually, on 6th September, the Russians had to admit they did shoot down the aircraft, but said that it had been on an illegal spying mission for the United States of America. It wasn't their fault.

On 7th September President Reagan called the incident a 'crime against humanity' and an 'act of barbarism' committed by the Soviet Union. The United

States was trying to mobilise global condemnation of the Soviet Union on the floor of the UN General Assembly.

On 15th September Reagan ordered the Federal Aviation Administration to ban all Aeroflot aircraft from US airspace, effectively stopping all direct travel between the USSR and the USA.

Throughout all this, Sasha was on the phone to her mother every day, utterly distraught at the actions of her homeland and at the direct vilification she was experiencing as a Russian in America. What had been an abstract concept, a matter of theoretical discussion between her and her classmates, became a very real animosity between the two competing systems - socialism and capitalism. Sasha knew the theories, obviously, but having lived in the West for more than two years the day-to-day reality of Soviet life was becoming a fading and very selective memory. What was stirring in her, and what she was struggling with, was her love for Russia, not communism or the Soviet system. Steven was trying to be supportive, but he advised her not to be outspoken or even admit that she was Russian if challenged. With her slight accent she could pass for just about any European nationality. She was furious.

"So you're telling me I must *deny* who I am, just because of the senseless actions of crazy old men who have nothing to do with me!" she shouted at Steven, their first ever argument.

"Just until this blows over, Lexa, people are mad at Russia. They have no way of showing it to Russia, so if they know you're a Russian they're going to turn on you, even if it isn't your fault or anything to do with you. Most Americans don't know what the Soviet Union is, let alone what it means, they just think of it as 'Russia', period. Americans died on that plane too, which makes it worse."

"I need to see my Mama and Papa. Mama sounds so upset!"

"No, you don't! You need to stay here with me. This is our home, your home. We'll go and see them in a few weeks like we planned. Also, when you phone them bear in mind that people could be listening in. Your dad's a Russian diplomat, so everyone will think he's a spy and the FBI will be monitoring him. That's why he didn't come up here with your mom when we moved in. They've got enough to worry about without you running home and needing to be looked after."

Sasha swore at him in Russian for a good two minutes before she calmed down.

"My dad is *not* a spy!" she said.

Chapter 37 - Washington DC, September 1983

Wednesday again and the secret joint intelligence and security meeting convened at FBI headquarters. The Special Agent in Charge was smiling, which meant the FBI had some success to report this time. The SAC invited the Senior Special Agent from counterespionage to start.

"In the past few weeks we've trawled every seaport, airport, train station, bus depot and car-rental office in the country, as instructed. I can't begin to tell you how many that is, or what it's been costing the federal government. As far as Koenig is concerned, it's inconclusive, no sightings, but we have recovered his passport. It's a Federal Republic of Germany one, complete with all the correct immigration stamps and work permits for the USA, still valid. It was in a trash can by the highway heading north out of Seattle; a bum found it and was trying to sell it. Some sheriff's department has had it in its evidence locker for weeks. So, I think we can conclude that Koenig has changed his identity and left the US of A for pastures new. I'm satisfied that he is a Soviet agent. We've circulated his description and fingerprints to all our Legal Attachés and friendly law-enforcement agencies, plus Interpol.

"On the biggest fishing expedition ever, we have just one other item of interest - great interest. You may recall that Viktor Gumnov fell off the radar for a few days. We couldn't find him on flight manifests or train or bus stations anywhere near DC. We did find an image of him at Dulles Airport, at least we're almost certain it's him - it's not the best quality picture. We're pretty sure he boarded a domestic flight, and we've narrowed it down to the most likely few. One of these was to Seattle at 8am on the morning he went missing. We think he boarded that flight using the name Donald Anson. It appears to be completely fictitious, there's no one in the US with that name around the right age, ethnicity or description. In Seattle he managed to avoid all the cameras, but he did get himself a rental car from Hertz. He paid cash with a large deposit and a Florida driver's licence in the name of Anson. The licence is undoubtedly fake. He had the car for a little less than 48 hours. He returned it nearly out of gas with almost 300 miles added. That's enough for him to get to Vancouver or Portland and back, or anywhere in between. We have no trace of him crossing into Canada. Our agents are combing every inch of Washington State and Oregon. We'll find out where he went.

"So, we have Ewald Koenig and Viktor Gumnov, using an assumed name, in the same area at the same time, just before Koenig makes a run for it. In my book, that's a connection. It makes Gumnov an agent, an active KGB officer, especially in light of previous suggestions that that's what he is."

"Good work, Phil," the SAC said, "I've spoken to State and they've grounded Gumnov, pulled his travel authorisation. If he goes further than 20 miles from DC, other than to go to Pioneer Point, he'll be stopped and questioned. I've put an overt tail on him, just so he's aware. His wings are clipped. His case is being referred to Secretary Schultz who will decide whether to expel him or not. Now, Langley?"

"We've been occupied with the fall-out from the Korean massacre, as the President is calling it," the lead

CIA analyst started. "We have no doubt that the Korean airliner was deliberately shot down by the Soviets, but we're not sure why. Excessive zeal maybe, or a SNAFU, either way Moscow tried to deny it and then cover it up before coming clean. Moscow station is saying that there are strong indicators that the Soviets are gearing up militarily. Our stations in other Warsaw Pact countries and our imagery are telling us a similar story, a build-up of both national and Soviet troops, movements of tactical nuclear weapons, repositioning of warplanes and ships. Things are very tense.

"We've heard of an incident just a couple of days ago at one of the air-defence bases outside Moscow. Luckily, it went our way. A duty officer at the Serphukov base disregarded an alert of a single incoming missile, and he also disregarded an alert of a further four incoming missiles. In the report we intercepted he said to his boss that in all his training every attack scenario featured multiple missiles, tens or hundreds, so he assumed that a single missile or even four must be a false alarm. The thing is that Serphukov, being so close to Moscow, is one of the sites where an alert should automatically trigger an immediate response. The duty guy, a Lieutenant Colonel, was either incredibly smart and made the right call, or incredibly stupid and still made the right call. The Soviets are still trying to decide whether to shoot him or decorate him.

"Our assessment is that the alert was a technical fault, which we shouldn't regard as a good thing. It makes you wish we could send some of our technical people over there to fix the system for the Soviets so we don't get nuked because of a loose wire in some computer.

"The Soviets are hyper-sensitive just now. They don't like the global outrage and universal condemnation over KAL-007, even some of their own allies are siding with the UN majority over it. As we all know, Able Archer 83 is coming up in a few weeks. It's only a four-day exercise, but this one isn't going to look like any of the previous ones. It's been in the planning for a couple of years, and Defense say they're not going to change it now - they say it would need to be called off rather than altered at this stage. POTUS won't allow that. We're expecting the Soviets to be very, very jumpy when they start to see how it's panning out, especially the long radio silences and new communication code configurations.

"In normal times our ambassador to Moscow would have a fireside chat with Gromyko and everything would be accepted on trust - except there is no trust anymore. The ambassador will deliver the message anyway, but they won't believe him, and who can blame them? Our ambassador in Moscow wouldn't be told if we were planning to nuke the Soviets anyway, for obvious reasons.

"We're working with the British to find a way to get the message to Moscow that Able Archer *is* just an exercise and get the Soviets to believe it before any real shooting starts. For those reasons we haven't been putting too much effort into finding Ewald Koenig or whatever his name really is. I'll take your report on Gumnov to our Director; he'll want to let the Brits know."

"Thanks," said the SAC. "Before you go, is there any more on Grachev?"

"The guy with the timely heart attack? We are certain he *hasn't* had a heart attack. He was in a Georgian restaurant in Moscow demolishing large slabs of meat and drinking buckets of red wine and vodka the day after he landed. Our assessment, and again it is an assessment, is that his sudden departure was prompted by the need to get a very important message back to Moscow securely and quickly. We know they avoid the risk of signal leakage for anything important that isn't 'Immediate' level urgent. We have some low-level coverage of the Lubyanka, and we know Grachev, who is actually a Major General - that's a one-star in their system - in the KGB and therefore was the most senior KGB officer in the US, senior even to the *rezident*, had a long meeting with a Lieutenant General (a two-star) Sergei Baranov. Baranov heads up a special unit reporting directly to the Chairman of the KGB himself. He was Andropov's man, and very trusted by the Kremlin. We have no idea what they spoke about, unfortunately."

The meeting broke up. The SAC's good humour had been deflated by the CIA input. The analyst had spoken more frankly than was usual, which in his experience meant only one thing: the Agency was seriously worried.

******

He was alone in the dungeon. He was seeking solace, peace and quiet. He missed Leonid, and in a strange way he missed Huey too. Now he was on his own, separate from the others from Head Office in the embassy, separate too from the regular foreign service diplomats. His SSOD work had been curtailed, as much by the ambassador as by the Americans, and he found himself unable to do anything that he wanted to do. He was confined to Washington DC; he couldn't go to the sea. He didn't even want to fish on the Potomac, not now.

They were there again this morning. Two burly men in a standard government-issue Crown Victoria sedan, making no effort to conceal their presence. In normal times he would have complained to the State Department about unwarranted harassment of a diplomat, but these weren't normal times. As he pulled out of the parking lot at his Alexandria apartment block the Crown Victoria followed him. It kept two cars behind. At one set of traffic lights he went through as they turned red. The men looked angry, so he pulled over and waited for them to catch up before resuming his drive to the embassy. He waved at them; they waved back. In the office he sought out Nikolai Semyanov, the KGB *rezident*, to tell them about the overt tail he had grown.

"You're not alone, comrade," Semyanov had said, "I'm more concerned about the people who haven't got a tail on them. The feds are everywhere."

After an hour in the dungeon with his thoughts he decided to go home. They were waiting outside, drinking coffee and eating sandwiches.

As he pulled out of the embassy courtyard, he rolled down his window.

"I'm going home now," he shouted across to them.

"Be right with you," the burly man in the passenger seat replied.

Natasha was surprised to see him.

"Are you ill?" she asked.

"I don't know, maybe. Maybe just worn out. Is it time to go home now?"

"You tell me, Viktor. It's your work that brought us here. If it's done, maybe it is time to go home."

"I can't go yet, but I want you to leave."

"What do you mean, leave?" she demanded.

"Not leave me, just leave here. Go back to Moscow. It's not safe here anymore."

"Look, Viktor, I read the papers, I talk to other people at the embassy. If it's not safe here it's not safe in Moscow either. You think there'll be a war, don't you?"

"I need to try to stop it, but yes, I think there could be a war, and soon."

"But you're staying here? You expect me to go home on my own, to Moscow. To leave you here in Washington, to leave Sasha in Boston? You want us all to die alone, not together?"

"I don't want any of us to die. Maybe it won't happen, not if I can talk to the right people and if I can make Moscow listen."

"What is wrong with you Viktor? Talk to *me*!"

"I can't, Nata, believe me. I wish I could. I'm going to swim in the pool."

"Run away, Viktor! Go and swim in a cold pool, rather than talk to your wife! One thing, though, I'm not going anywhere without you. If you're staying here, so am I!"

He changed into his swimming trunks and a robe. He went down to the garden pool, which was deserted. Natasha was right, the water was cold but he needed the shock; he needed to feel a physical sensation. He couldn't bear to be without Natasha, but he also couldn't bear to be with her as she perished in a malignant disaster he had designed and engineered. He couldn't even think about Sasha, his daughter, his only child, and what would happen to her when the tsunami hit Boston and dragged her and her new husband and their new apartment and their unborn babies to the bottom of the sea.

That night he didn't sleep. He got up so he wouldn't disturb Natasha and he sat in his dressing gown on the chilly balcony, looking at the distant glow of Capitol Hill and the lights on the airplanes landing at and leaving National Airport. He resisted for a long while, then went to fetch a large Irish whiskey.

In the morning he would tell the FBI men that he was staying home. To be with his wife.

The Russia desk at MI6 was buzzing. The strange request from the CIA at Langley was perplexing and unusual. The Americans were pleading for help, help from the British, which wasn't the way it normally worked. Specifically, they stated that they had figured out that the British must have a well-placed asset within the Soviet intelligence system, probably the KGB and equally probably in London. The implication was that it wouldn't take the CIA too much time to work out who it was. They wanted MI6 to task their asset with conveying a credible message to Moscow about Exercise Able Archer '83, the NATO practice drill for an impending nuclear war between them and the Soviet Union. The message was simple, but also very complex. Able Archer '83 is *just an exercise!* It is not the beginning of World War III. It is not a pre-emptive strike to incapacitate the Soviet Union. The Soviet Union *must not* retaliate against the perceived threat. The Russia desk had been ordered to do their best to comply with the US request, and quickly. That's why they were busy trawling through classified documents that could safely be used to support the asset's message and creating other fake ones that Moscow might find compelling. The more experienced Russia hands were sceptical. If the boot was on the other foot and the Russians sent a similar message, would they believe it? Never!

An urgent sign was left for Agent Sunbeam, the KGB *rezident* at the Soviet Embassy in London. His handlers waited patiently in the safe house, an anonymous apartment in a featureless block in the back streets of Chelsea, for the agent to arrive. They were prepared for a long wait. It was late in the evening by the time Agent Sunbeam arrived, kitted out in evening dress.

"I'm sorry I'm late, gentlemen," the agent said, "I was required to be at an embassy dinner. I don't have long, but I do need a drink."

One of the handlers went to the kitchen and came back with a tray of three whisky tumblers, a bottle and a jug of water.

"Glad you could make it, Oleg," the senior handler said. "How is the temperature in Moscow?"

"I take it you're not asking about the weather," Gordievsky said. "My information is that Marshal Ustinov has ordered a full alert in all branches of the military, and he's initiated the plan for a retaliatory nuclear strike aimed initially at NATO forces in Europe, followed immediately by a full ICBM launch on the United States. Everything will be ready in a few days at the latest."

"We need you to persuade him, and everyone else who needs to be persuaded, that the NATO manoeuvres are just that, a pre-planned exercise involving all the NATO partners. This year it will be more elaborate, but it is an exercise nonetheless."

"I would like to be able to do that, Charles, but they're not going to accept my word alone. And I'm not sure I can just accept your word either, no offence."

"Understood, Oleg. We can and will provide documents to support the message. We would also want to arrange a chance meeting for you with a senior government figure, at Chatham House for example, at which you might hear the same message from a different horse's mouth. Would that work?"

"I trust you with my life, Charles. I hope I can trust you with the lives of my countrymen. I will do my best; I can only try. Now, give me the details, and another whisky."

******

In Washington the family was enjoying a few days together. Sasha and Steven had driven down from Boston. Brendan Rourke had relieved Steven of his, or rather his father's, beloved pickup truck but had replaced it with a second-hand but still very smart and serviceable compact Subaru station wagon. Sasha, with her brand-new Massachusetts driver's licence, drove it proudly into the parking lot at the Alexandria apartment block.

The four of them had dinner together, prepared by Natasha and Sasha while Steven and Viktor chatted about oceanology over a beer. It was simple Russian food, which Sasha said she had been missing. Although she was very good at eating, the kitchen was not her natural habitat and Sasha was thinking about learning how to cook. Even a simple *solyanka* - a soupy stew - was beyond her at the moment.

"Mama, there are these things called microwaves. You just get something out of the freezer and stick it in a metal box for a few minutes and that's dinner. Steven seems happy with it. I just haven't got around to being a wizard in the kitchen yet."

"I'm sure Steven would be happy if you fed him sawdust," Natasha said, "your father was for the first

300

year and a half after we got married. You'll need to learn to cook for when the novelty wears off. I'll let you have some easy recipes, and next time I come up to see you we'll stock up on spices and some basics for the larder. It's my secret, but a lot of the Russian dishes I 'cook' come out of cans and packets I buy from the Polish deli over in Arlington. Your dad doesn't know."

After dinner Steven went out to meet one of his brothers who was in town. Sasha sat with her father by the heater on the balcony. It wasn't yet too cold to sit out.

"How's Boston?" he asked her.

"I love it, apart from the idiots who get hostile when they know I'm Russian. The apartment is in South Boston, that's an Irish part, and now that I'm a Rourke I fit in well enough. The apartment is small and cosy, but I'm worried that it's going to be like an oven in the summer. There's no aircon, but Stepan's dad said he'll fix it if the landlord says it's OK. There isn't any work at the University just now - people have gone off learning Russian. I'll find something though, we'll be fine."

"And how is it living with someone who isn't family?" he asked her.

"He is family. He's my family, yours too."

"I'm sorry, that's not what I meant. I meant you've always liked your own space, and we've always tried to let you have it."

"It's good; it's different. I suppose that's growing up, isn't it? Papa, can I ask you something?"

"Sure."

"Are you a spy?"

"What is a spy, Sasha?"

"Someone who spies on other people, prying, secretive and sneaky."

"I work at the embassy, for the government. I'm Russian and a Soviet citizen. Part of my job is to get information that our government wants or needs. It's part of every Soviet civil servant's job to do that. In the Foreign Service it can be quite difficult to get information because the Americans are suspicious of our motives, so sometimes I need to find things out without asking direct questions. Is that prying, or being secretive and sneaky?"

"Not the way you say it, but I suppose it depends on what information you want."

"I only want information that our country needs."

"You haven't answered my question, have you?"

"I think I have; maybe you just haven't heard what I said."

Sasha looked at her father, then she went across the balcony to him and held his hand in hers. She looked worried and almost fearful. He felt his eyes welling up. He shook his head vigorously.

"Time to go in, Sasha. I'm getting cold, and I want another sip of the whiskey that Steven brought me from Brendan," he paused. "Sasha, will you promise me one thing?"

"If I can."

"Your mother and I will probably be going back to Moscow quite soon. I - we - want you to stay safe and well, and to be happy. We like Steven and his family, and you must try to be as good a daughter to them as you have been to us. Be a good wife to Steven too, I know he'll be a good husband. The thing I want you to promise it this: when we're back in Russia we'll call you whenever we can. If I or your mother ever say to you on the phone that Uncle Vanya sends his love it means you are in great danger. If one of us says that to you, you both have to get in your car immediately and drive north and west as far as you can, as fast as you possibly can. Will you do that?"

"Uncle Vanya, as in Chekhov, where we used to live?"

"Yes."

"Why will we need to get in the car and drive? You mean head for the hills?"

"I can't explain now. Things are happening here, in Moscow, in Europe. Just promise me you'll do it. For your mother and me."

"You're scaring me, Papa."

"I don't want to. It's just that in my work I may get to know things sooner than some other people. You're all we have. Like I said, we want you to be safe."

Sasha looked at him for the longest time, seeing a side of her father that she had never been aware of before.

"I hope you never have to talk to me about Uncle Vanya. I never liked him anyway," Sasha smiled sadly and held his hand a while longer, suddenly all grown up.

His ticket had come through. He had found out that Zbigniew Brzezinski was giving a late afternoon talk on international relations at Georgetown University on Tuesday 1st November, and he wanted to go. Not to hear the great man's views necessarily, but to try to get an opportunity to speak to him. He hadn't wanted to call Brzezinski's office and be fobbed off by an aide.

Shortly before 3pm he walked out of the embassy. He waved to the two burly men in the Crown Victoria that was parked illegally across 16th Street. He had decided to walk and walk quickly, knowing it would annoy his very visible FBI shadows. It was chilly and overcast, but he didn't mind that. Down to M Street and turn right. Along and across the bridge over Rock Creek Valley to the place where M Street merges with Pennsylvania Avenue. He stopped for a coffee at an Italian place near the junction of M Street and Wisconsin Avenue, gesturing to the pink and puffing FBI men that they could join him if they wanted. They ignored his unspoken invitation.

He found the Riggs Library at the university easily enough, showed his ticket and took a seat on the end of a row not too far from the front. He looked around at the ornate shelves of books and the elaborate ceilings. It was an impressive place; you could almost smell the knowledge it held. In another life, another universe, he might have been a professor at an American or Russian university. Or on reflection, he would prefer a European one. Sasha had once told him that as far as she could make out, a European university taught you how to think, an American one what to think, and a Soviet one not to think at all. She might just be right.

Brzezinski took the podium after a glowing but unnecessary introduction by the Dean of the School of Foreign Service. He spoke fluently and without notes about the current tense situation between the western world and the Soviet Union, his conclusion being that there had been a collective and long-running failure of diplomacy which caused a subsequent breakdown in trust, such that it had been, between the two sides. The rhetorical grandstanding required of the current elected populist leader of a democratic nation had been interpreted as a genuine expression of policy and intent, an impression that good diplomats could and should have been able to deflect. The urgent task now was to start again, and to rebuild a degree of trust, or at least comprehension, which would allow the respective adversaries to plough their own dogmatic furrows in peace until reality could intervene. Brzezinski said all this without causing any immediate offence to the Reaganite elements in the audience, most of whom would have to think about it for quite a while before a penny dropped. It was a great speech.

Afterwards Brzezinski stood for a while exchanging greetings with a few people he knew. Brzezinski caught sight of him and went over.

"Viktor, good to see you," he said.

"You too, Mr Brzezinski," he replied, "it was a very interesting speech, sir."

"If you're going to keep calling me sir and Mr Brzezinski, I'm going to have to get formal with you too, Lieutenant Colonel Gumnov. I said to call me Zbig, didn't I?"

"You did. You know what I am, then?"

"I do, Viktor. It saddens me in a way, but everyone serves the way they can, isn't that so? You would have been a good diplomat - I mean a proper one, not a KGB officer in a cover role. But I'm glad you're here, we need to talk. Will you walk with me outside for a while?"

"We'll have company. I have two FBI men following me around like faithful dogs."

"Give me a moment, will you."

Brzezinski beckoned one of his aides over and spoke quickly and quietly to her. She took out a notebook and wrote something down before hurrying away.

"Sorry about that," Brzezinski said, "I asked her to call Bill Webster over at the Bureau and get him to stand his guys down for the evening. I said to tell him you were with me, and they could find you again tomorrow morning at your apartment. Let's go."

He led the way out of the hall towards the Healy Lawn. Sure enough, the FBI men followed for a while, then they melted away. He looked at their retreating backs.

"I'm impressed, sir. Sorry, Zbig."

"One of the few remaining privileges I have left, I still know the private numbers of most of the people who matter in this town, one of them being the Director of the FBI. You never know when that sort of thing will be useful. We last spoke, when was it, a year ago? As I recall I told you then that the risks of a misunderstanding were very great and very real. Do you remember?"

"Of course," he said, "it's what I do."

"So you do," said Brzezinski. "I was hoping to run into you again, and if I hadn't seen you today, I would have called you. Secretary Schultz and I have been talking about you; he has your file on his desk, complete with a request from the Directors of both the FBI and the CIA that you be expelled. He set out the case they're making, and he and I agree that it is very circumstantial. The only evidence they have for now is a grainy picture of someone who looks quite like you renting a car from Hertz at Seattle airport and another picture of someone who looks a bit like you walking across the departure hall at Dulles airport. I'm no lawyer, but I don't think that's illegal. He's under a lot of pressure, though. He's going to suggest that you be invited to leave the US in a few weeks, after the Able Archer exercise.

"George asked me to talk to you about that too. I'm saying that so you know it's not just me speaking to you, I'm repeating what the Secretary of State, the *current* Secretary of State, told me. And he's repeating what the President of the United States, POTUS, told him at the same time he told the Secretary of Defense. The message is this: Able Archer '83 is an exercise. It's a complex, highly scripted scenario involving all NATO members in a simulation of the final preparations for a nuclear war with the Soviet Union. A *simulation*. In the original script the heads of government of NATO member states were going to participate in person, play their roles as if it were real. The president, George Schultz and Cap Weinberger have now agreed that this would not be a good idea and they're asking the others to reconsider as well. They can't tell them not to play, and it looks like Kohl and Thatcher still fancy a piece of the dramatic action and want to participate. The exercise has been two years in the planning, and it's too late to change the playbook now. It's important for you to know that because there are elements of this exercise that your side won't have seen before. They mustn't be alarmed, and they *must not* respond. One concrete thing they should note is reference to Pershing II missiles being deployed; they aren't in Europe yet. It's a sign they can see for themselves that this is just an exercise.

"The president has considered, and dismissed, the suggestion that he ask NATO to cancel the exercise. The White House, not just the president, is aware of the risks of a misunderstanding of NATO actions and intentions. Official messaging will be sent through various NATO ambassadors to the Soviet Union and your Warsaw Pact allies, but the assumption, probably correct in my opinion, is that there isn't enough trust for them to be believed. That's why I'm taking the unusual and rather desperate measure of asking you, Viktor Gumnov, to make sure that my sincere message is delivered to someone, anyone, in Moscow who will believe it and who can make Andropov and Ustinov and all the others believe it too."

Brzezinski paused as he processed what he'd just been told.

"Your daughter, Alexandra, has recently married an American boy and she's going to live in the US. I think that will give you an additional incentive, not that I think you need one, to do your damnedest to make your leaders understand what I'm telling you. I didn't mention your daughter to imply any kind of threat, by the way. If you know me at all you know I wouldn't do that."

A few seconds passed.

"Thank you Zbig," he said eventually, "you're saying you won't visit the sins of the father on the daughter."

"Pretty much."

"I passed on our last conversation to someone in Moscow who believed what you said then. Did you know what my job was a year ago?"

"I didn't, but I kind of guessed. I was only told when I saw Secretary Schultz a few days ago. We're old pals and I'd mentioned our meetings to him."

"Why are you asking me to do this?"

"Because I know you're a decent man. We have decent men and women in our intelligence services too. I think you get it; I think you believe me. It's not going to be easy for you. As a long-term student of Soviet and Russian history I know Moscow, and curiously for a supposedly revolutionary state, it's far more conservative than here. You have a rigid hierarchy, one in which the leaders only get to hear what people around them think they want to hear. In this country if the people think their leaders are assholes, they get to tell them every four years - and boy do they know it! It means our leaders have to listen to the people and speak to them; if they don't, they get fired or worse, ignored. Do your best, Viktor. A lot of people will be depending on it. I expect I'll see you at the Thanksgiving reception the First Lady will be holding, as long as the world is still here. You take care now."

Brzezinski turned and walked off into the gathering twilight. He sat down for a few minutes on a cold damp bench and tried to take in what he had just been told. As he walked back to the embassy, he was composing in his head the telegram he would send that night to Leonid Grachev in Moscow, marked Top Secret and Immediate. He hoped to God, if there was one, that Leonid would know what to do and who to speak to.

He would also call Natasha to tell her he'd be late home.

Chapter 40 - Moscow, November 1983

His telegram landed on Leonid's desk in the Lubyanka just before lunch on 2nd November. He read it several times, and he understood that Viktor must have thought it important enough to send it to him as it was. Anything marked Top Secret and Immediate was prioritised by the NSA and the British and anyone else with the necessary electronic interception equipment and decryption capability, including some of their own Warsaw Pact allies and comrades in different Soviet departments. When he'd digested the contents fully, Leonid picked up the phone and called Baranov's office.

Baranov read the telegram twice. He put it down and removed his glasses. Reaching for his bottom drawer he pulled out two glasses and a bottle of his ever-present Armenian *konjac*.

"Chairman Chebrikov has sent down an edict about this sort of thing. He says he needs intelligence, not analysis and opinion, although he's not as blind as Fedorchuk was. But if *Chapai* is right, we need to get this to Andropov. Fortunately, we have the same message from a different source. The London *rezident* has submitted a similar report, obviously excluding references to the VRYaN mayhem your man has devised for the USA. The London report states that there is documentary evidence to support the assertion that what is planned is just an exercise. The *rezident* says he joined a chance discussion between a British defence minister, not the top one, and an academic at this Chatham House place in London. Before they knew who he was he heard them say that NATO realises that the exercise is a risk, but it could not be cancelled at this late stage. The minster was reassuring the academic that it is going to be an exercise, not the real thing. I can take this to Chebrikov or go to see Andropov. Yuri Vladimirovich still calls me late at night to find out what's really going on here. On balance, I think I'll bypass Chebrikov - he's out of town anyway and I'll send him a request asking to see him when he gets back.

"I think Andropov can persuade Ustinov and Gromyko, and Chebrikov will do what he's told. The military high command is something different. Normally I'd have faith in Ustinov's ability to keep the Generals under control but Standing Orders do give a degree of autonomy to field-based units in times of crisis. All it would take is for a field commander to think that Moscow was incapacitated and he could launch his tactical nuclear missiles. Excuse me Leonid, I'm just thinking out loud. To get Ustinov to issue an order to all field commanders explicitly telling them not to obey Standing Orders and not to initiate any action without a direct order from the centre will take some doing.

"As for *Chapai's* other request, or should it be demand, to ditch VRYaN in its entirety, now is definitely not the time. Andropov will need to keep it up his sleeve; having the option of initiating a plan to disable the Americans for a considerable time will be a useful bargaining chip for him with the hard-liners. I agree with him and presumably you; *Chapai's* plan must not be allowed to happen, but we cannot expect our leaders to concede that at this stage.

"I'll call Andropov's office. Be at your desk at all times until I call you; you will be coming with me to see him, wherever and at whatever time it is going to be. If this goes wrong, I won't be going down alone. Thank you, Leonid."

Leonid went back to his office, pausing to use the bathroom along the way. He might not have another chance for quite a while. He sent an aide to the cafeteria for sandwiches and coffee, and he called for the latest newspapers from London and Washington. He sat down for a long wait.

The call came very late in the evening.

"Leonid, we're going to see him now. Be downstairs in five minutes."

They rode in Baranov's official car. The road north out of Moscow to the state *dacha,* the *gosdacha*, near Zavidovo where Andropov was currently ensconced was deserted, but even so it took almost two hours to cover the 130 kilometres. They passed through the security cordon and were led to a waiting room, incongruously elegant in its pre-revolutionary style. The house itself was large and set in extensive grounds. It was an old Imperial hunting lodge, one of the first to be 'liberated' by the Bolsheviks and taken into state ownership. The Party leader and his elite coterie, the most equal among all equals, enjoyed its opulent luxury as often as they could. It was now the official country residence of the General Secretary of the Communist Party of the Soviet Union and the Chairman of the Council of Ministers. Andropov kept them waiting until 2am.

When they were called into his presence, they saw that Andropov was wearing a dressing gown and looked extremely tired. He needed a shave probably as much as he needed some sleep. His pallor made him look greyer than usual, which was not easy.

"Comrades," Andropov spoke very quietly, almost a whisper, "I am told you need to see me urgently. I must tell you, Comrade Sergei Stepanovich, that your Chairman is not at all happy that you have come to see me without speaking to him first. Somebody must have told him you were coming. I have lied for you; I told Comrade Chebrikov that it is a personal family matter, you and I being old friends. I do hope that you're not going to put me in a difficult position. Who is your friend?"

"Comrade Yuri Vladimirovich, may I present Major General Grachev, formerly the head of the undeclared unit at our embassy in Washington. He brings news from the agent we have spoken about before, the one I call *Chapai*. The information which Comrade Leonid Petrovich has corroborates that provided by our *rezident* in London about the forthcoming NATO charade."

"I remember him now. Please explain, Comrade Major General," Andropov whispered.

"Comrade General Secretary," Leonid began, "my officer, *Chapai*, has made extensive contacts among people with influence and connections in Reagan's inner circle in Washington. One of these is the former National Security Advisor to President Carter."

"The Polish fellow?" Andropov asked.

"Yes, Zbigniew Brzezinski. Brzezinski is now a distinguished academic, but he remains a close confidant of the present NSA, William Clark, as well as many others in the current administration. *Chapai* spoke with Brzezinski just two days ago. Brzezinski told him that *Chapai's* cover is blown, and he will soon be asked to leave the United States, not expelled as such but invited to leave. In the meantime, his movements are being openly watched by American agents. Brzezinski asked *Chapai* to get a message to the 'right people' in Moscow, people who you and Marshal Ustinov and Comrade Gromyko would trust. *Chapai* sent a telegram to me, which arrived this morning. I have discussed it at length with General Baranov.

"The message is that you are to be assured that the exercise that NATO will be starting on 7th November and concluding on 11th November, which they are calling Able Archer '83, is just an exercise. It is to be a simulation of the final stages of preparation for a nuclear attack on the Soviet Union by NATO, using the American's new Pershing II missiles. The exercise will be very realistic, with consistent military communication security drills and new encryption procedures. Much of the exercise will be carried out in radio silence.

"In his telegram, *Chapai* states that reference to Pershing II missiles is significant. As yet they have not arrived in the European theatre of operations, although they are on their way. *Chapai* states that Brzezinski was asked by Secretary of State George Schultz, and indirectly by Reagan himself, to pass this message on. They know that official communications to our government through the American, British or other NATO ambassadors would probably not be believed, which is why they are taking what Brzezinski has called an 'unusual and desperate measure'.

"Washington is very concerned about another 'misunderstanding'. They are concerned that unless we are aware of the true purpose of the exercise the Soviet Union and its allies will assume that it is the commencement of a real attack and the beginning of a nuclear war, which will of course require a response."

"If they are so concerned, why don't they change it or cancel the exercise altogether?" Andropov asked.

"According to *Chapai*, they say it is too late to make changes at this stage, the exercise is due to commence on 7th November and orders have been sent out. Cancellation is not a politically viable option for the Americans or most of the NATO governments."

"I see," said Andropov, "and they have chosen to start their ludicrous war games on the commemoration day of our October Revolution, the day we parade our forces in Red Square to show our people that we are a strong and proud socialist nation. They could use these war games as a smokescreen to launch missiles aimed directly at Red Square to eliminate most of the Politburo and High Command, not to mention the troops and equipment and the spectators."

"*Chapai's* message is that the United States detests the socialist system, and it will continue to work against it economically and politically, but not militarily. In his words, the Americans think a nuclear war would be 'bad for business'."

"That has a ring of truth about it, Grachev," Andropov said. "I will speak to Ustinov and Gromyko, and to Chebrikov. The Revolution Day parade must go ahead, and Ustinov will be there. I will not, and nor will the key commanders and Politburo members I will need around me on that day. Do not respond to this

Chapai, other than to acknowledge receipt of his message, nor to the *resident* in London. I will not have Washington and London think they can bring me or the Soviet Union to heel with messages sent through spies. There is too great a smell of co-ordination about these messages. They are similar but not identical, and they come from different directions, but I suspect they originate from the same mind. We know that the Americans have exposed *Chapai*. I think you need to have a close look at your man in London, Comrade General Baranov. I do not like or trust coincidences such as this.

"I accept the assurance you have brought me, but with reservations. My orders to Ustinov and to the army, navy and air force, will be to respond immediately and conclusively if a single missile launch is detected in the area of the exercise. It will be a hair-trigger situation. Comrade Gromyko will communicate that officially to all NATO states through official Foreign Ministry channels. It is up to the Americans and NATO to make sure there are no more 'misunderstandings'. Is there anything else?"

"No, Comrade Yuri Vladimirovich," said Baranov, "thank you for seeing us. I felt it was important that we spoke."

"It was, it is," said Andropov, "but, Sergei Stepanovich, I caution you to think very carefully before excluding your chain of command in future. You can push our friendship so far, but I will not tolerate you undermining the proper function of the Committee for State Security. I am sure you will understand my meaning. Now, I am going to try to get a few hours' sleep. Have a safe journey back to Moscow."

They drove back to Moscow in virtual silence. Dawn was breaking as they neared the city. It was 3rd November.

It was 16th November, 10am. He sat at his desk in the Soviet Embassy in Washington watching the light snow fall outside. On his desk were five documents, laid out side by side. Good news and bad.

The first, undated, from Leonid Grachev, said simply that his words had been passed to the right people. The fact that the world had not ended between 7th and 11th November had already suggested that this was probably the case, but it was good to know.

The second, dated 12th November, was from the head of KGB personnel in Moscow. He congratulated Viktor on his exemplary service, and he was delighted to inform the esteemed Comrade Lieutenant Colonel that he had been nominated by Comrade Lieutenant General Baranov for an award of the Order of the Red Banner for his exceptional contribution to the security of the Soviet Union. The nomination had been accepted by Chairman Chebrikov.

The third, dated 11th November, was from Craig Durov at the State Department. Durov expressed regret at the news that his post had been abolished and he stated that, in pursuance of the relevant treaties and regulations, his and Natasha's visas would be revoked in fourteen days. They would need to leave the United States on or before Friday 25th November, the day after Thanksgiving.

The fourth was from Ambassador Brevnov, dated 15th November, stating coldly that the position of head of the SSOD offices in Washington and San Francisco were being amalgamated into one position, to be based on the West Coast where people tended to be more receptive to friendly overtures from the Soviet Union. The incumbent in San Francisco would remain in post, but his services in Washington were no longer required.

The final one was an invitation from the First Lady's office, asking him if he could attend a Thanksgiving eve drinks reception on 23rd November.

He called Natasha, who was in the library working, and said they were going for an early but very long lunch. Later, a little woozy from too much wine, they took a taxi to Alexandria. He noticed that the FBI car was no longer there. They had planned to start packing - Natasha had taken the news stoically - but instead they had ended up in bed for one of the best afternoons they'd had in a long time.

"I'm glad, in a way," Natasha said, "that we're going home. You've not been yourself for months. I think it's time."

"What about Sasha and Steven?" he asked.

"I'll miss them," Natasha said, "but our fledgling has grown feathers and flown from our nest. She's a married woman now, with her own life. I hope we'll be able to see them and talk to them. Maybe they can come to Russia. I'm assuming that our 'departure' means it will be difficult for you to get permission to come back."

"You're probably right. I might be able to get a Canadian visa, though, and we could meet them there. Europe will be easier, for us at least. We'll drive up to Boston tomorrow and spend a couple of days there. We can pack up next week and get flights arranged. We have to go with KLM to Amsterdam then on to

Moscow now that Aeroflot has been banned. At least it will be more comfortable."

******

They took a couple of days to drive north, enjoying a long last look at the New England countryside. Sasha was initially tearful, Steven sombre, but he and Natasha jollied them out of it. They had a great dinner down by the water at Faneuil Hall Market, and Natasha made sure that Sasha had all she needed to make a few experimental *solyankas* for her unsuspecting husband. Sasha said she would come down to Washington for their last few days and drive them to the airport on Friday. Maybe they could see the Rourkes for a Thanksgiving dinner?

And that's what happened. He went into the office one last time, shredded the contents of his personal safe and handed in his and Natasha's embassy passes. He kept the keys to the Lincoln, instructing the transport officer to come and get it from Alexandria on the morning of 25th November.

On 23rd November he made his way to the Hyatt Hotel, as he had for the last two Thanksgiving receptions. This time the First Lady was there, and he got to meet her briefly; they didn't say much to each other. Brzezinski was circulating and approached him.

"We can't go on meeting like this," Brzezinski said.

"We won't," he had said, "I'm being sent home. We're leaving on Friday."

"I'd heard. I'll be sorry to see you go. Maybe our paths will cross again some time. For now, I want to say thanks. Thanks for the conversations, thanks for telling the right people what we spoke about. You must be quite persuasive. Things are still tense; the Pershing II deployment started today, and I'm sure Moscow won't like that, but they'll get over it."

Brzezinski signalled to a passing waitress and got two glasses of champagne and handed one to him.

"A toast," he said, "and nothing to do with red flags or white flags. Simply this: to understanding each other."

He nodded. They drank.

"Would you have done it, Zbig?" he asked the statesman.

"Done what? Cast the first stone? Fired the first missile? What do you think, Viktor?"

"I think I believe what you told me before."

"What was Operation Ryan all about?"

"It's not Ryan, it's VRYaN," he gave Brzezinski the words of the acronym, "it was just in case."

"I know enough Russian to know what it means. I hope it's never needed, and that anything that came out of it is quickly forgotten."

"I agree. Let's hope everyone else does too. It's not over yet, the conflict between us. Will there be a nuclear war, Zbig?"

Brzezinski smiled at the Soviet agent. He shook his head slowly from side to side.

"See you around, Viktor," were the last words he said as he turned and walked away.

******

They spent Thursday at York with Steven's family. Sasha stayed there, but he and Natasha drove home for their last night in Alexandria. The KLM flight left Dulles at 9am and got to Amsterdam in time for a late evening connection. They were booked through on KLM all the way, business class. Leonid had fixed it. Sasha drove them and their two suitcases, the same ones they had when they'd arrived in June 1981, a lifetime ago. Sasha choked back her tears and hugged her parents as they were about to go through to the departure lounge.

"Call me? When you get to Moscow, no matter what time it is here. We're going back to Boston and we'll be there before you land."

"We will, darling," said Natasha.

"*Au revoir*, Lexa," he said, "I love you. Give our love to Stepan too."

"Me too, Papa. Don't mention me to Uncle Vanya, please. I don't want to hear from him, ever."

He smiled and hugged his daughter.

"Lexa suits you," he said.

"My Stepan has good taste."

The flight was long and uneventful, and mercifully quiet and sober. When they disembarked at Sheremetyevo the quietness and sobriety vanished.

"We're home, Nata," he said, absorbing the chaos.

Leonid was waiting for them. He grinned from ear to ear and hugged them both. Katya was there too, despite the hour, and she did the same. They all rode home in a service car to their new apartment, in the same block where Leonid lived. Leonid and Katya escorted them up and went in with them. They didn't stay.

"Welcome home, both of you. Katya and I have missed you. Come to dinner tomorrow and you can tell us all about Washington."

As he saw them to the door, he pulled Leonid gently aside.

"Did they agree to abandon the VRYaN plan, Leonid?"

"Not yet. Like I said to you once, we need to play a long game. We'll get there, don't worry. Sleep well. I'll see you tomorrow."

He didn't sleep well. He told Natasha it was jet lag and he sat in semi-darkness in the unfamiliar lounge. He had tried to sleep, and he was exhausted. But whenever he closed his eyes all he saw was Sasha's drowning, terrified face as she clung to her husband Stepan in their last moments as the tsunami engulfed them.

Also by Jo Calman in the Kelso series:

A Transfer of Power

A Price for Mercy

An Inner Circle

An Undeclared Contest

www.jo-calman.com

Printed in Great Britain
by Amazon